LITTLE HER

AND OTHER STORIES

Thomas Mann was born in 1875 in the ancient Hanseatic town of Lübeck, of a line of prosperous and influential merchants. His father, head of the ancestral firm, had been senator and twice mayor of the free city; his mother was of Germanic-Creole heritage. Brought up in the company of five brothers and sisters, Mann completed his education under the discipline of North German schoolmasters and entered an insurance office in Munich at the age of nineteen. During this time he secretly wrote his first tale, *Fallen*, and shortly afterwards left the insurance office to study art and literature at the University of Munich. Then, after spending a year in Rome, he devoted himself exclusively to writing.

He was only twenty-five when *Buddenbrooks*, his first major novel, was published. Before it was banned and burned by Hitler, it had sold over a million copies in Germany alone. His second great novel, *The Magic Mountain*, was published in 1924 after twelve years of labour. In 1926 the chance request of a Munich artist for an introduction to a portfolio of Joseph drawings was the genesis of the tetralogy *Joseph and His Brothers*, the first volume of which was published in 1933. He was awarded the Nobel Prize for literature in 1929.

In 1933 Thomas Mann left Germany to live for a time in Switzerland. Then, after several previous visits, in 1938 he settled in the United States, living first in Princeton, New Jersey, and later in California, where he wrote *Dr Faustus* and *The Holy Sinner*. Among the honours he received in the USA was his appointment as a Fellow of the Library of Congress. He revisited his native country in 1949 and returned to Switzerland in 1952, where *The Black Swan* and *Confessions of Felix Krull* were written, and where he died in 1955.

BY THOMAS MANN

Buddenbrooks
Tristan (including *Tontö Kroger*)
Royal Highness
Death in Venice
The Infant Prodigy
The Magic Mountain
Disorder and Early Sorrow
Mario and the Magician
Joseph and His Brothers
Lotte in Weimar
The Transposed Heads
Doctor Faustus
The Holy Sinner
The Black Swan
Confessions of Felix Krull
Stories of a Lifetime Volumes I and II

Reflections of a Non-Political Man
A Sketch of My Life
Order of the Day
An Exchange of Letters
The Coming Victory of Democracy
Essays of Three Decades
Last Essays
Letters to Paul Amann
The Letters of Thomas Mann Volumes 1 and II

Thomas Mann

LITTLE HERR FRIEDEMANN

and Other Stories

MINERVA

Published by Minerva 1997

2 4 6 8 10 9 7 5 3 1

Copyright © Martin Secker & Warburg Ltd 1961

First published in Great Britain by
Martin Secker & Warburg 1961

Minerva
Random House, 20 Vauxhall Bridge Road,
London SW1V 2SA

Random House Australia (Pty) Limited
20 Alfred Street, Milsons Point, Sydney
New South Wales 2061, Australia

Random House New Zealand Limited
18 Poland Road, Glenfield,
Auckland 10, New Zealand

Random House South Africa (Pty) Limited
Endulini, 5A Jubilee Road, Parktown 2193,
South Africa

Random House UK Limited Reg. No. 954009

A CIP catalogue record for this book
is available from the British Library

ISBN 0 7493 8687 8

Papers used by Random House UK Ltd are natural, recy-
clable products made from wood grown in sustainable
forests. The manufacturing processes conform to the
environmental regulations of the country of origin

Printed and bound in Great Britain by
Cox & Wyman, Reading, Berkshire

CONTENTS

DISILLUSIONMENT
(1896)

I CONFESS that I was completely bewildered by the conversation which I had with this extraordinary man. I am afraid that I am even yet hardly in a state to report it in such a way that it will affect others as it did me. Very likely the effect was largely due to the candour and friendliness with which an entire stranger laid himself open to me.

It was some two months ago, on an autumnal afternoon, that I first noticed my stranger on the Piazza di San Marco. Only a few people were abroad; but on the wide square the standards flapped in the light sea-breeze in front of that sumptuous marvel of colour and line which stood out with luminous enchantment against a tender pale-blue sky. Directly before the centre portal a young girl stood strewing corn for a host of pigeons at her feet, while more and more swooped down in clouds from all sides. An incomparably blithe and festive sight.

I met him on the square and I have him in perfect clarity before my eye as I write. He was rather under middle height and a little stooped, walking briskly and holding his cane in his hands behind his back. He wore a stiff black hat, a light summer overcoat, and dark striped trousers. For some reason I mistook him for an Englishman. He might have been thirty years old, he might have been fifty. His face was smooth-shaven, with a thickish nose and tired grey eyes; round his mouth played constantly an inexplicable and somewhat simple smile. But from time to time he would look searchingly about him, then stare upon the ground, mutter a few words to himself, give his head a shake and fall to smiling again. In this fashion he marched perseveringly up and down the square.

After that first time I noticed him daily; for he seemed to have no other business than to pace up and down, thirty, forty, or fifty times, in good weather and bad, always alone and always with that extraordinary bearing of his.

On the evening which I mean to describe there had been a concert by a military band. I was sitting at one of the little tables which spread out into the piazza from Florian's café; and when after the concert the concourse of people had begun to disperse, my unknown, with his accustomed absent smile, sat down in a seat left vacant near me.

The evening drew on, the scene grew quieter and quieter, soon all the tables were empty. Hardly any strollers were left, the majestic square was wrapped in peace, the sky above it thick with stars; a great half-moon hung above the splendid spectacular façade of San Marco.

I had been reading my paper, with my back to my neighbour, and was about to surrender the field to him when I was obliged instead to turn in his direction. For whereas I had not heard a single sound, he now suddenly began to speak.

'You are in Venice for the first time, sir?' he asked, in bad French. When I essayed to answer in English he went on in good German, speaking in a low, husky voice and coughing often to clear it.

'You are seeing all this for the first time? Does it come up to your expectations? Surpasses them, eh? You did not picture it as finer than the reality? You mean it? You would not say so in order to seem happy and enviable? Ah!' He leaned back and looked at me, blinking rapidly with a quite inexplicable expression.

The ensuing pause lasted for some time. I did not know how to go on with this singular conversation and once more was about to depart when he hastily leaned towards me.

'Do you know, my dear sir, what disillusionment is?' he asked in low, urgent tones, both hands leaning on his stick. 'Not a miscarriage in small, unimportant matters, but the great and general disappointment which everything, all of life, has in store? No, of course, you do not know. But from my youth up I have carried it about with me; it has made me lonely, unhappy, and a bit queer, I do not deny that.

'You could not, of course, understand what I mean, all at once. But you might; I beg of you to listen to me for a few minutes. For if it can be told at all it can be told without many words.

'I may begin by saying that I grew up in a clergyman's family, in quite a small town. There reigned in our home a punctilious cleanliness and the pathetic optimism of the scholarly atmosphere. We breathed a strange atmosphere, compact of pulpit rhetoric, of large words for good and evil, beautiful and base, which I bitterly hate, since perhaps they are to blame for all my sufferings.

'For me life consisted utterly of those large words; for I knew no more of it than the infinite, insubstantial emotions which they called up in me. From man I expected divine virtue or hair-raising wickedness; from life either ravishing loveliness or else consummate horror; and I was full of avidity for all that and of a profound, tormented yearning for a larger reality, for experience of no matter what kind, let it be glorious and intoxicating bliss or unspeakable undreamed-of anguish.

'I remember, sir, with painful clearness the first disappointment of my life; and I would beg you to observe that it had not at all to do with the miscarriage of some cherished hope, but with an unfortunate occurrence. There was a fire at night in my parents' house, when I was hardly more than a child. It had spread insidiously until the whole small storey was in flames up to my chamber door, and the stairs would soon have been on fire as well. I discovered it first, and I remember that I went rushing through the house shouting over and over: "Fire, fire!" I know exactly what I said and what feeling underlay the words, though at the time it could scarcely have come to the surface of my consciousness. "So this," I thought, "is a fire. This is what it is like to have the house on fire. Is this all there is to it?"

'Goodness knows it was serious enough. The whole house burned down, the family was only saved with difficulty, and I got some burns. And it would be wrong to say that my fancy could have painted anything much worse than the actual burning of my parents' house. Yet some vague, formless idea of an event even more frightful must have existed somewhere within me, by comparison with which the reality seemed flat. This fire was the first great event in my life. It left me defrauded of my hope of fearfulness.

'Do not fear lest I go on to recount my disappointments to you in detail. Enough to tell you that I zealously fed my magnificent expectations of life with the matter of a thousand books and the works of all the poets. Ah, how I have learned to hate them, those poets who chalked up their large words on all the walls of life – because they had no power to write them on the sky with pencils dipped in Vesuvius! I came to think of every large word as a lie or a mockery.

'Ecstatic poets have said that speech is poor: "Ah, how poor are words," so they sing. But no, sir. Speech, it seems to me, is rich, is extravagantly rich compared with the poverty and limitations of life. Pain has its limits: physical pain in unconsciousness and mental in torpor; it is not different with joy. Our human need for communication has found itself a way to create sounds which lie beyond these limits.

'Is the fault mine? Is it down my spine alone that certain words can run so as to awaken in me intuitions of sensations which do not exist?

'I went out into that supposedly so wonderful life, craving just one, one single experience which should correspond to my great expectations. God help me, I have never had it. I have roved the globe over, seen all the best-praised sights, all the works of art upon which have been lavished the most extravagant words. I have stood in front of these and said to myself: "It is beautiful. And yet – is that all? Is it no more beautiful than that?"

'I have no sense of actualities. Perhaps that is the trouble. Once, somewhere in the world, I stood by a deep, narrow gorge in the mountains. Bare rock went up perpendicular on either side, and far below the water roared past. I looked down and thought to myself: "What if I were to fall?" But I knew myself well enough to answer: "If that were to happen you would say to yourself as you fell: 'Now you are falling, you are actually falling. Well and what of it?'"

'You may believe me that I do not speak without experience of life. Years ago I fell in love with a girl, a charming, gentle creature, whom it would have been my joy to protect and cherish. But she loved me not, which was not surprising, and she married another. What other experience can be so painful as this? What tortures are greater than the dry agonies of baffled lust? Many a night I lay wide-eyed and wakeful; yet my greatest torture resided in the thought: "So this is the greatest pain we can suffer. Well, and what then – is this all?"

'Shall I go on to tell you of my happiness? For I have had my happiness as well and it too has been a disappointment. No, I need not go on; for no heaping up of bald examples can make clearer to you that it is life in general, life in its dull, uninteresting, average course which has disappointed me – disappointed, disappointed!

'What is man? asks young Werther – man, the glorious half-god? Do not his powers fail him just where he needs them most? Whether he soars upwards in joy or sinks down in anguish, is he not always brought back to bald, cold consciousness precisely at the point where he seeks to lose himself in the fullness of the infinite?

'Often I have thought of the day when I gazed for the first time at the sea. The sea is vast, the sea is wide, my eyes roved far and wide and longed to be free. But there was the horizon. Why a horizon, when I wanted the infinite from life?

'It may be narrower, my horizon, than that of other men. I have said that I lack a sense of actualities – perhaps it is that I have too much. Perhaps I am too soon full, perhaps I am too soon done with things. Am I acquainted in too adulterated a form with both joy and pain?

'I do not believe it; and least of all do I believe in those whose views of life are based on the great words of the poets – it is all lies and poltroonery. And you may have observed, my dear sir, that there are human beings so vain and so greedy of the admiration and envy of others that they pretend to have experienced the heights of happiness but never the depths of pain?

'It is dark and you have almost ceased to listen to me; so I can the more easily confess that I too have tried to be like these men and make myself appear happy in my own and others' eyes. But it is some years since that the bubble of this vanity was pricked. Now I am alone, unhappy, and a little queer, I do not deny it.

'It is my favourite occupation to gaze at the starry heavens at night – that being the best way to turn my eyes away from earth and from life. And perhaps it may be pardoned in me that I still cling to my distant hopes? That I dream of a freer life, where the actuality of my fondest anticipations is revealed to be without any torturing residue of disillusionment? Of a life where there are no more horizons?

'So I dream and wait for death. Ah, how well I know it already, death, that last disappointment! At my last moment I shall be saying to myself: "So this is the great experience – well, and what of it? What is it after all?"

'But it has grown cold here on the piazza, sir – that I can still feel – ha ha! I have the honour to bid you a very good night.'

LITTLE HERR FRIEDEMANN
(1897)

I T was the nurse's fault. When they first suspected, Frau Consul Friedemann had spoken to her very gravely about the need of controlling her weakness. But what good did that do? Or the glass of red wine which she got daily besides the beer which was needed for the milk? For they suddenly discovered that she even sank so low as to drink the methylated spirit which was kept for the spirit lamp. Before they could send her away and get someone to take her place, the mischief was done. One day the mother and sisters came home to find that little Johannes, then about a month old, had fallen from the couch and lay on the floor, uttering an appallingly faint little cry, while the nurse stood beside him quite stupefied.

The doctor came and with firm, gentle hands tested the little creature's contracted and twitching limbs. He made a very serious face. The three girls stood sobbing in a corner and the Frau Consul in the anguish of her heart prayed aloud.

The poor mother, just before the child's birth, had already suffered a crushing blow: her husband, the Dutch Consul, had been snatched away from her by sudden and violent illness, and now she was too broken to cherish any hope that little Johannes would be spared to her. But by the second day the doctor had given her hand an encouraging squeeze and told her that all immediate danger was over. There was no longer any sign that the brain was affected. The facial expression was altered, it had lost the fixed and staring look. ... Of course, they must see how things went on – and hope for the best, hope for the best.

The grey gabled house in which Johannes Friedemann grew up stood by the north gate of the little old commercial city. The front door led into a large flag-paved entry, out of which a stair with a white wooden balustrade led up into the second storey. The faded wall-paper in the living-room had a landscape pattern, and straight-backed chairs and sofas in dark-red plush stood round the heavy mahogany table.

Often in his childhood Johannes sat here at the window, which always had a fine showing of flowers, on a small footstool at his mother's feet, listening to some fairy-tale she told him, gazing at her smooth grey head, her mild and gentle face, and breathing in the faint scent she exhaled. She showed him the picture of his father, a kindly man with grey side-whiskers – he was now in heaven, she said, and awaiting them there.

Behind the house was a small garden where in summer they spent much of their time, despite the smell of burnt sugar which came over from the refinery close by. There was a gnarled old walnut tree in whose shade little Johannes would sit, on a low wooden stool, cracking walnuts, while Frau Friedemann and her three daughters, now grown women, took refuge from the sun under a grey canvas tent. The mother's gaze often strayed from her embroidery to look with sad and loving eyes at her child.

He was not beautiful, little Johannes, as he crouched on his stool industriously cracking his nuts. In fact, he was a strange sight, with his pigeon breast, humped back, and disproportionately long arms. But his hands and feet were delicately formed, he had soft red-brown eyes like a doe's, a sensitive mouth, and fine, light-brown hair. His head, had it not sat so deep between his shoulders, might almost have been called pretty.

When he was seven he went to school, where time passed swiftly and uniformly. He walked every day, with the strut deformed people often have, past the quaint gabled houses and shops to the old schoolhouse with the vaulted arcades. When he had done his preparation he would read in his books with the lovely title-page illustrations in colour, or else work in the garden, while his sisters kept house for their invalid mother. They went out too, for they belonged to the best society of the town; but unfortunately they had not married, for they had not much money nor any looks to recommend them.

Johannes too was now and then invited out by his schoolmates, but it is not likely that he enjoyed it. He could not take part in their games, and they were always embarrassed in his company, so there was no feeling of good fellowship.

There came a time when he began to hear certain matters talked about, in the courtyard at school. He listened wide-eyed and large-eared, quite silent, to his companions' raving over this or that little girl. Such things, though they entirely engrossed the attention of these others, were not, he felt, for him; they belonged in the same category as the ball games and gymnastics. At times he felt a little sad. But at length he had become quite used to standing on one side and not taking part.

But after all it came about – when he was sixteen – that he felt suddenly drawn to a girl of his own age. She was the sister of a classmate of his, a blond, hilarious hoyden, and he met her when calling at her brother's house. He felt strangely embarrassed in her neighbourhood; she too was embarrassed and treated him with such artificial cordiality that it made him sad.

One summer afternoon as he was walking by himself on the wall outside the town, he heard a whispering behind a jasmine bush and peeped cautiously through the branches. There she sat on a bench beside a long-legged, red-haired youth of his acquaintance. They had their arms about each other and he was imprinting on her lips a kiss, which she returned amid giggles. Johannes looked, turned round, and went softly away.

His head was sunk deeper than ever between his shoulders, his hands trembled, and a sharp pain shot upwards from his chest to his throat. But he choked it down, straightening himself as well as he could. 'Good,' said he to himself. 'That is over. Never again will I let myself in for any of it. To the others it brings joy and happiness, for me it can only mean sadness and pain. I am done with it. For me that is all over. Never again.'

The resolution did him good. He had renounced, renounced for ever. He went home, took up a book, or else played on his violin, which despite his deformed chest he had learned to do.

At seventeen Johannes left school to go into business, like everybody else he knew. He was apprenticed to the big lumber firm of Herr Schlievogt down on the river-bank. They were kind and considerate, he on his side was responsive and friendly, time passed with peaceful regularity. But in his twenty-first year his mother died, after a lingering illness.

This was a sore blow for Johannes Friedemann, and the pain of it endured. He cherished this grief, he gave himself up to it as one gives oneself to a great joy, he fed it with a thousand childhood memories; it was the first important event in his life and he made the most of it.

Is not life in and for itself a good, regardless of whether we may call its content 'happiness'? Johannes Friedemann felt that it was so, and he loved life. He, who had renounced the greatest joy it can bring us, taught himself with infinite, incredible care to take pleasure in what it had still to offer. A walk in the springtime in the parks surrounding the town; the fragrance of a flower; the song of a bird – might not one feel grateful for such things as these?

And that we need to be taught how to enjoy, yes, that our education is always and only equal to our capacity for enjoyment – he knew that too, and he trained himself. Music he loved, and attended all the concerts that were given in the town. He came to play the violin not so badly himself, no matter what a figure of fun he made when he did it; and took delight in every beautiful soft tone he succeeded in producing. Also, by much reading he came in time to possess a literary taste the like of which did not exist in the place. He kept up with the new books, even the foreign ones; he knew how to savour the seductive rhythm of a lyric or the ultimate flavour of a subtly told tale – yes, one might almost call him a connoisseur.

He learned to understand that to everything belongs its own enjoyment and that it is absurd to distinguish between an experience which is 'happy' and one which is not. With a right good will he accepted each emotion as it came, each mood, whether sad or gay. Even he cherished the unfulfilled desires, the longings. He loved them for their own sakes and told himself that with fulfilment the best of them would be past. The vague, sweet, painful yearning and hope of quiet spring evenings – are they not richer in joy than all the fruition the sum-

mer can bring? Yes, he was a connoisseur, our little Herr Friedemann.

But of course they did not know that, the people whom he
met on the street, who bowed to him with the kindly, com-
passionate air he knew so well. They could not know that this
unhappy cripple, strutting comically along in his light overcoat and shiny top hat – strange to say, he was a little vain –
they could not know how tenderly he loved the mild flow of
his life, charged with no great emotions, it is true, but full of a
quiet and tranquil happiness which was his own creation.

But Herr Friedemann's great preference, his real passion,
was for the theatre. He possessed a dramatic sense which was
unusually strong; at a telling theatrical effect or the catastrophe
of a tragedy his whole small frame would shake with emotion.
He had his regular seat in the first row of boxes at the opera-
house; was an assiduous frequenter and often took his sisters
with him. Since their mother's death they kept house for their
brother in the old home which they all owned together.

It was a pity they were unmarried still; but with the decline
of hope had come resignation – Friederike, the eldest, was seventeen years further on than Herr Friedemann. She and her sister
Henriette were over-tall and thin, whereas Pfiffi, the youngest,
was too short and stout. She had a funny way, too, of shaking
herself as she talked, and water came in the corners of her mouth.

Little Herr Friedemann did not trouble himself overmuch
about his three sisters. But they stuck together loyally and were
always of one mind. Whenever an engagement was announced
in their circle they with one voice said how very gratifying that
was.

Their brother continued to live with them even after he became independent, as he did by leaving Herr Schlievogt's firm
and going into business for himself, in an agency of sorts, which
was no great tax on his time. His offices were in a couple of
rooms on the ground floor of the house so that at mealtimes
he had but the pair of stairs to mount – for he suffered now
and then from asthma.

His thirtieth birthday fell on a fine warm June day, and after dinner he sat out in the grey canvas tent, with a new head-rest embroidered by Henriette. He had a good cigar in his mouth and a good book in his hand. But sometimes he would put the latter down to listen to the sparrows chirping blithely in the old nut tree and look at the clean gravel path leading up to the house between lawns bright with summer flowers.

Little Herr Friedemann wore no beard, and his face had scarcely changed at all, save that the features were slightly sharper. He wore his fine light-brown hair parted on one side.

Once, as he let the book fall on his knee and looked up into the sunny blue sky, he said to himself: 'Well, so that is thirty years. Perhaps there may be ten or even twenty more, God knows. They will mount up without a sound or a stir and pass by like those that are gone; and I look forward to them with peace in my heart.'

Now, it happened in July of the same year that a new appointment to the office of District Commandant had set the whole town talking. The stout and jolly gentleman who had for many years occupied the post had been very popular in social circles and they saw him go with great regret. It was in compliance with goodness knows what regulations that Herr von Rinnlingen and no other was sent hither from the capital.

In any case the exchange was not such a bad one. The new Commandant was married but childless. He rented a spacious villa in the southern suburbs of the city and seemed to intend to set up an establishment. There was a report that he was very rich – which received confirmation in the fact that he brought with him four servants, five riding and carriage horses, a landau and a light hunting-cart.

Soon after their arrival the husband and wife left cards on all the best society, and their names were on every tongue. But it was not Herr von Rinnlingen, it was his wife who was the centre of interest. All the men were dazed, for the moment too dazed to pass judgement; but their wives were quite prompt and definite in the view that Gerda von Rinnlingen was not their sort.

'Of course, she comes from the metropolis, her ways would

naturally be different,' Frau Hagenström, the lawyer's wife, said, in conversation with Henriette Friedemann. 'She smokes, and she rides. That is of course. But it is her manners – they are not only free, they are positively brusque, or even worse. You see, no one could call her ugly, one might even say she is pretty; but she has not a trace of feminine charm in her looks or gestures or her laugh – they completely lack everything that makes a man fall in love with a woman. She is not a flirt – and goodness knows I would be the last to disparage her for that. But it is strange to see so young a woman – she is only twenty-four – so entirely wanting in natural charm. I am not express-ing myself very well, my dear, but I know what I mean. All the men are simply bewildered. In a few weeks, you will see, they will be disgusted.'

'Well,' Fräulein Friedemann said, 'she certainly has every-thing she wants.'

'Yes,' cried Frau Hagenström, 'look at her husband! And how does she treat him? You ought to see it – you will see it! I would be the first to approve of a married woman behaving with a certain reserve towards the other sex. But how does she behave to her own husband? She has a way of fixing him with an ice-cold stare and saying "My dear friend!" with a pitying expression that drives me mad. For when you look at him – upright, correct, gallant, a brilliant officer and a splendidly pre-served man of forty! They have been married four years, my dear.'

Herr Friedemann was first vouchsafed a glimpse of Frau von Rinnlingen in the main street of the town, among all the rows of shops, at midday, when he was coming from the Bourse, where he had done a little bidding.

He was strolling along beside Herr Stephens, looking tiny and important, as usual. Herr Stephens was in the wholesale trade, a huge stocky man with round side-whiskers and bushy eyebrows. Both of them wore top hats; their overcoats were un-buttoned on account of the heat. They tapped their canes along the pavement and talked of the political situation; but half-way down the street Stephens suddenly said:

'Deuce take it if there isn't the Rinnlingen driving along.'

'Good,' answered Herr Friedemann in his high, rather sharp voice, looking expectantly ahead. 'Because I have never yet set eyes on her. And here we have the yellow cart we hear so much about.'

It was in fact the hunting-cart which Frau von Rinnlingen was herself driving today with a pair of thoroughbreds; a groom sat behind her, with folded arms. She wore a loose beige coat and skirt and a small round straw hat with a brown leather band, beneath which her well-waved red-blond hair, a good, thick crop, was drawn into a knot at the nape of her neck. Her face was oval, with a dead-white skin and faint bluish shadows lurking under the close-set eyes. Her nose was short but well-shaped, with a becoming little saddle of freckles; whether her mouth was as good or not could not be told, for she kept it in continual motion, sucking the lower and biting the upper lip.

Herr Stephens, as the cart came abreast of them, greeted her with a great show of deference; little Herr Friedemann lifted his hat too and looked at her with wide-eyed attention. She lowered her whip, nodded slightly, and drove slowly past, looking at the houses and shop-windows.

After a few paces Herr Stephens said:

'She has been taking a drive and was on her way home.'

Little Herr Friedemann made no answer, but stared before him at the pavement. Presently he started, looked at his companion, and asked: 'What did you say?'

And Herr Stephens repeated his acute remark.

Three days after that Johannes Friedemann came home at midday from his usual walk. Dinner was at half past twelve, and he would spend the interval in his office at the right of the entrance door. But the maid came across the entry and told him that there were visitors.

'In my office?' he asked.

'No, upstairs with the mistresses.'

'Who are they?'

'Herr and Frau Colonel von Rinnlingen.'

'Ah,' said Johannes Friedemann. 'Then I will –'

And he mounted the stairs. He crossed the lobby and laid his hand on the knob of the high white door leading into the 'landscape room'. And then he drew back, turned round, and slowly returned as he had come. And spoke to himself, for there was no one else there, and said: 'No, better not.'

He went into his office, sat down at his desk, and took up the paper. But after a little he dropped it again and sat looking to one side out of the window. Thus he sat until the maid came to say that luncheon was ready; then he went up into the dining-room where his sisters were already waiting, and sat down in his chair, in which there were three music-books.

As she ladled the soup Henriette said:

'Johannes, do you know who were here?'

'Well?' he asked.

'The new Commandant and his wife.'

'Indeed? That was friendly of them.'

'Yes,' said Pfiffi, a little water coming in the corners of her mouth. 'I found them both very agreeable.'

'And we must lose no time in returning the call,' said Friederike. 'I suggest that we go next Sunday, the day after tomorrow.'

'Sunday,' Henriette and Pfiffi said.

'You will go with us, Johannes?' asked Friederike.

'Of course he will,' said Pfiffi, and gave herself a little shake. Herr Friedemann had not heard her at all; he was eating his soup, with a hushed and troubled air. It was as though he were listening to some strange noise he heard.

Next evening *Lohengrin* was being given at the opera, and everybody in society was present. The small auditorium was crowded, humming with voices and smelling of gas and perfumery. And every eye-glass in the stalls was directed towards box thirteen, next to the stage; for this was the first appearance of Herr and Frau von Rinnlingen and one could give them a good looking-over.

When little Herr Friedemann, in flawless dress clothes and glistening white pigeon-breasted shirt-front, entered his box, which was number thirteen, he started back at the door, making a gesture with his hand towards his brow. His nostrils dilated feverishly. Then he took his seat, which was next to Frau von Rinnlingen's.

She contemplated him for a little while, with her under lip stuck out; then she turned to exchange a few words with her husband, a tall, broad-shouldered gentleman with a brown, good-natured face and turned-up moustaches.

When the overture began and Frau von Rinnlingen leaned over the balustrade Herr Friedemann gave her a quick, searching side glance. She wore a light-coloured evening frock, the only one in the theatre which was slightly low in the neck. Her sleeves were full and her white gloves came up to her elbows. Her figure was statelier than it had looked under the loose coat; her full bosom slowly rose and fell and the knot of red-blond hair hung low and heavy at the nape of her neck.

Herr Friedemann was pale, much paler than usual, and little beads of perspiration stood on his brow beneath the smoothly parted brown hair. He could see Frau von Rinnlingen's left arm, which lay upon the balustrade. She had taken off her glove and the rounded, dead-white arm and ringless hand, both of them shot with pale blue veins, were directly under his eye – he could not help seeing them.

The fiddles sang, the trombones crashed, Telramund was slain, general jubilation reigned in the orchestra, and little Herr Friedemann sat there motionless and pallid, his head drawn in between his shoulders, his forefinger to his lips and one hand thrust into the opening of his waistcoat.

As the curtain fell, Frau von Rinnlingen got up to leave the box with her husband. Johannes Friedemann saw her without looking, wiped his handkerchief across his brow, then rose suddenly and went as far as the door into the foyer, where he turned, came back to his chair, and sat down in the same posture as before.

When the bell rang and his neighbours re-entered the box he felt Frau von Rinnlingen's eyes upon him, so that finally against his will he raised his head. As their eyes met, hers did not swerve aside; she continued to gaze without embarrassment until he himself, deeply humiliated, was forced to look away.

He turned a shade paler and felt a strange, sweet pang of anger and scorn. The music began again.

Towards the end of the act Frau von Rinnlingen chanced to drop her fan; it fell at Herr Friedemann's feet. They both stooped at the same time, but she reached it first and gave a little mocking smile as she said: 'Thank you.'

Their heads were quite close together and just for a second he got the warm scent of her breast. His face was drawn, his whole body twitched, and his heart thumped so horribly that he lost his breath. He sat without moving for half a minute, then he pushed back his chair, got up quietly, and went out.

He crossed the lobby, pursued by the music; got his top hat from the cloak-room, his light overcoat and his stick, went down the stairs and out of doors.

It was a warm, still evening. In the gas-lit street the gabled houses towered towards a sky where stars were softly beaming. The pavement echoed the steps of a few passers-by. Someone spoke to him, but he heard and saw nothing; his head was bowed and his deformed chest shook with the violence of his breathing. Now and then he murmured to himself:

'My God, my God!'

He was gazing horror-struck within himself, beholding the havoc which had been wrought with his tenderly cherished, scrupulously managed feelings. Suddenly he was quite over-powered by the strength of his tortured longing. Giddy and drunken he leaned against a lamp-post and his quivering lips uttered the one word: 'Gerda!'

The stillness was complete. Far and wide not a soul was to be seen. Little Herr Friedemann pulled himself together and went on, up the street in which the opera-house stood and which ran steeply down to the river, then along the main street north-wards to his home.

How she had looked at him! She had forced him, actually, to cast down his eyes! She had humiliated him with her glance. But was she not a woman and he a man? And those strange brown eyes of hers — had they not positively glittered with unholy joy?

Again he felt the same surge of sensual, impotent hatred

mount up in him; then he relived the moment when her head
had touched his, when he had breathed in the fragrance of her
body – and for the second time he halted, bent his deformed
torso backwards, drew in the air through clenched teeth, and
murmured helplessly, desperately, uncontrollably:

'My God, my God!'

Then went on again, slowly, mechanically, through the
heavy evening air, through the empty echoing street until
he stood before his own house. He paused a minute in the
entry, breathing the cool, dank inside air; then he went into his
office.

He sat down at his desk by the open window and stared
straight ahead of him at a large yellow rose which somebody
had set there in a glass of water. He took it up and smelt it with
his eyes closed, then put it down with a gesture of weary sadness. No, no. That was all over. What was even that fragrance
to him now? What any of all those things that up to now had
been the well-springs of his joy?

He turned away and gazed into the quiet street. At intervals
steps passed and the sound died away. The stars stood still and
glittered. He felt so weak, so utterly tired to death. His head was
quite vacant, and suddenly his despair began to melt into a
gentle, pervading melancholy. A few lines of a poem flickered
through his head, he heard the *Lohengrin* music in his ears,
he saw Frau von Rinnlingen's face and her round white arm on
the red velvet – then he fell into a heavy fever-burdened sleep.

Often he was near waking, but feared to do so and managed
to sink back into forgetfulness again. But when it had grown
quite light, he opened his eyes and looked round him with a
wide and painful gaze. He remembered everything, it was as
though the anguish had never been intermitted by sleep.

His head was heavy and his eyes burned. But when he had
washed up and bathed his head with cologne he felt better and
sat down in his place by the still open window. It was early,
perhaps only five o'clock. Now and then a baker's boy passed;
otherwise there was no one to be seen. In the opposite house the

blinds were down. But birds were twittering and the sky was luminously blue. A wonderfully beautiful Sunday morning.

'A feeling of comfort and confidence came over little Herr Friedemann. Why had he been distressing himself? Was not everything just as it had been? The attack of yesterday had been a bad one. Granted. But it should be the last. It was not too late, he could still escape destruction. He must avoid every occasion of a fresh seizure, he felt sure he could do this. He felt the strength to conquer and suppress his weakness.

It struck half past seven and Friederike came in with the coffee, setting it on the round table in front of the leather sofa against the rear wall.

'Good morning, Johannes,' said she; 'here is your breakfast.'

'Thanks,' said little Herr Friedemann. And then: 'Dear Friederike, I am sorry, but you will have to pay your call without me, I do not feel well enough to go. I have slept badly and have a headache – in short, I must ask you –'

'What a pity!' answered Friederike. 'You must go another time. But you do look ill. Shall I lend you my menthol pencil?'

'Thanks,' said Herr Friedemann. 'It will pass.' And Friederike went out.

Standing at the table he slowly drank his coffee and ate a croissant. He felt satisfied with himself and proud of his firmness. When he had finished he sat down again by the open window, with a cigar. The food had done him good and he felt happy and hopeful. He took a book and sat reading and smoking and blinking into the sunlight.

Morning had fully come, wagons rattled past, there were many voices and the sound of the bells on passing trams. With and among it all was woven the twittering and chirping; there was a radiant blue sky, a soft mild air.

At ten o'clock he heard his sisters cross the entry; the front door creaked, and he idly noticed that they passed his window. An hour went by. He felt more and more happy.

A sort of hubris mounted in him. What a heavenly air – and how the birds were singing! He felt like taking a little walk. Then suddenly, without any transition, yet accompanied by a terror namelessly sweet came the thought: 'Suppose I were to go to her!' And suppressing, as though by actual muscular effort, every warning voice within him, he added with blissful resolution: 'I will go to her!'

He changed into his Sunday clothes, took his top hat and his stick, and hurried with quickened breath through the town and into the southern suburbs. Without looking at a soul he kept raising and dropping his head with each eager step, completely rapt in his exalted state until he arrived at the avenue of chestnut trees and the red brick villa with the name of Commandant von Rinnlingen on the gate-post.

But here he was seized by a tremor, his heart throbbed and pounded in his breast. He went across the vestibule and rang at the inside door. The die was cast, there was no retreating now. 'Come what come may,' thought he, and felt the stillness of death within him.

The door suddenly opened and the maid came towards him across the vestibule; she took his card and hurried away up the red-carpeted stair. Herr Friedemann gazed fixedly at the bright colour until she came back and said that her mistress would like him to come up.

He put down his stick beside the door leading into the salon and stole a look at himself in the glass. His face was pale, the eyes red, his hair was sticking to his brow, the hand that held his top hat kept on shaking.

The maid opened the door and he went in. He found himself in a rather large, half-darkened room, with drawn curtains. At his right was a piano, and about the round table in the centre stood several arm-chairs covered in brown silk. The sofa stood along the left-hand wall, with a landscape painting in a heavy gilt frame hanging above it. The wall-paper too was dark in tone. There was an alcove filled with potted palms.

A minute passed, then Frau von Rinnlingen opened the portières on the right and approached him noiselessly over the thick brown carpet. She wore a simply cut frock of red and black plaid. A ray of light, with motes dancing in it, streamed from the alcove and fell upon her heavy red hair so that it shone like gold. She kept her strange eyes fixed upon him with a searching gaze and as usual stuck out her under lip.

'Good morning, Frau Commandant,' began little Herr Friedemann, and looked up at her, for he came only as high as her chest. 'I wished to pay you my respects too. When my sisters did so I was unfortunately out ... I regretted sincerely ...'

He had no idea at all what else he should say; and there she stood and gazed ruthlessly at him as though she would force him to go on. The blood rushed to his head. 'She sees through me,' he thought, 'she will torture and despise me. Her eyes keep flickering. ...'

But at last she said, in a very high, clear voice:

'It is kind of you to have come. I have also been sorry not to see you before. Will you please sit down?'

She took her seat close beside him, leaned back, and put her arm along the arm of the chair. He sat bent over, holding his hat between his knees. She went on:

'Did you know that your sisters were here a quarter of an hour ago? They told me you were ill.'

'Yes,' he answered, 'I did not feel well enough to go out, I thought I should not be able to. That is why I am late.'

'You do not look very well even now,' said she tranquilly, not shifting her gaze. 'You are pale and your eyes are inflamed. You are not very strong, perhaps?'

'Oh,' said Herr Friedemann, stammering, 'I've not much to complain of, as a rule.'

'I am ailing a good deal too,' she went on, still not turning her eyes from him, 'but nobody notices it. I am nervous, and sometimes I have the strangest feelings.'

She paused, lowered her chin to her breast, and looked up expectantly at him. He made no reply, simply sat with his dreamy gaze directed upon her. How strangely she spoke, and how her clear and thrilling voice affected him! His heart beat more quietly and he felt as though he were in a dream. She began again:

'I am not wrong in thinking that you left the opera last night before it was over?'

'Yes, madam.'

'I was sorry to see that. You listened like a music-lover –
though the performance was only tolerable. You are fond of
music, I am sure. Do you play the piano?'

'I play the violin, a little,' said Herr Friedemann. 'That is,
really not very much –'

'You play the violin?' she asked, and looked past him con-
sideringly. 'But we might play together,' she suddenly said. 'I
can accompany a little. It would be a pleasure to find somebody here – would you come?'

'I am quite at your service – with pleasure,' said he, stiffly.
He was still as though in a dream. A pause ensued. Then suddenly her expression changed. He saw it alter for one of cruel,
though hardly perceptible mockery, and again she fixed him
with that same searching, uncannily flickering gaze. His face
burned, he knew not where to turn; drawing his head down
between his shoulders he stared confusedly at the carpet, while
there shot through him once more that strangely sweet and
torturing sense of impotent rage.

He made a desperate effort and raised his eyes. She was looking over his head at the door. With the utmost difficulty he
fetched out a few words:

'And you are so far not too dissatisfied with your stay in our
city?'

'Oh, no,' said Frau Rinnlingen indifferently. 'No, certainly
not; why should I not be satisfied? To be sure, I feel a little
hampered, as though everybody's eyes were upon me, but – oh,
before I forget it,' she went on quickly, 'we are entertaining a
few people next week, a small, informal company. A little
music, perhaps, and conversation. ... There is a charming garden at the back, it runs down to the river. You and your sisters
will be receiving an invitation in due course, but perhaps I
may ask you now to give us the pleasure of your company?'

Herr Friedemann was just expressing his gratitude for the
invitation when the door-knob was seized energetically from
without and the Commandant entered. They both rose and
Frau von Rinnlingen introduced the two men to each other.
Her husband bowed to them both with equal courtesy. His
bronze face glistened with the heat.

He drew off his gloves, addressing Herr Friedemann in a powerful, rather sharp-edged voice. The latter looked up at him with large vacant eyes and had the feeling that he would presently be clapped benevolently on the shoulder. Heels together, inclining from the waist, the Commandant turned to his wife and asked, in a much gentler tone:

'Have you asked Herr Friedemann if he will give us the pleasure of his company at our little party, my love? If you are willing I should like to fix the date for next week and I hope that the weather will remain fine so that we can enjoy ourselves in the garden.'

'Just as you say,' answered Frau von Rinnlingen, and gazed past him.

Two minutes later Herr Friedemann got up to go. At the door he turned and bowed to her once more, meeting her expressionless gaze still fixed upon him.

He went away, but he did not go back to the town; unconsciously he struck into a path that led away from the avenue towards the old ruined fort by the river, among well-kept lawns and shady avenues with benches.

He walked quickly and absently, with bent head. He felt intolerably hot, as though aware of flames leaping and sinking within him, and his head throbbed with fatigue.

It was as though her gaze still rested on him — not vacantly as it had at the end, but with that flickering cruelty which went with the strange still way she spoke. Did it give her pleasure to put him beside himself, to see him helpless? Looking through and through him like that, could she not feel a little pity?

He had gone along the river-bank under the moss-grown wall; he sat down on a bench within a half-circle of blossoming jasmine. The sweet, heavy scent was all about him; the sun brooded upon the dimpling water.

He was weary, he was worn out; and yet within him all was tumult and anguish. Were it not better to take one last look and then to go down into that quiet water; after a brief struggle to be free and safe at peace? Ah, peace, peace — that was what

he wanted! Not peace in an empty and soundless void, but a
gentle, sunlit peace, full of good, of tranquil thoughts.

All his tender love of life thrilled through him in that moment, all his profound yearning for his vanished 'happiness'.
But then he looked about him into the silent, endlessly indifferent peace of nature, saw how the river went its own way in
the sun, how the grasses quivered and the flowers stood up
where they blossomed, only to fade and be blown away; saw
how all that was bent submissively to the will of life; and there
came over him all at once that sense of acquaintance and understanding with the inevitable which can make those who know it
superior to the blows of fate.

He remembered the afternoon of his thirtieth birthday and
the peaceful happiness with which he, untroubled by fears or
hopes, had looked forward to what was left of his life. He had
seen no light and no shadow there, only a mild twilight radi-
ance gently declining into the dark. With what a calm and
superior smile had he contemplated the years still to come – how
long ago was that?

Then this woman had come, she had to come, it was his fate
that she should, for she herself was his fate and she alone. He
had known it from the first moment. She had come – and
though he had tried his best to defend his peace, her coming
had roused in him all those forces which from his youth up he
had sought to suppress, feeling, as he did, that they spelled
torture and destruction. They had seized upon him with frightful, irresistible power and flung him to the earth.

They were his destruction, well he knew it. But why struggle,
then, and why torture himself? Let everything take its course.
He would go his appointed way, closing his eyes before the
yawning void, bowing to his fate, bowing to the overwhelming,
anguishingly sweet, irresistible power.

The water glittered, the jasmine gave out its strong pun-
gent scent, the birds chattered in the tree-tops that gave glimpses
among them of a heavy, velvety-blue sky. Little hump-backed
Herr Friedemann sat long upon his bench; he sat bent over, holding his head in his hands.

Everybody agreed that the Rinnlingens entertained very well. Some thirty guests sat in the spacious dining-room, at the long, prettily decorated table, and the butler and two hired waiters were already handing round the ices. Dishes clattered, glasses rang, there was a warm aroma of food and perfumes. Here were comfortable merchants with their wives and daughters; most of the officers of the garrison; a few professional men, lawyers and the popular old family doctor – in short, all the best society.

A nephew of the Commandant, on a visit, a student of mathematics, sat deeply in conversation with Fräulein Hagenström, whose place was directly opposite Herr Friedemann's, at the lower end of the table. Johannes Friedemann sat there on a rich velvet cushion, beside the unbeautiful wife of the Colonial Director and not far off Frau von Rinnlingen, who had been escorted to table by Consul Stephens. It was astonishing, the change which had taken place in little Herr Friedemann in these few days. Perhaps the incandescent lighting in the room was partly to blame; but his cheeks looked sunken, he made a more crippled impression even than usual, and his inflamed eyes, with their dark rings, glowed with an inexpressibly tragic light. He drank a great deal of wine and now and then addressed a remark to his neighbour.

Frau von Rinnlingen had not so far spoken to him at all; but now she leaned over and called out:

'I have been expecting you in vain these days, you and your fiddle.'

He looked vacantly at her for a while before he replied. She wore a light-coloured frock with a low neck that left the white throat bare; a Maréchal Niel rose in full bloom was fastened in her shining hair. Her cheeks were a little flushed, but the same bluish shadows lurked in the corners of her eyes.

Herr Friedemann looked at his plate and forced himself to make some sort of reply; after which the school superintendent's wife asked him if he did not love Beethoven, and he had to answer that too. But at this point the Commandant, sitting at the head of the table, caught his wife's eye, tapped on his glass and said:

'Ladies and gentlemen, I suggest that we drink our coffee in the next room. It must be fairly decent out in the garden too, and whoever wants a little fresh air, I am for him.'

Lieutenant von Deidesheim made a tactful little joke to cover the ensuing pause, and the table rose in the midst of laughter. Herr Friedemann and his partner were among the last to quit the room; he escorted her through the 'old German' smoking-room to the dim and pleasant living-room, where he took his leave.

He was dressed with great care: his evening clothes were irreproachable, his shirt was dazzlingly white, his slender, well-shaped feet were encased in patent-leather pumps, which now and then betrayed the fact that he wore red silk stockings.

He looked out into the corridor and saw a good many people descending the steps into the garden. But he took up a position at the door of the smoking-room, with his cigar and coffee, where he could see into the living-room.

Some of the men stood talking in this room, and at the right of the door a little knot had formed round a small table, the centre of which was the mathematics student, who was eagerly talking. He had made the assertion that one could draw through a given point more than one parallel to a straight line; Frau Hagenström had cried that this was impossible, and he had gone on to prove it so conclusively that his hearers were constrained to behave as though they understood.

At the rear of the room, on the sofa beside the red-shaded lamp, Gerda von Rinnlingen sat in conversation with young Fräulein Stephens. She leaned back among the yellow silk cushions with one knee slung over the other, slowly smoking a cigarette, breathing out the smoke through her nose and sticking out her lower lip. Fräulein Stephens sat stiff as a graven image beside her, answering her questions with an assiduous smile.

Nobody was looking at little Herr Friedemann, so nobody saw that his large eyes were constantly directed upon Frau von Rinnlingen. He sat rather droopingly and looked at her. There was no passion in his gaze nor scarcely any pain. But there was something dull and heavy there, a dead weight of impotent, involuntary adoration.

Some ten minutes went by. Then as though she had been secretly watching him the whole time, Frau von Rinnlingen approached and paused in front of him. He got up as he heard her say:

'Would you care to go into the garden with me, Herr Friedemann?'

He answered:

'With pleasure, madam.'

'You have never seen our garden?' she asked him as they went down the steps. 'It is fairly large. I hope that there are not too many people in it; I should like to get a breath of fresh air. I got a headache during supper; perhaps the red wine was too strong for me. Let us go this way.' They passed through a glass door, the vestibule, and a cool little courtyard, whence they gained the open air by descending a couple more steps.

The scent of all the flower-beds rose into the wonderful, warm, starry night. The garden lay in full moonlight and the guests were strolling up and down the white gravel paths, smoking and talking as they went. A group had gathered round the old fountain, where the much-loved old doctor was making them laugh by sailing paper boats.

With a little nod Frau von Rinnlingen passed them by, and pointed ahead of her, where the fragrant and well-cared for garden blended into the darker park.

'Shall we go down this middle path?' asked she. At the beginning of it stood two low, squat obelisks.

In the vista at the end of the chestnut alley they could see the river shining green and bright in the moonlight. All about them was darkness and coolness. Here and there side paths branched off, all of them probably curving down to the river. For a long time there was not a sound.

'Down by the water,' she said, 'there is a pretty spot where I often sit. We could stop and talk a little. See the stars glittering here and there through the trees.'

He did not answer, gazing, as they approached it, at the

river's shimmering green surface. You could see the other bank and the park along the city wall. They left the alley and came out on the grassy slope down to the river, and she said:

'Here is our place, a little to the right, and there is no one there.'

The bench stood facing the water, some six paces away, with its back to the trees. It was warmer here in the open. Crickets chirped among the grass, which at the river's edge gave way to sparse reeds. The moonlit water gave off a soft light.

For a while they both looked in silence. Then he heard her voice; it thrilled him to recognize the same low, gentle, pensive tone of a week ago, which now as then moved him so strangely:

'How long have you had your infirmity, Herr Friedemann? Were you born so?'

He swallowed before he replied, for his throat felt as though he were choking. Then he said, politely and gently:

'No, *gnädige Frau*. It comes from their having let me fall, when I was an infant.'

'And how old are you now?' she asked again.

'Thirty years old.'

'Thirty years old,' she repeated. 'And these thirty years were not happy ones?'

Little Herr Friedemann shook his head, his lips quivered.

'No,' he said, 'that was all lies and my imagination.'

'Then you have thought that you were happy?' she asked.

'I have tried to be,' he replied, and she responded:

'That was brave of you.'

A minute passed. The crickets chirped and behind them the boughs rustled lightly.

'I understand a good deal about unhappiness,' she told him. 'These summer nights by the water are the best thing for it.'

He made no direct answer, but gestured feebly across the water, at the opposite bank, lying peaceful in the darkness.

'I was sitting over there not long ago,' he said.

'When you came from me?' she asked. He only nodded.

Then suddenly he started up from his seat, trembling all over; he sobbed and gave vent to a sound, a wail which yet seemed like a release from strain, and sank slowly to the ground before

her. He had touched her hand with his as it lay beside him on
the bench, and clung to it now, seizing the other as he knelt before her, this little cripple, trembling and shuddering; he buried
his face in her lap and stammered between his gasps in a voice
which was scarcely human:

'You know, you understand ... let me ... I can no longer ...
my God, oh, my God!'

She did not repulse him, neither did she bend her face towards him. She sat erect, leaning a little away, and her close-set
eyes, wherein the liquid shimmer of the water seemed to be
mirrored, stared beyond him into space.

Then she gave him an abrupt push and uttered a short, scornful laugh. She tore her hands from his burning fingers, clutched
his arm, and flung him sidewise upon the ground. Then she
sprang up and vanished down the wooded avenue.

He lay there with his face in the grass, stunned, unmanned,
shudders coursing swiftly through his frame. He pulled himself
together, got up somehow, took two steps, and fell again, close
to the water. What were his sensations at this moment? Perhaps
he was feeling that same luxury of hate which he had felt before
when she had humiliated him with her glance, degenerated
now, when he lay before her on the ground and she had treated
him like a dog, into an insane rage which must at all costs find
expression even against himself – a disgust, perhaps of himself,
which filled him with a thirst to destroy himself, to tear himself
to pieces, to blot himself utterly out.

On his belly he dragged his body a little farther, lifted its
upper part, and let it fall into the water. He did not raise his
head nor move his legs, which still lay on the bank.

The crickets stopped chirping a moment at the noise of the
little splash. Then they went on as before, the boughs lightly
rustled, and down the long alley came the faint sound of laughter.

THE DILETTANTE

(1897)

IT can all be summed up, beginning, middle, and end – yes, and
fitting valediction too, perhaps – in the one word: 'disgust'. The
disgust which I now feel for everything and for life as a whole;
the disgust that chokes me, that shatters me, that hounds me out
and pulls me down, and that one day may give me strength to
break the whole fantastic and ridiculous situation across my
knee and finish with it once and for all. I may go on for another
month or so, perhaps for six months or a year; eat and drink
and fill my days somehow or other. Outwardly my life may pro-
ceed as peacefully, regularly, and mechanically as it has been doing all this winter, in frightful contrast to the process of dry rot
and dissolution going on within. It would seem that the more
placid, detached, and solitary a man's outer life, the more
strenuous and violent his inner experiences are bound to be. It
comes to the same thing: if you take care not to be a man of
action, if you seek peace in solitude, you will find that life's
vicissitudes fall upon you from within and it is upon that stage
you must prove yourself a hero or a fool.

I have bought this new note-book in order to set down my
story in it – but to what end, after all? Perhaps just to fill in the
time? Out of interest in the psychological, and to soothe myself
with the conviction that it all had to be? There is such consola-
tion in the inevitable! Or perhaps in order to give myself a temporary illusion of superiority and therewith a certain indifference to fate? For even indifference, as I know full well, might be
a sort of happiness.

It lies so far behind me, the little old city with its narrow,
irregular, gabled streets, its Gothic churches and fountains, its
busy, solid, simple citizens, and the big patrician house, hoary
with age, where I grew up!

It stood in the centre of the town and had lasted out four

generations of well-to-do, respected business men and their families. The motto over the front door was *'Ora et labora'*. You entered through a large flagged court, with a wooden gallery, painted white, running round it up above; and mounted the stairs to a good-sized lobby and a dark little columned hall, whence you had access, through one of the tall white-enamelled doors, to the drawing-room, where my mother sat playing the piano.

The room was dull, for thick dark-red curtains half-shrouded the windows. The white figures of gods and goddesses on the wall hangings stood out plastically from their blue background and seemed as though listening to the deep, heavy first notes of a Chopin nocturne which was her favourite piece. She always played it very slowly, as though to enjoy to the full each melancholy cadence. The piano was old and its resonance had suffered; but by using the soft pedal you could give the notes a veiled, dull silvery sound and so produce quite extraordinary effects.

I would sit on the massive, straight-backed mahogany sofa listening, and watching my mother as she played. She was small and fragile and wore as a rule a soft, pale-grey gown. Her narrow face was not beautiful, it was more like that of a quiet, gentle, dreamy child, beneath the parted, slightly waved indefinitely blond hair. Sitting at the piano, her head a little on one side, she looked like one of those touching little angels who sit in old pictures at the Madonna's feet and play on their guitars.

When I was little she often used to tell me, in her low, deprecatory voice, such fairy-tales as nobody else knew; or she would simply put her hands on my head as it lay in her lap and sit there motionless, not saying a word. Those, I think, were the happiest, peacefullest days of my life. – Her hair did not grey, she became no older; only her figure grew more fragile with the years and her face thinner, stiller, and more dreaming.

But my father was a tall, broad-shouldered gentleman, in fine black broadcloth trousers and coat, with a white waistcoat on which his gold eye-glasses dangled. He wore grey mutton-chop whiskers, with a firm round chin coming out between them, smooth-shaven like his upper lip. Between his brows stood permanently two horizontal folds. He was a powerful man, of great influence in public affairs. I have seen men leave his presence, some with quickened breath and sparkling eyes, others quite broken and in despair. For it sometimes happened that I, and I suppose my mother and my two elder sisters as well, were witnesses at such scenes – either because our father wanted to rouse my ambitions and stimulate me to get on in the world, or else, as I have since suspected, because he needed an audience. He had a way of leaning back in his chair, with one hand thrust into the opening of his waistcoat, and looking after the favoured or the disappointed man, which even as a child led me vaguely to such a conclusion.

I sat in my corner looking at my father and mother, and it was as though I would choose between them: whether I would spend my life in deeds of power or in dreamy musing. And always in the end my eyes would rest upon my mother's quiet face.

Not that I could have been at all like her outwardly, for my occupations were for the most part quite lively and bustling. One of them I still remember, which I vastly preferred to any sort of game with my schoolmates. Even now, at thirty, I still recall it with a heightened sense of pleasure.

I owned a large and well-equipped puppet theatre, and I would shut myself in alone with it to perform the most wonderful musical dramas. My room was in the second storey and had two dark and grisly-bearded ancestral portraits hanging on the wall. I would draw the curtains and set a lamp near the theatre, for it heightened the atmosphere to have artificial light. I, as conductor, took my place directly in front of the stage, my left hand resting upon a large round pasteboard box which was the sole visible orchestral instrument.

The performers would now enter; I had drawn them myself with pen and ink, cut them out, and fitted them into little wooden blocks so that they could stand up. There were the most beautiful ladies, and gentlemen in overcoats and top hats.

'Good evening, ladies and gentlemen,' I would say. 'Everybody all right? I got here betimes, for there was still some work to do. But it is quite time for you to go to your dressing-rooms.'

They went behind the stage and soon came back transfigured, in the gayest and most beautiful costumes, to look through the peep-hole which I had cut in the curtain and see if there was a good house. The house was in fact not so bad; and I rang the bell to let myself know that the performance was about to begin, lifted my baton, and paused to enjoy the sudden stillness which my gesture evoked. Another motion called up the dull warning rumble of the drums with which the overture began – this I performed with my left hand on the top of the box. Then came in the horns, clarinets, and flutes; these I reproduced with my own voice in most inimitable fashion, and so it went on until upon a powerful crescendo the curtain rose and the play began, in a setting of gloomy forest or glittering palace hall.

I would mentally sketch out the drama beforehand and then improvise the details as I went along. The shrilling of the clarinets, the beating of the drums accompanied singing of great passion and sweetness; I chanted splendid bombastic verse with more rhyme than reason; in fact it seldom had any connected meaning, but rolled magnificently on, as I drummed with my left hand, performed both song and accompaniment with my own voice, and directed with my right hand both music and acting down to the minutest detail. The applause at the end of each act was so enthusiastic that there were repeated curtain calls, and even the conductor had sometimes to rise from his seat and bow low in pride and gratitude.

Truly, when after such a strenuous performance I put my toy theatre away, all the blood in my body seemed to have risen to my head and I was blissfully exhausted as is a great artist at the triumphant close of a production to which he has given all that is in him. Up to my thirteenth or fourteenth year this was my favourite occupation.

I recall so very little of my childhood and boyhood in the great house, where my father conducted his business on the ground floor, my mother sat dreaming in her easy-chair, and my sisters, who were two and three years older than I, bustled about in kitchen and laundry.

I am clear that I was an unusually brisk and lively lad. I was well born, I was an adept in the art of imitating my schoolmasters, I knew a thousand little play-acting tricks and had a quite superior use of language – so that it was not hard for me to be popular and respected among my mates. But lessons were a different matter; I was too busy taking in the attitudes and gestures of my teachers to have attention left over for what they were saying, while at home my head was too full of my verses, my theatre, and all sorts of airy trifles to be in a state to do any serious work.

'You ought to be ashamed,' my father would say, the furrows in his brow getting deeper as he spoke, when I brought him my report into the drawing-room after dinner and he perused it with one hand stuck in his waistcoat. 'It does not make very good reading for me and that's a fact. Will you kindly tell me what you expect will become of you? You will never get anywhere in life like this.'

Which was depressing; but it did not prevent me from reading aloud to my parents and sisters after the evening meal a poem which I had written during the afternoon. My father laughed so that his pince-nez bounced about all over his waistcoat. 'What sort of fool's tricks are those?' he cried again and again. But my mother drew me to her and stroked my hair. 'It is not bad at all, my dear,' she said. 'I find there are some quite pretty lines in it.'

Later on, when I was at an older stage, I taught myself a way of playing the piano. Being attracted by the black keys, I began with the F-sharp major chords, explored modulations over into other scales, and by assiduous practice arrived at a certain skill in various harmonies without time or tune, but imparting all possible expressiveness to my mystical billows of sound.

My mother said that my attack displayed a taste for piano, and she got a teacher for me. The lessons went on for six months, but I had not sufficient manual dexterity or sense of rhythm to succeed.

Well, the years passed, and despite my troubles at school I found life very jolly. In the circle of my relatives and friends I was high-spirited and popular, being amiable out of sheer pleasure in playing the amiable part; though at the same time I began instinctively to look down on all these people, finding them arid and unimaginative.

One afternoon, when I was some eighteen years old and about to enter the highest class at school, I overheard a little conversation between my parents. They were sitting together at the round table in the sitting-room and did not see me dawdling by the window in the adjacent dining-room, staring at the pale sky above the gabled roofs. I heard my own name and slipped across to the half-open white-enamelled folding doors.

My father was leaning back in his chair with his legs crossed and the financial newspaper in one hand while with the other he slowly stroked his chin between the mutton-chops. My mother sat on the sofa with her placid face bent over her embroidery. The lamp was on the table between.

My father said: 'It is my view that we ought to take him out of school and apprentice him to some good well-known firm.'

'Oh!' answered my mother looking up in dismay. 'Such a gifted child!'

My father was silent for a moment, meticulously brushing a speck from his coat. Then he lifted his shoulders and put out his hands, palms up. Said he:

'If you think, my love, that it takes no brains to be a business man you are much mistaken. And besides, I realize to my regret that the lad is accomplishing absolutely nothing at school. His gifts to which you refer are of the dilettante variety — though let me hasten to add that I by no means underestimate the value of that sort of thing. He can be very charming when he likes; he knows how to flatter and amuse his company, and he needs to please and be successful. Many a man has before now made a fortune with this equipment. Possessing it, and in view of his indifference to other fields of endeavour, he is not unadapted to a business career in the larger sense.'

My father leaned back in some self-satisfaction, took a cigarette out of his case, and slowly lighted it.

'You are quite right,' said my mother, looking about the room with a saddened face. 'Only I have often thought and to some extent hoped that we might make an artist of him. I suppose it is true that no importance can be attached to his musical talent, which has remained undeveloped; but have you noticed that since he went to that art exhibition he has been doing a little drawing? It does not seem at all bad to me.'

My father blew out smoke from his cigarette, sat erect, and said curtly:

'That is all stuff and nonsense. Anyhow, we can easily ask him.'

I asked myself. What indeed did I really want? The prospect of any sort of change was most welcome to me. So in the end I put on a solemn face and said that I was quite ready to leave school and become a business man. I was apprenticed to the wholesale lumber business of Herr Schlievogt, down on the river-bank.

The change was only superficial, of course. I had but the most moderate interest in the lumber business; I sat in my revolving chair under the gas burner in the dark, narrow counting-room, as remote and indifferent as on the bench at school. This time I had fewer cares – that was the great difference.

Herr Schlievogt was a stout man with a red face and stiff grey nautical beard; he troubled himself very little about me, being mostly in the mills, at some distance from the counting-house and yards. The clerks treated me with respect. I had social relations with but one of them, a talented and self-satisfied young man of good family whom I had known when I was at school. His name was Schilling. He made as much fun of everything in the world as I did, but he displayed a lively interest in the lumber business and every day gave utterance to his firm resolve that he would some day and somehow become a rich man.

As for me, I mechanically performed my necessary tasks and for the rest spent my time sauntering among the workmen in the yards, between the stacks of lumber, looking at the river beyond the high wooden lattice, where now and then a freight train rolled past, and thinking about some theatre or concert I had lately attended or some book which I had read.

For I read a great deal, read everything I could lay my hands on, and my capacity for impressions was great. I had an emotional grasp of each character created by an author; in each one I thought to see myself, and identified myself wholly with the atmosphere of a book – until it was the turn of a new one to have its effect upon me. I would sit in my room – with a book on my knee instead of the toy theatre to occupy me – and look up at my two ancestral portraits while I savoured the style of the book in which I was then absorbed, my brain filled with an unproductive chaos of half-thoughts and fanciful imaginings.

My sisters had married in quick succession. When I was not at the office I would often go down to the drawing-room, where my mother sat, now almost always alone. She was a little ailing, her face had grown even more childlike and placid, and when she played Chopin to me or I showed her a new sequence of harmonies which I had discovered, she would ask me whether I was content and happy in my calling. – And there was no doubt that I was happy.

I was not much more than twenty, my choice of a career was still provisional, and the idea was not foreign to me that I need not always spend my life with Herr Schlievogt or with some bigger lumber-dealer. I knew that one day I could free myself, leave my gabled birthplace, and live somewhere more in accordance with my tastes: read good and well-written novels, attend the theatre, make a little music. Was I not happy? Did I not eat excellently well, go dressed in the best? And as in my schooldays I realized that there were poor and badly dressed boys who behaved with subservience to me and my like, so now I was stimulated by the consciousness that I belonged to the upper classes, the rich and enviable ones, born to look down with benevolent contempt upon the unlucky and dissatisfied. Why should I not be happy? Let things take their course. And there was a certain charm in the society of these relations and friends. It gave me a blithe feeling of superiority to smile at their limitations and yet to gratify my desire to please by behaving towards them with the extreme of affability. I basked in the sunshine of their somewhat puzzled approbation – puzzled because while they approved, they vaguely discerned elements of contradiction and extravagance.

A change began to take place in my father. Each day when he came to table at four o'clock the furrows on his brow seemed to have got deeper. He no longer thrust his hand imposingly between his waistcoat buttons, his bearing was depressed and self-conscious. One day he said to me:

'You are old enough now to share with me the cares which are undermining my health. And it is even my duty to acquaint you with them, to prevent you from cherishing false expectations. You know that I made considerable sacrifices to give your sisters their marriage portions. And of late the firm has lost a deal of money as well. I am an old man, and a discouraged one; I do not feel that things will change much for the better. I must ask you to realize that you will be flung upon your own resources.'

These things he said some two months before his death. One day he was found sitting in his arm-chair in the office, waxen-faced, paralysed, and unable to articulate. A week later the whole town attended his funeral.

My mother sat by the table in the drawing-room, fragile and silent, with her eyes mostly closed. My sisters and I hovered about her; she would nod and smile, but still be motionless and silent, her hands in her lap and her strange, wide, melancholy gaze directed at one of the white deities on the wall. Gentlemen in frock-coats would come in to tell her about the progress of the liquidation; she would nod and smile and shut her eyes again.

She played Chopin no more. When she passed her pale, delicate hand over her smoothly parted hair it would tremble with fatigue and weakness. Scarcely six months after my father's death, she laid herself down and died, without a murmur, without one struggle for life.

So it was all over now – and what was there to hold me to the place? For good or ill, the business of the firm had been liquidated; I turned out to have fallen heir to some hundred thousand marks, enough to make me independent. I had no duties and on some ground or other had been declared unfit for service.

There was no longer any bond between me and those among whom I had grown up. Their point of view was too one-sided for me to share it, and on their side they regarded me with more and more puzzled eyes. Granted that they knew me for what I was, a perfectly useless human being – as such, indeed, did I know myself. But I was cynical and fatalistic enough to look on the bright side of what my father had called my dilettante talents, self-satisfied enough to want to enjoy life in my own way.

I drew my little competence out of the bank and almost without any formal farewell left my native town to pursue my travels.

I remember as though they were a beautiful, far-away dream those next three years, in which I surrendered myself greedily to a thousand new, rich, and varied sensations. How long ago was it that I spent a New Year's Day amid snow and ice among the monks at the top of the Simplon Pass? How long since I was sauntering across the Piazza Erbe in Verona? Since I entered the Piazza di San Pietro from the Borgo San Spirito, trod for the first time beneath the colonnades, and let my gaze stray abashed into the distances of that mammoth square? Since I looked down from Corso Vittorio Emmanuele on the city of Naples, white in the brilliant light, and saw far off across the bay the charming silhouette of Capri, veiled in deep-blue haze? All that was some six years ago, hardly more.

I lived very carefully within my means, in simple lodgings or in modest pensions. But what with travelling and the difficulty of giving up all at once the good bourgeois comforts I was used to, my expenses were after all not small. I had set apart for my travels the sum of fifteen thousand marks out of my capital – but I overstepped this limit.

For the rest I fared very well among the people with whom I came into contact: disinterested and often very attractive characters, to whom of course I could not be the object of respect that I had been in my former surroundings, but from whom, on the other hand, I need not fear disapproving or questioning looks.

My social gifts sometimes made me genuinely popular – I recall for instance a scene in Pensione Minelli at Palermo, where there was a circle of French people of all ages. One evening I improvised for them 'a music drama by Richard Wagner' with a lavishness of tragic gesture, recitative, and rolling harmonies, finishing amid enormous applause. An old gentleman hurried up to me; he had scarcely a hair on his head, his sparse white muttonchops straggled down across his grey tweed jacket. He seized my hands, tears in his eyes, and cried:

'But it is amazing! Amazing, my dear sir! I swear to you that not for thirty years have I been so pricelessly entertained. Permit me to thank you from the bottom of my heart. But you must, you certainly must become an actor or a musician!'

Truly, on such an occasion I felt something of the arrogance of a great painter who draws a caricature on the table-cloth to amuse his friends. – But after dinner I sat down alone in the salon and spent a sad and solitary hour trying sustained chords on the piano in an effort to express the mood evoked in me by the sight of Palermo.

Leaving Sicily, I had just touched the African coast, then gone on into Spain. In the country near Madrid, on a gloomy, rainy winter afternoon, I felt the first time the desire – and the necessity – for a return to Germany. For aside from the fact that I began to crave a settled and regular life, I saw without any prolonged calculation that however carefully I lived I should have spent twenty thousand marks before my return.

I did not hesitate many days before setting out on the long journey through France, which was protracted to nearly six months by lengthy sojourns in this place and that. I recall with painful distinctness the summer evening of my arrival at the capital city in the centre of Germany which even before setting out on my travels I had selected as my home. Hither I had now come: a little wiser, equipped with a little experience and know-ledge, and full of childish joy at the prospect of here setting up my rest and establishing – carefree, independent, and in enjoy-ment of my modest means – a life of quiet and contemplation.

The spot was not badly chosen. It is a city of some size, yet not so bustling as a metropolis, nor marred by a too obtrusive business life. It has some fine old squares and its atmosphere is not lacking in either elegance or vivacity. Its suburbs are charm-ing; best of all I liked the well-laid-out promenade leading up to the Lerchenberg, a long ridge against which most of the town is built. From this point there is an extended view over houses, churches, and the river winding gently away into the distance. From some positions, and especially when the band is playing on a summer afternoon and carriages and pedestrians are moving to and fro, it recalls the Pincio. – But I will return to this promenade later on.

It would be hard to overestimate the peculiar pleasure I drew from the arrangement of the bedroom and sitting-room I had taken in a busy quarter in the centre of the city. Most of our family effects had passed into the possession of my sisters, but enough was left for my needs: adequate and even handsome furniture, my books, and my two ancestral portraits, even the old grand piano, which my mother had willed to me.

When everything had been placed and the photographs which I had acquired on my travels were hung on the walls or arranged on the heavy mahogany writing-desk and the bow-front chest of drawers, and when ensconced in my new fastness I sat down in an arm-chair by the window to survey by turns my abode within and the busy street life outside, my comfort and pleasure were no small thing. And yet – I shall never forget the moment – besides my satisfaction and confidence something else stirred in me, a faint sense of anxiety and unrest, a faint consciousness of being on the defensive, of rousing myself against some power that threatened my peace: the slightly depressing thought that I had now for the first time left behind the temporary and provisional and exchanged it for the definite and fixed.

I will not deny that these and like sensations repeated themselves from time to time. But must they not come, now and then, those afternoon hours in which one sits and looks out into the growing twilight, perhaps into a slowly falling rain, and becomes prey to gloomy foreboding? True, my future was secure. I had entrusted the round sum of eighty thousand marks to the bank, the interest came to about six hundred marks the quarter – my God, but the times are bad! – so that I could live decently, buy books, and now and then visit the theatre or enjoy some lighter kind of diversion.

My days in fact conformed very well to the ideal which I had always had in view. I got up at about ten, breakfasted, and spent the rest of the morning at the piano or reading some book or magazine. Then I strolled up the street to my little restaurant, ate my dinner, and took a long walk, through the city streets, to a gallery, the suburbs, or the Lerchenberg. I came back and resumed the same occupations: read, played the piano, amused myself with drawings of a sort, or wrote a letter, slowly and carefully. Perhaps I attended the theatre or a concert after my evening meal; if not, I sat in a café and read the papers until bedtime. That was a good day, with a solid and gratifying content, when I had discovered a motif on the piano which seemed to me new and pleasing, or when I had carried away from a painting in the gallery or from the book I had read some fine and abiding impression.

I must say too that my programme was seriously conceived with the view of giving my days as much ideal content as possible. I ate modestly, had as a rule only one suit at a time; in short, I limited my material demands in order to be able to get a good seat at the opera or concert, to buy the latest books or visit this or that art exhibition.

But the days went by, they turned into weeks and months – of boredom? Yes, I confess it. One has not always a book at hand which will absorb one for hours on end. I might sit all the morning at the piano and have no success with my improvisations. I would be seated at the window smoking cigarettes and feel stealing over me a distaste of all the world, myself included. I would be possessed by fear, spring up and go out of doors, there to shrug my shoulders and watch with a superior smile the business men and labourers on the street, who lacked the spiritual and material gifts which would fit them for the enjoyment of leisure.

But is a man of seven-and-twenty able seriously to believe – no matter how likely it is – that his days are now fixed and unchangeable up to the end? A span of blue sky, the twitter of a bird, some half-vanished dream of the night before – everything has power to suffuse his heart with undefined hopes and fill it with the solemn expectation of some great and nameless joy. –

I dawdled from one day to the next – aimless, dreamy, occupied with this or that little thing to look forward to, even if it were only the date of a forthcoming publication, with the lively conviction that I was certainly very happy even though now and again weary of my solitude.

They were not precisely infrequent, those hours in which I was painfully conscious of my lack of contact with my kind. That I had none needs no explanation. I was not in touch with society – neither the first circles nor the second. To introduce myself as a *fêtard* among the gilded youth, I lacked means for that, God knew – and on the other hand, bohemia? But I was well brought up, I wear clean linen and a whole suit, and it does not amuse me to carry on anarchistic conversations with shabby young people at tables sticky with absinthe. In short, there was no one sphere to which I could naturally gravitate, and the chance connexions I made from time to time were few, slight, and superficial – though this was largely my own fault, for I held back, I know, being insecure myself and unpleasantly aware that I could not make clear even to a drunken painter exactly who and what I was.

Besides, of course, I had given up society; I had broken with it when I took the liberty of going my own way regardless of its claims upon me. So if in order to be happy I needed 'people', then I had to ask myself whether I should not have been by now busy and useful making money as a business man in a large way and becoming the object of respect and envy.

But meanwhile? The fact remained that my philosophic isolation disturbed me far too much. It refused to fit in with my conception of happiness, with the consciousness or conviction that I was happy – and from this conviction I was utterly unable to part. That I was not happy, that I was in fact unhappy – certainly that was unthinkable. And there the matter rested, until the next time came, when I found myself sitting alone, withdrawn and remote, alarmingly morose – and, in short, in an intolerable state.

But are happy people morose? I thought of my home life in the limited circle where I had moved in the pleasing consciousness of my own talents and parts, sociable, charming, my eyes

bright with fun and mockery and good feeling of a rather con-
descending sort; viewed as a little odd and yet quite generally
liked. Then I had been happy, despite Herr Schlievogt and the
lumber business, whereas now –?

But some vastly interesting book would appear, a new French
novel, which I would spend the money to buy and, sitting in my
comfortable arm-chair, would enjoy my leisure. Three hundred
unexplored pages of charming blague and literary art! Certainly
life was going as I would have it. Was I asking myself whether
I was happy? Such a question is sheer rubbish, nothing else.

So ends another day, undeniably a full one, thank God!
Evening is here, the curtains are drawn, the lamp burns on
the writing-table, it is nearly midnight. I might go to bed, but I
remain sprawled in my arm-chair with idle hands, gazing up at
the ceiling in order to concentrate on the vague gnawing and
boring of an indefinite ache which I know not how to dispel.

I have spent the past hours immersed in a great work of art:
one of those tremendous and ruthless works of genius which
rack and deafen, enrapture and shatter the reader with their
decadent and dilettante splendours. My nerves still quiver, my
imagination is rampant, my mind seethes with strange fancies,
with moods mingled of yearning, religious fervour, triumph,
and a mystical peace. And with all that the compulsion, which
for ever urges them upwards and outwards, to display them, to
share them, to 'make something of them'.

Suppose I were an artist in very truth, capable of giving utterance to my feelings in music, in verse, in sculpture – or best of
all, to be honest, in all of them at once? It is true that I can do a
little of everything. For instance, I can sit at my piano in my
quiet little room and express the fullness of my feelings, to my
heart's content – ought that not to be enough? Of course, if I
needed 'people' in order to be happy, then I could understand.
But supposing that I set store by success, by recognition, praise,
fame, envy, love? My God, when I recall that scene at Palermo
I have to admit to myself that something like that at this
moment would be a great encouragement to me now!

If I am honest with myself I cannot help admitting the sophistical and ridiculous distinction between the two kinds of happiness, inward and outward. Outward happiness – of what does it consist? There are men, the favourites of the gods, it would seem, whose happiness is genius and their genius happiness; children of light, who move easily through life with the reflection and image of the sun in their eyes; easy, charming, amiable, while all the world surrounds them with praise, admiration, envy, and love – for even envy is powerless to hate them. And they mingle in the world like children, capricious, arrogant, spoiled, friendly as the sunshine, as certain of their genius and their joy as though it were impossible things should be otherwise.

As for me, weak though I may be, I confess that I should like to be like them. Rightly or wrongly I am possessed with the feeling that I once belonged among them – but what matter? For when I am honest with myself I know that the real point is what one thinks of oneself, to what one gives oneself, to what one feels strong enough to give oneself!

Perhaps the truth is that I resigned my claim to this 'outward happiness' when I withdrew myself from the demands of society and arranged my life to do without people. But of my inward satisfaction there is no doubt at all – it cannot, it must not be doubted; for I repeat, with emphasis of desperation, that happy I must and will be, for I conceive too profoundly of happiness as a virtue, as genius, refinement, charm; and of unhappiness as something ugly, mole-like, contemptible – in a word, absurd – to be able to be unhappy and still preserve my self-respect.

I could not permit myself to be unhappy, could not stand the sight of myself in such a role. I should have to hide in the dark like a bat or an owl and gaze with envy at the children of light. I should have to hate them with a hatred which would be nothing but a festered love – and I should have to despise myself!

Hide in the dark! Ah, there comes to my mind all that I have been thinking and feeling these many months about my philosophic isolation – and my fit takes me again, my familiar, my too-much-feared fear! I am conscious of anger against some force which threatens me.

Certainly I found consolations, ameliorations, oblivion for the time and for another time and yet another. But my fear always returned, returned a thousand times in the course of the months and the years.

There are autumn days that are like a miracle. Summer is past, the trees are yellow and brown, all day the wind whistles round the corners, and turbid water fills all the gutters. You have come to terms with the time of year; you have come home, so to speak, to sit by the stove and let the winter go over your head. Then one morning you wake to see with unbelieving eyes a narrow strip of luminous blue shine through your bedroom curtains. You spring astonished out of bed and open the window, a tremulous wave of sunshine streams towards you, while through all the street noises you hear the blithe twitter of a bird. It is as though the fresh light atmosphere of an early October day were to breathe the ineffably sweet and spicy air which belongs to the promiseful winds of May. It is spring – obviously, despite the calendar, a day in spring. You fling on your clothes to hurry through the streets and into the country, out under the open sky.

Now, such an unhoped-for blessing of a day there was, some four months ago – we are now in the month of February. And on that day I saw a lovely sight. I had got up before nine, in a bright and joyful mood, possessed by vague hopes of change, of unexpected and happy events. I took the road to the Lerchenberg, mounting the right side of the hill and following along the ridge on the main road, close to the low stone parapet, in order to keep in sight all the way – it takes perhaps half an hour – the view over the slightly terraced city on the slope below, the river winding and glittering in the sun, and the green hilly landscape dim in the distance.

Hardly anyone was up here. The benches were empty, here and there among the trees a white statue looked out; a faded leaf straggled down. Watching the bright panorama as I walked, I went on undisturbed until I had reached the end of the ridge, where my road slanted down among old chestnut trees. Then I heard the ringing of horses' hoofs and the rolling of a wagon coming on at a lively trot. It would pass me at about the middle of the descent, so I moved to one side and stood still.

It was a small, light, two-wheeled cart drawn by two large, briskly snorting, glossy light bays. A young lady of nineteen or twenty years held the reins, seated beside a dignified elderly gentleman with bushy white eyebrows and moustaches brushed up *à la russe*. A servant in plain black and silver livery adorned the seat behind.

The pace of the horses had been slowed down at the top of the descent, which seemed to have made one of them nervous; it swung out sidewise from the shaft, tucked down its head, and braced its forelegs, trembling. The old gentleman leaned over to help his companion, drawing in one rein with his elegantly gloved hand. The driving seemed to have been turned over to her only temporarily and half as a game; at least she seemed to do it with a childish air of mingled importance and inexperience. She made a vexed little motion of the head as she tried to quiet the shying and stumbling animal.

She was slender and brunette. Her hair was gathered to a firm knot in the back of her neck, but lay loose and soft on brow and temples so that I could see the single bright brown strands; atop it perched a round dark straw hat trimmed with a ribbon bow. For the rest she wore a short dark-blue jacket and a simple skirt of light-grey cloth. The brunette skin of her finely formed oval face looked freshened and rosy in the morning air; the most attractive features in it were the long, narrow eyes, whose scarcely visible iris was a shining black, above which arched brows so even that they looked as though they were drawn with a pen. The nose was perhaps a little long and the mouth might have been smaller, though the lips were clear-cut and fine. It was charming to see the gleaming white well-spaced teeth of her upper jaw, which, in her efforts to control the struggling horse, she pressed hard upon her lower lip, lifting her chin, which was almost as round as a child's.

It would not be true to say that this face possessed any striking or exceptional beauty. What it had was youth, the charm of gaiety and freshness, polished, as it were, refined and heightened by ease, well-being, and luxurious living-conditions. Certainly those bright narrow eyes, now looking in displeasure at the refractory horse, would assume next minute their accustomed expression of happy security. The sleeves of her jacket, which were wide at the shoulders, came close round the slender wrists and she had an enchantingly dainty and elegant way of holding the reins in her slim ungloved white hands.

I stood by the edge of the path unnoted as the cart drove past, and walked slowly on when the horses quickened their pace again and took it out of sight. I felt pleasure and admiration, but at the same time a strange and poignant pain – was it envy, love, self-contempt? I did not dare to think.

The image in my mind as I write is that of a beggar, a poor wretch standing at a jeweller's window and staring at a costly jewel within. The man will not even feel any conscious desire to possess the stone, the bare idea would make him laugh at his own absurdity.

It came about quite by chance that I saw this same young lady again, only a week later, at the opera, during a performance of Gounod's *Faust*. Hardly had I entered the brightly lighted auditorium to betake myself to my seat in the stalls when I became aware of her seated at the old gentleman's side in a proscenium box on the other side of the stage. To my surprise I felt a little startled and confused, and in consequence perhaps averted my eyes, letting them rove over the other tiers and boxes. It was only when the overture had begun that I summoned resolution to look at the pair more closely.

The old gentleman wore a buttoned-up frock-coat and a black tie. He leaned back in his seat with dignified calm, one of his brown-gloved hands resting on the ledge in front of him while the other slowly stroked his beard or the close-cropped grey hair. The young girl – undoubtedly his daughter – leaned forward with lively interest, clasping her fan with both hands and resting them on the velvet upholstery of the ledge. Now and then with a quick gesture she tossed back the bright, soft brown hair from her brow and temples.

She wore a light-coloured silk blouse with a bunch of violets in her girdle. In the bright light her narrow eyes seemed to sparkle even more than before; and the position of the lips and mouth which I had noticed proved to be habitual with her; for she constantly set her even, shining, well-spaced white teeth on her under lip and drew the chin upwards a little. This innocent little face quite devoid of coquetry, the detached and merrily roving glance, the delicate white throat, confined only by a ribbon the colour of her blouse, the gesture with which she called the old gentleman's attention to something in the stalls, on the stage, or in a box – all this gave the impression of an unspeakably refined and charming child, though it had nothing touching about it and did not arouse any of those emotions of pity which we sometimes feel for children. It was childlike in an elevated, tempered, and superior way that rested upon a security born of physical well-being and good breeding. Her evident high spirits did not have their source in pride, but in an inward and unconscious poise.

Gounod's music, spirited and sentimental by turns, seemed not a bad accompaniment to this young lady's appearance. I listened without looking at the stage, lost in a mild and pensive mood which without the music might have been more painful than it was. But after the first act there disappeared from his place in the stalls a gentleman of between twenty-five and thirty years who presently with a very easy bow appeared in the box on which my eye was fastened. The old man put out his hand at once, the young lady gave him hers with a gay nod, and he carried it respectfully to his lips as they invited him to sit down.

I was quite ready to admit that this gentleman's shirt-front was the most incomparable I had ever had the pleasure of beholding. It was fully exposed, for the waistcoat was the narrowest of black strips; his dress coat was not fastened save by a single button which came below his middle, and it was cut out from the shoulders in a sweeping curve. A stand-up collar with turned-over points met the shirt-front beneath a wide black tie, and his studs were two large square black buttons, standing out on the admirably starched, dazzlingly white expanse of shirt, which however did not lack flexibility, for it had a pleasing little concavity in the neighbourhood of the waist and swelled out again just as pleasingly and glossily below.

Of course, this shirt-front was what took the eye; but there was a head atop, entirely round and covered with close-cropped very blond hair and boasting such adornments as a pair of eye-glasses without rims or cord, a rather weedy, waving blond moustache, and a host of little duelling scars running up to the temple on one cheek. For the rest the gentleman was faultlessly built and moved with assurance.

In the course of the evening – for he remained in the box – I noted two attitudes characteristic of him. If the conversation languished he sat leaning jauntily back with one leg cocked over the other and his opera-glasses on his knee, bent his head and stuck out his whole mouth as far as it would go, to plunge into absorbed contemplation of his moustache, quite hypnotized, it would seem, and turning the while his head slowly to and fro. On the other hand, taken up in a conversation with the young lady, he would, to be sure, respectfully alter the position of his legs; then leaning even farther back and seizing his chair with both hands, he would elevate his chin as high as possible and smile down upon his young neighbour with his mouth wide open, assuming an amiable and slightly superior air. What wonderfully happy self-confidence such a young man must rejoice in!

In all seriousness, I do not undervalue the possession. Upon none of his motions, however airily audacious, did the faintest self-consciousness ensue – he was buoyed up by his own self-respect. And why not? It was plain that he had made his way – not necessarily by pushing – and was on the straight road to a plain and profitable goal. He dwelt in the shade of good understanding with all the world and in the sunshine of general approbation. And so he sat there chatting with a young girl for whose pure and priceless charms he probably had an eye – and if he had he need feel no hesitation in asking for her hand. Certainly I have no desire to utter one contemptuous word in the direction of this young gentleman.

But as for me? I sat far off in the darkness below, sulkily observing that priceless and unobtainable young creature as she laughed and prattled happily with this unworthy male. Shut out, unregarded, disqualified, unknown, *hors ligne – déclassé*, pariah, a pitiable object even to myself!

I stopped on till the end and came on the three in the cloak-room, where they lingered a little getting their furs, chatting with this or that acquaintance, here a lady, there an officer. When they left, the young gentleman accompanied the young lady and her father, and I followed at a little remove through the vestibule.

It was not raining, there were a few stars in the sky, they did not take a cab. Talking easily, the three passed on ahead and I followed, timid, oppressed, tortured by my poignant, mocking, miserable feelings. – They had not far to go; not more than one turning and they stopped in front of a stately house with a plain façade, and father and daughter disappeared after a cordial leave-taking from their companion, who walked off with a brisk tread.

On the heavy, carved house-door was a plate with the name: Justizrat Rainer.

I am determined to see these notes to a finish, though my in-ward resistance is so great that I am tempted every minute to spring up and escape. I have dug and burrowed into this mess until I am perfectly exhausted. I am sick to death of it all.

Not quite three months since, I read in the paper that a charity bazaar was to be held in the Rathaus under the aus-pices of the best society in the city. I read the announcement attentively and made up my mind to go. 'She will be there,' I thought; 'perhaps she will have a stall, and nothing can prevent my speaking to her. After all I am a man of good birth and breeding, and if I like this Fräulein Rainer I am just as well qualified as the man with the shirt-front to address her and exchange a few light words.'

It was a windy, rainy afternoon when I betook myself to the Rathaus, before whose doors was a press of carriages and people. I made my way into the building, paid the entrance fee, left my hat and coat, and with some difficulty gained the broad and crowded staircase up to the first floor and so into the hall. I was greeted by a waft of heavy scent – wine, food, perfume, and pine needles – and a confused hurly-burly of laughter, talk, cries, and ringing gongs.

The immensely high and large space was gaily adorned with flags and garlands; along the walls and down the middle were the stalls, both open and closed, fantastically arrayed gentlemen acting as barkers in front of the latter and shouting at the top of their lungs. Ladies, likewise in costume, were everywhere selling flowers, embroideries, tobacco, and various refreshments. On the stage at the upper end, decorated with potted plants, a noisy band was in action, while a compact procession of people moved slowly forward in the narrow lanes between the rows of stalls.

A little confused by the noise of the music, the barkers, and the grab-bags, I joined the procession, and in no time at all, scarcely four paces from the entrance, I found her whom I sought. She was selling wine and lemonade and wore the bright-coloured skirt, the square white head-dress and short stays of the Albanian peasant costume, her tender arms bare to the elbow. She was looking rather flushed, leaning back against her serving-table, playing with her gaudy fan and talking with a group of gentlemen round the stall. Among them I saw at the first glance a well-known face – my gentleman of the shirt-front stood beside her at the table with four fingers of each hand thrust in the side pockets of his jacket.

I pushed my way over, meaning to approach her when she was less surrounded. This was a test: we should see whether I still had in me some remnant of the blithe self-assurance and conscious ability of yore, or whether my present moroseness and pessimism were only too well justified. What was it ailed me? Why did the sight of this girl – I confess it – make my cheeks burn with the same old mingled feelings of envy, yearning, chagrin, and bitter exasperation? A little straightforwardness, in the devil's name, a little gaiety and self-confidence, as befits a talented and happy man! With nervous eagerness I summoned the apt word, the light Italian phrase with which I meant to address her.

It took some time for me to make the circuit of the hall in that slowly moving stream of people; and when once more I stood in front of her booth all the gentlemen save one had gone. He of the shirt-front still leaned against her table, discoursing blithely with the fair vendeuse. I would take the liberty of interrupting their conversation. And turning quickly, I edged myself out of the stream and stood before her stall.

What happened? Ah, nothing at all, or hardly anything. The conversation broke off, the young man stepped aside and, holding his rimless, ribbonless pince-nez with all five fingers, stared at me through them and it, while the young lady swept me with a calm and questioning gaze – from my suit down to my boots. My suit was by no means new and my boots were muddy, as I was well aware. I was hot too, and very likely my hair was ruffled. I was not cool, I was not unconcerned, I was not equal to the occasion. Here was I, a stranger, not one of the elect, intruding and making myself absurd; hatred and helpless hapless misery prevented me from looking at her at all, and in desperation I carried through my stout resolve by saying gruffly, with a scowl and in a hoarse voice:

'I'd like a glass of wine.'

What matter whether she really did, as I thought, cast a quick mocking glance at her companion? We stood all three in silence as she gave me the wine; without raising my eyes, red and distraught with pain and fury, a wretched and ridiculous figure, I stood between the two, drank a few sips, laid the money on the table, and rushed out of the hall.

Since that moment it is all up with me; it added but little to my bitter cup when a few days later I read in the paper that Herr Justizrat Rainer had the honour to announce his daughter Anna's engagement to Herr Dr Alfred Witznagel.

Since that moment it is all up with me. My last remaining shreds of happiness and self-confidence have been blown to the winds, I can do no more. Yes, I am unhappy; I freely admit it, I seem a lamentable and absurd figure even to myself. And that I cannot bear. I shall make an end of it. Today, or tomorrow, or some time, I will shoot myself.

My first impulse, my first instinct, was a shrewd one: I would make copy of the situation, I would contribute my pathetic sickness to swell the literature of unhappy love. But that was all folly. One does not die of an unhappy love-affair. One revels in it. It is not such a bad pose. But what is destroying me is that hope has been destroyed with the destruction of all pleasure in myself.

Was I – if I might ask the question – was I in love with this girl? Possibly. ... But how – and why? Such love, if it existed, was a monstrosity born of a vanity which had long since become irritable and morbid, rasped into torment at sight of an unattainable prize. Love was the mere pretext, escape, and hope of salvation for my feelings of envy, hatred, and self-contempt.

Yes, it was all superficial. And had not my father once called me a dilettante?

No, I had not been justified, I less than most people, in keeping aloof and ignoring society – I, who am too vain to support her indifference or contempt, who cannot do without her and her applause. But here was not a matter of justification, rather one of necessity; and was it just my impractical dilettantism that made me useless for society? Ah, well, it was precisely my dilettantism that was killing me!

Indifference, I know, would be a sort of happiness. But I cannot be indifferent to myself, I am not in a position to look at myself with other eyes than those of 'people' – and all innocent as I am, I am being destroyed by my bad conscience. But is a bad conscience ever anything but a festering vanity?

There is only one kind of unhappiness: to suffer the loss of pleasure in oneself. No longer to be pleasant to oneself – that is the worst that can happen; and I have known it for such a long time! All else is the play of life, it enriches life; any other kind of suffering can leave one perfectly satisfied with oneself, one can get on quite well with it. It is the conflict in oneself, the suffering with a bad conscience, the struggle with one's vanity – it is these make you a pitiable and disgusting spectacle.

An old acquaintance of mine turned up, a man named Schilling, in whose company I had once served society by working in Herr Schlievogt's lumber-yard. He was in the city on business and came to see me: a cynical individual with his hands in his trouser pockets, black-rimmed pince-nez, and a convincingly tolerant shoulder-shrug. He arrived one evening and said: 'I am stopping for a few days.' We went to a wine-house.

He met me as though I were still the happy and self-satisfied individual he had known; and in the belief that he was merely confirming my own conviction he said:

'My God, young fellow, but you have done yourself well here! Independent, eh? And you are right too, deuce take me if you aren't! Man lives but once as they say, and that's all there is to it. You are the cleverer of us two, I must say. But you were always a bit of a genius.' And went on just as of yore, whole-heartedly recognizing my claims to superiority and being agree-able without suspecting for a moment that I on my side was afraid of his opinion.

I struggled desperately to retain his high opinion of me, to appear happy and self-satisfied. All in vain. I had not the back-bone, the courage, or the countenance; I was languid and ill at ease, I betrayed my insecurity – and with astonishing quickness he grasped the situation. He had been perfectly ready to grant my superiority – but it was frightful to see how he saw through me, was first astonished, then impatient, then cooled off and be-trayed his contempt and disgust with every word he spoke. He left me early and next day I received a curt note saying that after all he found he was obliged to go away.

It is a fact that everybody is much too preoccupied with him-self to form a serious opinion about another person. The world displays a readiness, born of indolence, to pay a man whatever degree of respect he himself demands. Be as you will, live as you like – but be bold about it, display a good conscience and nobody will be moral enough to condemn you. But once suffer yourself to become split, forfeit your own self-esteem, betray that you despise yourself, and your view will be blindly accepted by all and sundry. As for me, I am a lost soul.

I cease to write, fling the pen from me – full of disgust, full of disgust! I will make an end of it – alas, that is an attitude too heroic for a dilettante. In the end I shall go on living, eating, sleeping; I shall gradually get used to the idea that I am dull, that I cut a wretched and ridiculous figure.

Good God, who would have thought, who could have thought that such is the doom which overtakes the man born a dilettante!

TOBIAS MINDERNICKEL

(1897)

ONE of the streets running steeply up from the docks to the middle town was named Grey's Road. At about the middle of it, on the right, stood Number 47, a narrow, dingy-looking building no different from its neighbours. On the ground floor was a chandler's shop where you could buy overshoes and castor oil. Crossing the entry along a courtyard full of cats and mounting the mean and shabby, musty-smelling stair, you arrived at the upper storeys. In the first, on the left, lived a cabinet-maker; on the right a midwife. In the second, on the left a cobbler, on the right a lady who began to sing loudly whenever she heard steps on the stair. In the third on the left, nobody; but on the right a man named Mindernickel – and Tobias to boot. There was a story about this man; I tell it, because it is both puzzling and sinister, to an extraordinary degree.

Mindernickel's exterior was odd, striking, and provoking to laughter. When he took a walk, his meagre form moving up the street supported by a cane, he would be dressed in black from head to heels. He wore a shabby old-fashioned top hat with a curved brim, a frock-coat shining with age, and equally shabby trousers, fringed round the bottoms and so short that you could see the elastic sides to his boots. True, these garments were all most carefully brushed. His scrawny neck seemed longer because it rose out of a low turn-down collar. His hair had gone grey and he wore it brushed down smooth on the temples. His wide hat-brim shaded a smooth-shaven sallow face with sunken cheeks, red-rimmed eyes which were usually directed at the floor, and two deep, fretful furrows running from the nose to the drooping corners of the mouth.

Mindernickel seldom left his house – and this for a very good reason. For whenever he appeared in the street a mob of children would collect and sally behind him, laughing, mocking, singing – 'Ho, ho, Tobias!' they would cry, tugging at his coat-

tails, while people came to their doors to laugh. He made no de-
fence; glancing timidly round, with shoulders drawn up and
head stuck out, he continued on his way, like a man hurrying
through a driving rain without an umbrella. Even while they
were laughing in his face he would bow politely and humbly to
people as he passed. Farther on, when the children had stopped
behind and he was not known, and scarcely noted, his manner
did not change. He still hurried on, still stooped, as though a
thousand mocking eyes were on him. If it chanced that he
lifted his timid, irresolute gaze from the ground, you would see
that, strangely enough, he was not able to fix it steadily upon
anyone or anything. It may sound strange, but there seemed to
be missing in him the natural superiority with which the normal, perceptive individual looks out upon the phenomenal
world. He seemed to measure himself against each phenomenon,
and find himself wanting; his gaze shifted and fell, it grovelled
before men and things.

What was the matter with this man, who was always alone
and unhappy even beyond the common lot? His clothing belonged to the middle class; a certain slow gesture he had, of his
hand across his chin, betrayed that he was not of the common
people among whom he lived. How had fate been playing with
him? God only knows. His face looked as though life had hit
him between the eyes, with a scornful laugh. On the other hand,
perhaps it was a question of no cruel blow but simply that he
was not up to it. The painful shrinking and humility expressed
in his whole figure did indeed suggest that nature had denied
him the measure of strength, equilibrium, and backbone which
a man requires if he is to live with his head erect.

When he had taken a turn up into the town and come back to
Grey's Road, where the children welcomed him with lusty bawl-
ings, he went into the house and up the stuffy stair into his own
bare room. It had but one piece of furniture worthy the name, a
solid Empire chest of drawers with brass handles, a thing of
dignity and beauty. The view from the window was hopelessly
cut off by the heavy side wall of the next house; a flower-pot full
of earth stood on the ledge, but there was nothing growing in it.
Tobias Mindernickel went up to it sometimes and smelled at the

earth. Next to this room was a dark little bedchamber. Tobias on coming in would lay hat and stick on the table, sit down on the dusty green-covered sofa, prop his chin with his hand, and stare at the floor with his eyebrows raised. He seemed to have nothing else to do.

As for Tobias Mindernickel's character, it is hard to judge of that. Some favourable light seems to be cast by the following episode. One day this strange man left his house and was pounced upon by a troop of children who followed him with laughter and jeers. One of them, a lad of ten years, tripped over another child's foot and fell so heavily to the pavement that blood burst from his nose and ran from his forehead. He lay there and wept. Tobias turned at once, went up to the lad, and began to console him in a mild and quavering voice. 'You poor child,' said he, 'have you hurt yourself? You are bleeding – look how the blood is running down from his forehead. Yes, yes, you do look miserable, you weep because it hurts you so. I pity you. Of course, you did it yourself, but I will tie my handkerchief round your head. There, there! Now pull yourself together and get up.' And actually with the words he bound his own hand-kerchief round the bruise and helped the lad to his feet. Then he went away. But he looked a different man. He held himself erect and stepped out firmly, drawing longer breaths under his narrow coat. His eyes looked larger and brighter, he looked squarely at people and things, while an expression of joy so strong as to be almost painful tightened the corners of his mouth.

After this for a while there was less tendency to jeer at him among the denizens of Grey's Road. But they forgot his astonishing behaviour with the lapse of time, and once more the cruel cries resounded from dozens of lusty throats behind the bent and infirm man: 'Ho, ho, Tobias!'

One sunny morning at eleven o'clock Mindernickel left the house and betook himself through the town to the Lerchenberg, a long ridge which constitutes the afternoon walk of good society. Today the spring weather was so fine that even in the forenoon there were some carriages as well as pedestrians moving about. On the main road, under a tree, stood a man with a young hound on a leash, exhibiting it for sale. It was a muscular little animal about four months old, with black ears and black rings round its eyes.

Tobias at a distance of ten paces noticed this; he stood still, rubbed his chin with his hand, and considered the man, and the hound alertly wagging its tail. He went forward, circling three times round the tree, with the crook of his stick pressed against his lips. Then he stepped up to the man, and keeping his eye fixed on the dog, he said in a low, hurried tone: 'What are you asking for the dog?'

'Ten marks,' answered the man.

Tobias kept still a moment, then he said with some hesitation: 'Ten marks?'

'Yes,' said the man.

Tobias drew a black leather purse from his pocket, took out a note for five marks, one three-mark and one two-mark piece, and quickly handed them to the man. Then he seized the leash, and two or three people who had been watching the bargain laughed to see him as he gave a quick, frightened look about him and, with his shoulders stooped, dragged away the whimpering and protesting beast. It struggled the whole of the way, bracing its forefeet and looking up pathetically in its new master's face. But Tobias pulled, in silence, with energy and succeeded in getting through the town.

An outcry arose among the urchins of Grey's Road when Tobias appeared with the dog. He lifted it in his arms, while they danced round, pulling at his coat and jeering; carried it up the stair and bore it into his own room, where he set it on the floor, still whimpering. Stooping over and patting it with kindly condescension he told it:

'There, there, little man, you need not be afraid of me; that is quite unnecessary.'

He took a plate of cooked meat and potatoes out of a drawer and tossed the dog a part of it, whereat it ceased to whine and ate the food with loud relish, wagging its tail.

'And I will call you Esau,' said Tobias. 'Do you understand? That will be easy for you to remember.' Pointing to the floor in front of him he said, in a tone of command:

'Esau!'

And the dog, probably in the hope of getting more to eat, did come up to him. Tobias clapped him gently on the flank and said:

'That's right, good doggy, good doggy!'

He stepped back a few paces, pointed to the floor again, and commanded:

'Esau!'

And the dog sprang to him quite blithely, wagging its tail, and licked its master's boots.

Tobias repeated the performance with unflagging zest, some twelve or fourteen times. Then the dog got tired, it wanted to rest and digest its meal. It lay down, in the sagacious and charming attitude of a hunting dog, with both long, slender forelegs stretched before it, close together.

'Once more,' said Tobias. 'Esau!'

But Esau turned his head aside and stopped where he was.

'Esau!' Tobias's voice was raised, his tone more dictatorial still. 'You've got to come, even if you are tired.'

But Esau laid his head on his paws and came not at all.

'Listen to me,' said Tobias, and his voice was now low and threatening; 'you'd best obey or you will find out what I do when I am angry.'

But the dog hardly moved his tail.

Then Mindernickel was seized by a mad and extravagant fit of anger. He clutched his black stick, lifted up Esau by the nape of the neck, and in a frenzy of rage he beat the yelping animal, repeating over and over in a horrible, hissing voice:

'What, you do not obey me? You dare to disobey me?'

At last he flung the stick from him, set down the crying animal, and with his hands upon his back began to pace the room, his breast heaving, and flinging upon Esau an occasional proud and angry look. When this had gone on for some time, he stopped in front of the dog as it lay on its back, moving its fore-paws imploringly. He crossed his arms on his chest and spoke with a frightful hardness and coldness of look and tone – like Napoleon, when he stood before a company that had lost its standard in battle:

'May I ask you what you think of your conduct?'

And the dog, delighted at this condescension, crawled closer, nestled against its master's leg, and looked up at him bright-eyed.

For a while Tobias gazed at the humble creature with silent contempt. Then as the touching warmth of Esau's body communicated itself to his leg he lifted Esau up.

'Well, I will have pity on you,' he said. But when the good beast essayed to lick his face his voice suddenly broke with melancholy emotion. He pressed the dog passionately to his breast, his eyes filling with tears, unable to go on. Chokingly he said:

'You see, you are my only ... my only ...' He put Esau to bed, with great care, on the sofa, supported his own chin with his hand, and gazed at him with mild eyes, speechlessly.

Tobias Mindernickel left his room now even less often than before; he had no wish to show himself with Esau in public. He gave his whole time to the dog, from morning to night; feeding him, washing his eyes, teaching him commands, scolding him, and talking to him as though he were human. Esau, alas, did not always behave to his master's satisfaction. When he lay beside Tobias on the sofa, dull with lack of air and exercise, and gazed at him with soft, melancholy eyes, Tobias was pleased. He sat content and quiet, tenderly stroking Esau's back as he said:

'Poor fellow, how sadly you look at me! Yes, yes, life is sad, that you will learn before you are much older.'

But sometimes Esau was wild, beside himself with the urge to exercise his hunting instincts; he would dash about the room, worry a slipper, leap on the chairs, or roll over and over with sheer excess of spirits. Then Tobias followed his motions from afar with a helpless, disapproving, wandering air and a hateful, peevish smile. At last he would brusquely call Esau to him and say:

'That's enough now, stop dashing about like that – there is no reason for such high spirits.'

Once it even happened that Esau got out of the room and

bounced down the stairs to the street, where he at once began to chase a cat, to eat dung in the road, and jump up at the children frantic with joy. But when the distressed Tobias appeared with his wry face, half the street roared with laughter to see him, and it was painful to behold the dog bounding away in the other direction from his master. That day Tobias in his anger beat him for a long time.

One day, when he had had the dog for some weeks, Tobias took a loaf of bread out of the chest of drawers and began stooping over to cut off little pieces with his big bone-handled knife and let them drop on the floor for Esau to eat. The dog was frantic with hunger and playfulness: it jumped up at the bread, and the long-handled knife in the clumsy hands of Tobias ran into its right shoulder-blade. It fell bleeding to the ground.

In great alarm Tobias flung bread and knife aside and bent over the injured animal. Then the expression of his face changed, actually a gleam of relief and happiness passed over it. With the greatest care he lifted the wounded animal to the sofa – and then with what inexhaustible care and devotion he began to tend the invalid. He did not stir all day from its side, he took it to sleep on his own bed, he washed and bandaged, stroked and caressed and consoled it with unwearying solicitude.

'Does it hurt so much?' he asked. 'Yes, you are suffering a good deal, my poor friend. But we must be quiet, we must try to bear it.' And the look on his face was one of gentle and melancholy happiness.

But as Esau got better and the wound healed, so the spirits of Tobias sank again. He paid no more attention to the wound, confining his sympathy to words and caresses. But it had gone on well, Esau's constitution was sound; he began to move about once more. One day after he had finished off a whole plate of milk and white bread he seemed quite right again; jumped down from the sofa to rush about the room, barking joyously, with all his former lack of restraint. He tugged at the bedcovers, chased a potato round the room, and rolled over and over in his excitement.

Tobias stood by the flower-pot in the window. His arms

stuck out long and lean from the ragged sleeves and he mechanically twisted the hair that hung down from his temples. His figure stood out black and uncanny against the grey wall of the next building. His face was pale and drawn with suffering and he followed Esau's pranks unmoving, with a sidelong, jealous, wicked look. But suddenly he pulled himself together, approached the dog, and made it stop jumping about; he took it slowly in his arms.

'Now, poor creature,' he began, in a lachrymose tone – but Esau was not minded to be pitied, his spirits were too high. He gave a brisk snap at the hand which would have stroked him; he escaped from the arms to the floor, where he jumped mockingly aside and ran off, with a joyous bark.

That which now happened was so shocking, so inconceivable, that I simply cannot tell it in any detail. Tobias Mindernickel stood leaning a little forward, his arms hanging down; his lips were compressed, the balls of his eyes vibrated uncannily in their sockets. Suddenly with a sort of frantic leap, he seized the animal, a large bright object gleamed in his hand – and then he flung Esau to the ground with a cut which ran from the right shoulder deep into the chest. The dog made no sound, he simply fell on his side, bleeding and quivering.

The next minute he was on the sofa with Tobias kneeling before him, pressing a cloth on the wound and stammering:

'My poor brute, my poor dog! How sad everything is! How sad it is for both of us! You suffer – yes, yes, I know. You lie there so pathetic – but I am with you, I will console you – here is my best handkerchief –'

But Esau lay there and rattled in his throat. His clouded, questioning eyes were directed upon his master, with a look of complaining, innocence, and incomprehension – and then he stretched out his legs a little and died.

But Tobias stood there motionless, as he was. He had laid his face against Esau's body and he wept bitter tears.

LITTLE LIZZY

(1897)

THERE are marriages which the imagination, even the most practised literary one, cannot conceive. You must just accept them, as you do in the theatre when you see the ancient and doddering married to the beautiful and gay, as the given premisses on which the farce is mechanically built up.

Yes, the wife of Jacoby the lawyer was lovely and young, a woman of unusual charm. Some years – shall we say thirty years? – ago, she had been christened with the names of Anna, Margarete, Rosa, Amalie; but the name she went by was always Amra, composed of the initials of her four real ones; it suited to perfection her somewhat exotic personality. Her soft, heavy hair, which she wore parted on one side and brushed straight back above her ears from the narrow temples, had only the darkness of the glossy chestnut; but her skin displayed the dull, dark sallowness of the south and clothed a form which southern suns must have ripened. Her slow, voluptuous indolent presence suggested the harem; each sensuous, lazy movement of her body strengthened the impression that with her the head was entirely subordinate to the heart. She needed only to have looked at you once, with her artless brown eyes, lifting her brows in the pathetically narrow forehead, horizontally, in a quaint way she had, for you to be certain of that. But she herself was not so simple as not to know it too. Quite simply, she avoided exposing herself, she spoke seldom and little – and what is there to say against a woman who is both beautiful and silent? Yes, the word 'simple' is probably the last which should be applied to her. Her glance was artless; but also it had a kind of luxurious cunning – you could see that she was not dull, also that she might be a mischief-maker. In profile her nose was rather too thick; but her full, large mouth was utterly lovely, if also lacking in any expression save sensuality.

This disturbing phenomenon was the wife of Jacoby the lawyer, a man of forty. Whoever looked at him was bound to be amazed at the fact. He was stout, Jacoby the lawyer; but stout is not the word, he was a perfect colossus of a man! His legs, in their columnar clumsiness and the slate-grey trousers he always wore, reminded one of an elephant's. His round, fat-upholstered back was that of a bear, and over the vast round of his belly his funny little grey jacket was held by a single button strained so tight that when it was unbuttoned the jacket came wide open with a pop. Scarcely anything which could be called a neck united this huge torso with the little head atop. The head had narrow watery eyes, a squabby nose, and a wee mouth between cheeks drooping with fullness. The upper lip and the round head were covered with harsh, scanty, light-coloured bristles that showed the naked skin, as on an overfed dog. There was no doubt that Jacoby's fatness was not of a healthy kind. His gigantic body, tall as well as stout, was not muscular, but flabby. The blood would sometimes rush to his puffy face, then ebb away leaving it of a yellowish pallor; the mouth would be drawn and sour.

Jacoby's practice was a limited one; but he was well-to-do, partly from his wife's side; and the childless pair lived in a comfortable apartment in the Kaiserstrasse and entertained a good deal. This must have been Frau Amra's taste, for it is unthinkable that the lawyer could have cared for it; he participated with an enthusiasm of a peculiarly painful kind. This fat man's character was the oddest in the world. No human being could have been politer, more accommodating, more complaisant than he. But you unconsciously knew that this over-obligingness was somehow forced, that its true source was an inward insecurity and cowardice – the impression it gave was not very pleasant. A man who despises himself is a very ugly sight; worse still when vanity combines with his cowardice to make him wish to please. This was the case, I should say, with Jacoby: his obsequiousness was almost crawling, it went beyond the bounds of personal decency. He was quite capable of saying to a lady as he escorted her to table: 'My dear lady, I am a disgusting creature, but will you do me the honour?' No humour would be mingled with the remark; it was simply cloying, bitter, self-tortured – in a word, disgusting, as he said.

The following once actually happened: the lawyer was taking a walk, and a clumsy porter with a hand-cart ran over his foot. Too late the man stopped his cart and turned round – whereupon Jacoby, quite pale and dazed, his cheeks shaking up and down, took off his hat and stuttered: 'I b-beg your pardon.' A thing like that is infuriating. But this extraordinary colossus seemed perpetually to suffer from a plague of conscience. When he took a walk with his wife on the Lerchenberg, the Corso of the little city, he would roll his eyes round at Amra, walking with her wonderful elastic gait at his side, and bow so anxiously, diligently, and zealously in all directions that he seemed to be begging pardon of all the lieutenants they met for being in unworthy possession of such a beautiful wife. His mouth had a pathetically ingratiating expression, as though he wanted to disarm their scorn.

I have already hinted that the reason why Amra married Jacoby is unfathomable. As for him, he was in love with her, ardently, as people of his physical make-up seldom are, and with such anxious humility as fitted the rest of his character. Sometimes, late in the evening, he would enter their large sleeping-chamber with its high windows and flowered hangings – softly, so softly that there was no sound, only the slow shaking of floor and furniture. He would come up to Amra's massive bed, where she already lay, kneel down, and with infinite caution take her hand. She would lift her brows in a level line, in the quaint way she had, and look at her husband, abject before her in the dim light, with a look of malice and sensuality combined. With his puffy, trembling hands he would softly stroke back the sleeve and press his tragic fat face into the soft brown flesh of her wrist, where little blue veins stood out. And he would speak to her, in a shaking, half-smothered voice, as a sensible man in everyday life never speaks:

'Amra, my dear Amra! I am not disturbing you? You were not asleep yet? Dear God! I have been thinking all day how beautiful you are and how much I love you. I beg you to listen,

for it is so very hard to express what I feel: I love you so much
that sometimes my heart contracts and I do not know where to
turn. I love you beyond my strength. You do not understand
that, I know; but you believe it, and you must say, just one
single time, that you are a little grateful to me. For, you see,
such a love as mine to you is precious, it has its value in this
life of ours. And that you will never betray or deceive me, even
if you cannot love me, just out of gratitude for this love. I have
come to you to beg you, as seriously, as fervently as I can . . .'
here the lawyer's speech would be dissolved in sobs, in low,
bitter weeping, as he knelt. Amra would feel moved; she would
stroke her husband's bristles and say over and over, in the sooth-
ing, contemptuous singsong one uses to a dog who comes to lick
one's feet: 'Yes, yes, good doggy, good doggy!'

And this behaviour of Amra's was certainly not that of a
moral woman. For to relieve my mind of the truth which I
have so far withheld, she did already deceive her husband; she
betrayed him for the embraces of a gentleman named Alfred
Läutner, a gifted young musician, who at twenty-seven had
made himself a small reputation with amusing little compositions. He was a slim young chap with a provocative face, a
flowing blond mane, and a sunny smile in his eyes, of which
he was quite aware. He belonged to the present-day race of
small artists, who do not demand the utmost of themselves,
whose first requirement is to be jolly and happy, who employ
their pleasing little talents to heighten their personal charms.
It pleases them to play in society the role of the naïve genius.
Consciously childlike, entirely unmoral and unscrupulous,
merry and self-satisfied as they are, and healthy enough to enjoy even their disorders, they are agreeable even in their vanity,
so long as that has not been wounded. But woe to these
wretched little poseurs when serious misfortune befalls them,
with which there is no coquetting, and when they can no longer
be pleasant in their own eyes. They will not know how to be
wretched decently and in order, they do not know how to attack
the problem of suffering. They will be destroyed. All that is a
story in itself. But Herr Alfred Läutner wrote pretty things,
mostly waltzes and mazurkas. They would have been rather

too gay and popular to be considered music as I understand it, if each of them had not contained a passage of some originality, a modulation, a harmonic phrasing, some sort of bold effect that betrayed wit and invention, which was evidently the point of the whole and which made it interesting to genuine musicians. Often these two single measures would have a strange plaintive, melancholy tone which would come out abruptly in the midst of a piece of dance-music and as suddenly be gone.

Amra Jacoby was on fire with guilty passion for this young man, and as for him he had not enough moral fibre to resist her seductions. They met here, they met there, and for some years an immoral relation had subsisted between them, known to the whole town, who laughed at it behind the lawyer's back. But what did he think? Amra was not sensitive enough to betray herself on account of a guilty conscience, so we must take it as certain that, however heavy the lawyer's heart, he could cherish no definite suspicions.

Spring had come, rejoicing all hearts; and Amra conceived the most charming idea.

'Christian,' said she – Jacoby's name was Christian – 'let us give a party, a beer party to celebrate the new beer – of course quite simply, but let's have a lot of people.'

'Certainly,' said the lawyer, 'but could we not have it a little later?'

To which Amra made no reply, having passed on to the consideration of details.

'It will be so large that we cannot have it here, we must hire a place, some sort of outdoor restaurant where there is plenty of room and fresh air. You see that, of course. The place I am thinking of is Wendelin's big hall at the foot of the Lerchenberg. The hall is independent of the restaurant and brewery, connected by a passage only. We can decorate it for the occasion and set up long tables, drink our bock, and dance – we must have music and even perhaps some sort of entertainment. There is a little stage, as I happen to know, that makes it very suitable. It will be a very original party and no end of fun.'

The lawyer's face had gone a pale yellow as she spoke, and the corners of his mouth went down. He said:

'My dear Amra! How delightful it will be! I can leave it all too you, you are so clever. Make any arrangements you like.'

And Amra made her arrangements. She took counsel of various ladies and gentlemen, she went in person to hire the hall, she even formed a committee of people who were invited or who volunteered to co-operate in the entertainment. These were exclusively men, except for the wife of Herr Hildebrandt, an actor at the Hoftheater, who was herself a singer. Then there was Herr Hildebrandt, an Assessor Witznagel, a young painter, Alfred Läutner the musician, and some students brought in by Herr Witznagel, who were to do Negro dances.

A week after Amra had made her plan, this committee met in Amra's drawing-room in the Kaiserstrasse – a small, crowded, overheated room, with a heavy carpet, a sofa with quantities of cushions, a fan palm, English leather chairs, and a splay-legged mahogany table with a velvet cover, upon which rested several large illustrated morocco-bound volumes. There was a fireplace too, with a small fire still burning, and on the marble chimney-top were plates of dainty sandwiches, glasses, and two decanters of sherry. Amra reclined in one corner of the sofa under the fan palm, with her legs crossed. She had the beauty of a warm summer night. A thin blouse of light-coloured silk covered her bosom, but her skirt was of heavy dark stuff embroidered with large flowers. Sometimes she put up one hand to brush back the chestnut hair from her narrow forehead. Frau Hildebrandt sat beside her on the sofa; she had red hair and wore riding clothes. Opposite the two all the gentlemen formed a semicircle – among them Jacoby himself, in the lowest chair he could find. He looked unutterably wretched, kept drawing a long breath and swallowing as though struggling against increasing nausea. Herr Alfred Läutner was in tennis clothes – he would not take a chair, but leaned decoratively against the chimney-piece, saying merrily that he could not sit still so long.

Herr Hildebrandt talked sonorously about English songs. He was a most respectable gentleman, in a black suit, with a Roman

head and an assured manner – in short a proper actor for a
court theatre, cultured, knowledgeable, and with enlightened
tastes. He liked to hold forth in condemnation of Ibsen, Zola,
and Tolstoy, all of whom had the same objectionable aims. But
today he was benignly interested in the small affair under dis-
cussion.

'Do you know that priceless song "That's Maria!"?' He
asked. 'Perhaps it is a little racy – but very effective. And then'
so-and-so – he suggested other songs, upon which they came
to an agreement and Frau Hildebrandt said that she would
sing them. The young painter, who had sloping shoulders and a
very blond beard, was to give a burlesque conjuring turn. Herr
Hildebrandt offered to impersonate various famous characters.
In short, everything was developing nicely, the programme was
apparently arranged, when Assessor Witznagel, who had command of fluent gesture and a good many duelling scars, suddenly took the word.

'All very well, ladies and gentlemen, it looks like being most
amusing. But if I may say so, it still lacks something; it wants
some kind of high spot, a climax as it were, something a bit
startling, perhaps, to round the thing off. I leave it to you, I have
nothing particular in mind, I only think ...'

'That is true enough!' Alfred Läutner's tenor voice came
from the chimney-piece where he leaned. 'Witznagel is right.
We need a climax. Let us put our heads together!' He settled
his red belt and looked engagingly about him.

'Well, if we do not consider the famous characters as the
high spot,' said Herr Hildebrandt. Everybody agreed with the
Assessor. Something piquant was wanted for the principal number. Even Jacoby nodded, and murmured: 'Yes, yes, something
jolly and striking. ...' They all reflected.

At the end of a minute's pause, which was broken only by
stifled exclamations, an extraordinary thing happened. Amra
was sitting reclined among the cushions, gnawing as busily as a
mouse at the pointed nail of her little finger. She had a very
odd look on her face: a vacant, almost an irresponsible smile,
which betrayed a sensuality both tormented and cruel. Her eyes,
very bright and wide, turned slowly to the chimney-piece, where

for a second they met the musician's. Then suddenly she jerked her whole body to one side as she sat, in the direction of her husband. With both hands in her lap she stared into his face with an avid and clinging gaze, her own growing visibly paler, and said in her rich, slow voice:

'Christian, suppose you come on at the end as a *chanteuse*, in a red satin baby frock, and do a dance.'

The effect of these few words were tremendous. The young painter essayed to laugh good-humouredly; Herr Hildebrandt, stony-faced, brushed a crumb from his sleeve; his wife coloured up, a rare thing for her; the students coughed and used their handkerchiefs loudly; and Herr Assessor Witznagel simply left the field and got himself a sandwich. The lawyer sat huddled on his little chair, yellow in the face, with a terrified smile. He looked all round the circle, and stammered:

'But, my God ... I – I – I am not up to – not that I – I beg pardon, but ...'

Alfred Läutner had lost his insouciant expression; he even seemed to have reddened a little, and he thrust out his neck to peer searching into Amra's face. He looked puzzled and upset.

But she, Amra, holding the same persuasive pose, went on with the same impressiveness:

'And you must sing, too, Christian, a song which Herr Läutner shall compose, and he can accompany you on the piano. We could not have a better or more effective climax.'

There was a pause, an oppressive pause. Then this extraordinary thing happened, that Herr Läutner, as it were seized upon and carried away by his excitement, took a step forward and his voice fairly trembled with enthusiasm as he said:

'Herr Jacoby, that is a priceless idea, and I am more than ready to compose something. You must have a dance and song, anything else is unthinkable as a wind-up to our affair. You will see, it will be the best thing I have ever written or ever shall write. In a red satin baby frock. Oh, your wife is an artist, only an artist could have hit upon the idea! Do say yes, I beg of you. I will do my part, you will see, it will be an achievement.'

Here the circle broke up and the meeting became lively. Out of politeness, or out of malice, the company began to storm the lawyer with entreaties – Frau Hildebrandt went so far as to say, quite loudly, in her Brünnhilde voice:

'Herr Jacoby, after all, you are such a jolly and entertaining man!'

But the lawyer had pulled himself together and spoke, a little yellow, but with a strong effort at resolution:

'But listen to me, ladies and gentlemen – what can I say to you? It isn't my line, believe me. I have no comic gift, and besides . . . in short, no, it is quite impossible, alas!'

He stuck obstinately to his refusal, and Amra no longer insisted, but sat still with her absent look. Herr Läutner was silent too, staring in deep abstraction at a pattern in the rug. Herr Hildebrandt changed the subject, and presently the committee meeting broke up without coming to a final decision about the 'climax'.

On the evening of the same day Amra had gone to bed and was lying there with her eyes wide open; her husband came lumbering into the bedroom, drew a chair up beside the bed, dropped into it, and said, in a low, hesitating voice:

'Listen, Amra; to be quite frank, I am feeling very disturbed. I refused them today – I did not mean to be offensive – goodness knows I did not mean that. Or do you seriously feel that – I beg you to tell me.'

Amra was silent for a moment, while her brows rose slowly. Then she shrugged her shoulders and said:

'I do not know, my dear friend, how to answer you. You behaved in a way I should not have expected from you. You were unfriendly, you refused to support our enterprise in a way which they flatteringly considered to be indispensable to it. To put it mildly, you disappointed everybody and upset the whole company with your rude lack of compliance. Whereas it was your duty as host –'

The lawyer hung his head and sighed heavily. He said:

'Believe me, Amra, I had no intention to be disobliging. I do not like to offend anybody; if I have behaved badly I am ready to make amends. It is only a joke, after all, an innocent little dressing-up – why not? I will not upset the whole affair, I am ready to . . .'

The following afternoon Amra went out again to 'make preparations'. She drove to Number 78 Holzstrasse and went up to the second storey, where she had an appointment. And when she lay relaxed by the expression of her love she pressed her lover's head passionately to her breast and whispered:

'Write it for four hands. We will accompany him together while he sings and dances. I will see to the costume myself.'

And an extraordinary shiver, a suppressed and spasmodic burst of laughter went through the limbs of both.

For anyone who wants to give a large party out of doors Herr Wendelin's place on the slope of the Lerchenberg is to be recommended. You enter it from the pretty suburban street through a tall trellised gateway and pass into the parklike garden, in the centre of which stands a large hall, connected only by a narrow passage with restaurant, kitchen, and brewery. It is a large, brightly painted wooden hall, in an amusing mixture of Chinese and Renaissance styles. It has folding doors which stand open in good weather to admit the woodland air, and it will hold a great many people.

On this evening as the carriages rolled up they were greeted from afar by the gleam of coloured lights. The whole gateway, the trees, and the hall itself were set thick with lanterns, while the interior made an entrancing sight. Heavy garlands were draped across the ceiling and studded with paper lanterns. Hosts of electric lights hung among the decorations of the walls, which consisted of pine boughs, flags, and artificial flowers; the whole hall was brilliantly lighted. The stage had foliage plants grouped on either side, and a red curtain with a painted design of a presiding genius hovering in the air. A long row of decorated tables ran almost the whole length of the hall. And at these tables the guests of Attorney Jacoby were doing themselves well on cold roast veal and bock beer. There were certainly more than a hundred and fifty people: officers, lawyers, business men, artists, upper officials, with their wives and daughters. They were quite simply dressed, in black coats and light spring toilettes, for this was a jolly, informal occasion. The gentlemen carried their mugs in person to the big casks against one of the walls; the spacious, festive, brightly lighted room was filled with a heavy sweetish atmosphere of evergreen boughs, flowers, beer, food, and human beings; and there was a clatter and buzz of laughter and talk – the loud, simple talk and the high, good-natured, unrestrained, carefree laughter of the sort of people there assembled.

The attorney sat shapeless and helpless at one end of the table, near the stage. He drank little and now and then addressed a laboured remark to his neighbour, Frau Regierungsrat Havermann. He breathed offensively, the corners of his mouth hung down, he stared fixedly with his bulging watery eyes into the lively scene, with a sort of melancholy remoteness, as though there resided in all this noisy merriment something inexpressibly painful and perplexing.

Large fruit tarts were now being handed round for the company to cut from; they drank sweet wine with these, and the time for the speeches arrived. Herr Hildebrandt celebrated the new brew in a speech almost entirely composed of classical quotations, even Greek. Herr Witznagel, with florid gestures and ingenious turns of phrase, toasted the ladies, taking a handful of flowers from the nearest vase and comparing each flower to some feminine charm. Amra Jacoby, who sat opposite him in a pale-yellow silk frock, he called 'a lovelier sister of the Maréchal Niel'.

Then she nodded meaningfully to her husband, brushing back her hair from her forehead; whereupon the fat man arose and almost ruined the whole atmosphere by stammering a few words with painful effort, smiling a repulsive smile. Some half-hearted bravos rewarded him, then there was an oppressive pause, after which jollity resumed its sway. All smoking, all a little elevated by drink, they rose from table and with their own hands and a great deal of noise removed the tables from the hall to make way for the dancing.

It was after eleven and high spirits reigned supreme. Some of the guests streamed out into the brightly lighted garden to get the fresh air; others stood about the hall in groups, smoking, chatting, drawing beer from the kegs, and drinking it standing. Then a loud trumpet call sounded from the stage, summoning everybody to the entertainment. The band arrived and took its place before the curtain; rows of chairs were put in place and red programmes distributed on them; the gentlemen ranged themselves along the walls. There was an expectant hush.

The band played a noisy overture, and the curtains parted to reveal a row of Negroes horrifying to behold in their barbaric costumes and their blood-red lips, gnashing their teeth and emitting savage yells.

Certainly the entertainment was the crowning success of Amra's party. As it went on, the applause grew more and more enthusiastic. Frau Hildebrandt came on in a powdered wig, pounded with a shepherdess's crook on the floor and sang – in too large a voice – 'That's Maria!' A conjuror in a dress coat covered with orders performed the most amazing feats; Herr Hildebrandt impersonated Goethe, Bismarck, and Napoleon in an amazingly lifelike manner; and a newspaper editor, Dr Wiesensprung, improvised a humorous lecture which had as its theme bock beer and its social significance. And now the suspense reached its height, for it was time for the last, the mysterious number which appeared on the programme framed in a laurel wreath and was entitled: '*Little Lizzy*. Song and Dance. Music by Alfred Läutner.'

A movement swept through the hall, and people's eyes met as the band sat down at their instruments and Alfred Läutner came from the doorway where he had been lounging with a cigarette between his pouting lips to take his place beside Amra Jacoby at the piano, which stood in the centre of the stage in front of the curtains. Herr Läutner's face was flushed and he turned over his manuscript score nervously; Amra for her part was rather pale. She leaned one arm on the back of her chair and looked loweringly at the audience. The bell rang, the pianists played a few bars of an insignificant accompaniment, the curtains parted, little Lizzy appeared.

The whole audience stiffened with amazement as that tragic and bedizened bulk shambled with a sort of bear-dance into view. It was Jacoby. A wide, shapeless garment of crimson satin, without folds, fell to his feet; it was cut out above to make a repulsive display of the fat neck, stippled with white powder. The sleeves consisted merely of a shoulder puff, but the flabby arms were covered by long lemon-coloured gloves; on the head perched a high blond wig with a swaying green feather. And under the wig was a face, a puffy, pasty, unhappy, and desperately mirthful face, with cheeks that shook pathetically up and down and little red-rimmed eyes that strained in anguish towards the floor and saw nothing else at all. The fat man hoisted himself with effort from one leg to the other, while with his hands he either held up his skirts or else weakly raised his index fingers – these two gestures he had and knew no others. In a choked and gasping voice he sang; to the accompaniment of the piano.

The lamentable figure exhaled more than ever a cold breath of anguish. It killed every light-hearted enjoyment and lay like an oppressive weight upon the assembled audience. Horror was in the depths of all these spellbound eyes, gazing at this pair at the piano and at that husband there. The monstrous, unspeakable scandal lasted five long minutes.

Then came a moment which none of those present will forget as long as they live. Let us picture to ourselves what happened in that frightful and frightfully involved little instant of time.

You know of course the absurd little jingle called 'Lizzy'. And you remember the lines:

> I can polka until I am dizzy,
> I can waltz with the best and beyond,
> I'm the popular pet, little Lizzy,
> Who makes all the menfolks so fond –

which form the trivial and unlovely refrain to three longish stanzas. Alfred Läutner had composed a new setting to the verses I have quoted, and it was, as he had said it would be, his masterpiece. He had, that is, brought to its highest pitch his little artifice of introducing into a fairly vulgar and humorous piece of hack-work a sudden phrase of genuine art. The melody, in C-sharp major, had been in the first bars rather pretty and perfectly banal. At the beginning of the refrain the rhythm became livelier and dissonances occurred, which by means of the

constant accentuation of a B-natural made one expect a transition into F-sharp major. These dissonances went on developing
until the word 'beyond'; and after the 'I'm the' a culmination
into F-sharp major should have followed. Instead of which the
most surprising thing happened. That is, through a harsh turn,
by means of an inspiration which was almost a stroke of genius,
the key changed to F-major, and this little interlude which followed, with the use of both pedals on the long-drawn-out first
syllable of the word 'Lizzy', was indescribably, almost grue-
somely effective. It was a complete surprise, an abrupt assault
on the nerves, it shivered down the back, it was a miracle, a
revelation, it was like a curtain suddenly torn away to reveal
something nude.

And on the F-major chord Attorney Jacoby stopped dancing.
He stood still, he stood as though rooted to the stage with his
two forefingers lifted, one a little lower than the other. The
word 'Lizzy' stuck in his throat, he was dumb; almost at the
same time the accompaniment broke sharp off, and the incredible, absurd, and ghastly figure stood there frozen, with his
head thrust forward like a steer's, staring with inflamed eyes
straight before him. He stared into the brightly lighted,
decorated, crowded hall, in which, like an exhalation from all
these people, the scandal hung and thickened into visibility. He
stared at all these upturned faces, foreshortened and distorted
by the lighting, into these hundreds of pairs of eyes all directed
with the same knowing expression upon himself and the two
at the piano. In a frightful stillness, unbroken by the smallest
sound, his gaze travelled slowly and uneasily from the pair to
the audience, from the audience to the pair, while his eyes
widened more and more. Then knowledge seemed to flash
across his face, like a sudden rush of blood, making it red as
the frock he wore, only to give way to a waxen yellow pallor –
and the fat man collapsed, making the platform creak beneath
his weight.

For another moment the stillness reigned. Then there came
shrieks, hubbub ensued, a few gentlemen took heart to spring
upon the platform, among them a young doctor – and the curtains were drawn together.

Amra Jacoby and Alfred Läutner still sat at the piano. They had turned a little away from each other, and he, with his head bent, seemed to be listening to the echo of his F-major chord, while she, with her birdlike brain, had not yet grasped the situation, but gazed round her with vacant face.

The young doctor came back presently. He was a little Jewish gentleman with a serious face and a small pointed beard. Some people surrounded him at the door with questions — to which he replied with a shrug of the shoulders and the words:

'All over.'

THE WARDROBE

(1899)

It was cloudy, cool, and half-dark when the Berlin–Rome express drew in at a middle-sized station on its way. Albrecht van der Qualen, solitary traveller in a first-class compartment with lace covers over the plush upholstery, roused himself and sat up. He felt a flat taste in his mouth, and in his body the none-too-agreeable sensations produced when the train comes to a stop after a long journey and we are aware of the cessation of rhythmic motion and conscious of calls and signals from without. It is like coming to oneself out of drunkenness or lethargy. Our nerves, suddenly deprived of the supporting rhythm, feel bewildered and forlorn. And this the more if we have just roused out of the heavy sleep one falls into in a train.

Albrecht van der Qualen stretched a little, moved to the window, and let down the pane. He looked along the train. Men were busy at the mail van, unloading and loading parcels. The engine gave out a series of sounds, it snorted and rumbled a bit, standing still, but only as a horse stands still, lifting its hoof, twitching its ears, and awaiting impatiently the signal to go on. A tall, stout woman in a long raincoat, with a face expressive of nothing but worry, was dragging a hundred-pound suitcase along the train, propelling it before her with pushes from one knee. She was saying nothing, but looking heated and distressed. Her upper lip stuck out, with little beads of sweat upon it – altogether she was a pathetic figure. 'You poor dear thing,' van der Qualen thought. 'If I could help you, soothe you, take you in – only for the sake of that upper lip. But each for himself, so things are arranged in life; and I stand here at this moment perfectly carefree, looking at you as I might at a beetle that has fallen on its back.'

It was half-dark in the station shed. Dawn or twilight – he did not know. He had slept, who could say whether for two, five, or twelve hours? He had sometimes slept for twenty-four, or even more, unbrokenly, an extraordinarily profound sleep. He wore a half-length dark-brown winter overcoat with a velvet collar. From his features it was hard to judge his age: one might actually hesitate between twenty-five and the end of the thirties. He had a yellowish skin, but his eyes were black like live coals and had deep shadows round them. These eyes boded nothing good. Several doctors, speaking frankly as man to man, had not given him many more months. – His dark hair was smoothly parted on one side.

In Berlin – although Berlin had not been the beginning of his journey – he had climbed into the train just as it was moving off – incidentally with his red leather hand-bag. He had gone to sleep and now at waking felt himself so completely absolved from time that a sense of refreshment streamed through him. He rejoiced in the knowledge that at the end of the thin gold chain he wore round his neck there was only a little medallion in his waistcoat pocket. He did not like to be aware of the hour or of the day of the week, and moreover he had no truck with the calendars. Some time ago he had lost the habit of knowing the day of the month or even the month of the year. Everything must be in the air – so he put it in his mind, and the phrase was comprehensive though rather vague. He was seldom or never disturbed in this programme, as he took pains to keep all upsetting knowledge at a distance from him. After all, was it not enough for him to know more or less what season it was? 'It is more or less autumn,' he thought, gazing out into the damp and gloomy train shed. 'More I do not know. Do I even know where I am?'

His satisfaction at this thought amounted to a thrill of pleasure. No, he did not know where he was! Was he still in Germany? Beyond a doubt. In North Germany? That remained to be seen. While his eyes were still heavy with sleep the window of his compartment had glided past an illuminated sign; it probably had the name of the station on it, but not the picture of a single letter had been transmitted to his brain. In still dazed condition he had heard the conductor call the name two or three times, but not a syllable had he grasped. But out there in a twilight of which he knew not so much as whether it was

morning or evening lay a strange place, an unknown town. —
Albrecht van der Qualen took his felt hat out of the rack, seized
his red leather hand-bag, the strap of which secured a red and
white silk and wool plaid into which was rolled an umbrella
with a silver crook — and although his ticket was labelled
Florence, he left the compartment and the train, walked along
the shed, deposited his luggage at the cloakroom, lighted a
cigar, thrust his hands — he carried neither stick nor umbrella
— into his overcoat pockets, and left the station.

Outside in the damp, gloomy, and nearly empty square five
or six hackney coachmen were snapping their whips, and a man
with braided cap and long cloak is which he huddled shivering inquired politely: 'Hotel zum braven Mann?' Van der
Qualen thanked him politely and held on his way. The people
whom he met had their coat-collars turned up; he put his up too,
nestled his chin into the velvet, smoked, and went his way, not
slowly and not too fast.

He passed along a low wall and an old gate with two massive
towers; he crossed a bridge with statues on the railings and saw
the water rolling slow and turbid below. A long wooden boat,
ancient and crumbling, came by, sculled by a man with a long
pole in the stern. Van der Qualen stood for a while leaning over
the rail of the bridge. 'Here,' he said to himself, 'is a river; here
is *the* river. It is nice to think that I call it that because I do not
know its name.' —Then he went on.

He walked straight on for a little, on the pavement of a street
which was neither very narrow nor very broad; then he turned
off to the left. It was evening. The electric arc-lights came on,
flickered, glowed, sputtered, and then illuminated the gloom.
The shops were closing. 'So we may say that it is in every respect autumn,' thought van der Qualen, proceeding along the
wet black pavement. He wore no galoshes, but his boots were
very thick-soled, durable, and firm, and withal not lacking in
elegance.

He held to the left. Men moved past him, they hurried on
their business or coming from it. 'And I move with them,' he
thought, 'and am as alone and as strange as probably no man
has ever been before. I have no business and no goal. I have not

even a stick to lean upon. More remote, freer, more detached, no one can be, I owe nothing to anybody, nobody owes anything to me. God has never held out His hand over me, He knows me not at all. Honest unhappiness without charity is a good thing; a man can say to himself: I owe God nothing.'

He soon came to the edge of the town. Probably he had slanted across it at about the middle. He found himself on a broad suburban street with trees and villas, turned to his right, passed three or four cross-streets almost like village lanes, lighted only by lanterns, and came to a stop in a somewhat wider one before a wooden door next to a commonplace house painted a dingy yellow, which had nevertheless the striking feature of very convex and quite opaque plate-glass windows. But on the door was a sign: 'In this house on the third floor there are rooms to let.' 'Ah!' he remarked; tossed away the end of his cigar, passed through the door along a boarding which formed the dividing line between two properties, and then turned left through the door of the house itself. A shabby grey runner ran across the entry. He covered it in two steps and began to mount the simple wooden stair.

The doors to the several apartments were very modest too; they had white glass panes with woven wire over them and on some of them were name-plates. The landings were lighted by oil lamps. On the third storey, the top one, for the attic came next, were entrances right and left, simple brown doors without name-plates. Van der Qualen pulled the brass bell in the middle. It rang, but there was no sign from within. He knocked left. No answer. He knocked right. He heard light steps within, very long, like strides, and the door opened.

A woman stood there, a lady, tall, lean, and old. She wore a cap with a large pale-lilac bow and an old-fashioned, faded black gown. She had a sunken birdlike face and on her brow there was an eruption, a sort of fungus growth. It was rather repulsive.

'Good evening,' said van der Qualen. 'The rooms?'

The old lady nodded; she nodded and smiled slowly, without a word, understandingly, and with her beautiful long white hand made a slow, languid, and elegant gesture towards the

next, the left-hand door. Then she retired and appeared again
with a key. 'Look,' he thought, standing behind her as she unlocked the door; 'you are like some kind of banshee, a figure
out of Hoffmann, madam.' She took the oil lamp from its hook
and ushered him in.

It was a small, low-ceiled room with a brown floor. Its walls
were covered with straw-coloured matting. There was a window at the back in the right-hand wall, shrouded in long, thin
white muslin folds. A white door also on the right led into the
next room. This room was pathetically bare, with staring white
walls, against which three straw chairs, painted pink, stood out
like strawberries from whipped cream. A wardrobe, a washing-
stand with a mirror. ... The bed, a mammoth mahogany piece,
stood free in the middle of the room.

'Have you any objections?' asked the old woman, and passed
her lovely long, white hand lightly over the fungus growth on
her forehead. – It was as though she had said that by accident
because she could not think for the moment of a more ordinary
phrase. For she added at once: '– so to speak?'

'No, I have no objections,' said van der Qualen. 'The rooms
are rather cleverly furnished. I will take them. I'd like to have
somebody fetch my luggage from the station, here is the ticket.
You will be kind enough to make up the bed and give me some
water. I'll take the house key now, and the key to the apartment. ... I'd like a couple of towels. I'll wash up and go into
the city for supper and come back later.'

He drew a nickel case out of his pocket, took out some soap,
and began to wash his face and hands, looking as he did so
through the convex window-panes far down over the muddy,
gas-lit suburban streets, over the arc-lights and the villas. –
As he dried his hands he went over to the wardrobe. It was a
square one, varnished brown, rather shaky, with a simple
curved top. It stood in the centre of the right-hand wall exactly
in the niche of a second white door, which of course led into
the rooms to which the main and middle door on the landing
gave access. 'Here is something in the world that is well
arranged,' thought van der Qualen. 'This wardrobe fits into
the door niche as though it were made for it.' He opened the

wardrobe door. It was entirely empty, with several rows of hooks in the ceiling; but it proved to have no back, being closed behind by a piece of rough, common grey burlap, fastened by nails or tacks at the four corners.

Van der Qualen closed the wardrobe door, took his hat, turned up the collar of his coat once more, put out the candle, and set forth. As he went through the front room he thought to hear mingled with the sound of his own steps a sort of ringing in the other room: a soft, clear, metallic sound – but perhaps he was mistaken. As though a gold ring were to fall into a silver basin, he thought, as he locked the outer door. He went down the steps and out of the gate and took the way to the town.

In a busy street he entered a lighted restaurant and sat down at one of the front tables, turning his back to all the world. He ate a *soupe aux fines herbes* with croûtons, a steak with a poached egg, a compote and wine, a small piece of green gor-gonzola and half a pear. While he paid and put on his coat he took a few puffs from a Russian cigarette, then lighted a cigar and went out. He strolled for a while, found his homeward route into the suburb, and went leisurely back.

The house with the plate-glass windows lay quite dark and silent when van der Qualen opened the house door and mounted the dim stair. He lighted himself with matches as he went, and opened the left-hand brown door in the third storey. He laid hat and overcoat on the divan, lighted the lamp on the big writing-table, and found there his hand-bag as well as the plaid and umbrella. He unrolled the plaid and got a bottle of cognac, then a little glass and took a sip now and then as he sat in the arm-chair finishing his cigar. 'How fortunate, after all,' thought he, 'that there is cognac in the world!' Then he went into the bedroom, where he lighted the candle on the night-table, put out the light in the other room, and began to un-dress. Piece by piece he put down his good, unobtrusive grey suit on the red chair beside the bed; but then as he loosened his braces he remembered his hat and overcoat, which still lay on the couch. He fetched them into the bedroom and opened the wardrobe. . . . He took a step backwards and reached behind him to clutch one of the large dark-red mahogany balls which ornamented the bedposts. The room, with its four white walls, from which the three pink chairs stood out like strawberries from whipped cream, lay in the unstable light of the candle. But the wardrobe over there was open and it was not empty. Somebody was standing in it, a creature so lovely that Albrecht van der Qualen's heart stood still a moment and then in long, deep, quiet throbs resumed its beating. She was quite nude and one of her slender arms reached up to crook a forefinger round one of the hooks in the ceiling of the wardrobe. Long waves of brown hair rested on the childlike shoulders – they breathed that charm to which the only answer is a sob. The candlelight was mirrored in her narrow black eyes. Her mouth was a little large, but it had an expression as sweet as the lips of sleep when after long days of pain they kiss our brow. Her ankles nestled and her slender limbs clung to one another.

Albrecht van der Qualen rubbed one hand over his eyes and stared ... and he saw that down in the right corner the sacking was loosened from the back of the wardrobe. 'What –' said he ... 'won't you come in – or how should I put it – out? Have a little glass of cognac? Half a glass?' But he expected no answer to this and he got none. Her narrow, shining eyes, so very black that they seemed bottomless and inexpressive – they were directed upon him, but aimlessly and somewhat blurred, as though they did not see him.

'Shall I tell you a story?' she said suddenly in a low, husky voice.

'Tell me a story,' he answered. He had sunk down in a sitting posture on the edge of the bed, his overcoat lay across his knees with his folded hands resting upon it. His mouth stood a little open, his eyes half-closed. But the blood pulsated warm and mildly through his body and there was a gentle singing in his ears. She had let herself down in the cupboard and embraced a drawn-up knee with her slender arms, while the other leg stretched out before her. Her little breasts were pressed together by her upper arm, and the light gleamed on the skin of her flexed knee. She talked ... talked in a soft voice, while the candle-flame performed its noiseless dance.

Two walked on the heath and her head lay on his shoulder.

There was a perfume from all growing things, but the evening mist already rose from the ground. So it began. And often it was in verse, rhyming in that incomparably sweet and flowing way that comes to us now and again in the half-slumber of fever. But it ended badly; a sad ending: the two holding each other indissolubly embraced and, while their lips rest on each other, one stabbing the other above the waist with a broad knife – and not without good cause. So it ended. And then she stood up with an infinitely sweet and modest gesture, lifted the grey sacking at the right-hand corner – and was no more there.

From now on he found her every evening in the wardrobe and listened to her stories – how many evenings? How many days, weeks, or months did he remain in this house and in this city? It would profit nobody to know. Who would care for a miserable statistic? And we are aware that Albrecht van der Qualen had been told by several physicians that he had but a few months to live. She told him stories. They were sad stories, without relief; but they rested like a sweet burden upon the heart and made it beat longer and more blissfully. Often he forgot himself. – His blood swelled up in him, he stretched out his hands to her, and she did not resist him. But then for several evenings he did not find her in the wardrobe, and when she came back she did not tell him anything for several evenings and then by degrees resumed, until he again forgot himself.

How long it lasted – who knows? Who even knows whether Albrecht van der Qualen actually awoke on that grey afternoon and went into the unknown city; whether he did not remain asleep in his first-class carriage and let the Berlin–Rome express bear him swiftly over the mountains? Would any of us care to take the responsibility of giving a definite answer? It is all uncertain. 'Everything must be in the air ...'

THE WAY TO THE CHURCHYARD

(1901)

THE way to the churchyard ran along beside the highroad, ran beside it all the way to the end; that is to say, to the churchyard. On the other side of it were houses, new suburban houses, some of them still unfinished; after the houses came fields. The highroad was flanked by trees, gnarled beeches of considerable age, and half of it was paved and half not. But the way to the churchyard had a sprinkling of gravel, which made it seem like a pleasant foot-path. Between highroad and path ran a narrow dry ditch, filled with grass and wild flowers.

It was spring, it was nearly summer. The world was smiling, God's blue sky was filled with nothing but small, round, dense little morsels of cloud, tufted all over with funny little dabs of snowy white. The birds were twittering in the beeches, and a soft wind blew across the fields.

A wagon from the next village was going along the highroad towards the town, half on the paved, half on the unpaved part of the road. The driver's legs were hanging down both sides of the shaft, he was whistling out of tune. At the end of the wagon, with its back to the driver, sat a little yellow dog. It had a pointed muzzle and it gazed with an unspeakably solemn and collected air back over the way by which it had come. It was a most admirable little dog, good as gold, a pleasure to contemplate. But no, it does not belong to the matter in hand, we must pass it by. – A troop of soldiers came along, from the barracks close at hand; they marched in their own dust and sang. Another wagon passed, coming from the town and going to the next village. The driver was asleep and there was no dog; hence this wagon is devoid of interest. Two journeymen followed after it, one of them a giant, the other a hunchback. They walked barefoot, because they were carrying their boots on their backs; they shouted a good-natured greeting to the sleeping driver and went their way. Yes, this was but a moderate traffic, which pursued its ends without complications or incidents.

On the path to the churchyard walked a single figure, going slowly, with bent head, and leaning on a black stick. This man was named Piepsam, Praisegod Piepsam and no other name. I mention it expressly because of his ensuing most singular behaviour.

He wore black, for he was on his way to visit the graves of his loved ones. He had on a furry top hat with a wide brim, a frock-coat shiny with age, trousers both too tight and too short, and black kid gloves with all the shine rubbed off. His neck, a long, shrivelled neck with a huge Adam's apple, rose out of a frayed turn-over collar — yes, this turn-over collar was already rough at the corners. Sometimes the man raised his head to see how far away the churchyard still was; and then you got a glimpse of a strange face, a face, unquestionably, which you would not easily forget.

It was smooth-shaven and pallid. But a knobbly nose stuck out between the sunken cheeks, and this nose glowed with immoderate and unnatural redness and swarmed with little pimples, unhealthy excrescences which gave it an uneven and fantastic outline. The deep glow of the nose stood out against the dead paleness of the face; there was something artificial and improbable about it, as though he had put it on, like a carnival nose, and was wearing it as a sort of funereal joke. But it was no joke. — His mouth was big, with drooping corners, and he held it tightly compressed. His eyebrows were black, strewn with little white hairs, and when he glanced up from the ground he lifted them till they disappeared under the brim of his hat and you got a good view of the pathetically inflamed and red-rimmed eyes. In short, this was a face bound in the end to evoke one's pity.

Praisegod Piepsam's appearance was not enlivening, it fitted ill into the lovely afternoon; even for a man who was visiting the graves of his dear departed he looked much too depressed. His inner man, however, could one have seen within him, amply explained and justified the outward state. Yes, he was a bit depressed, a bit unhappy, a little hardly treated — is it so hard for happy people like yourselves to enter into his feelings? But the fact was, things were not going just a little badly with him, they were bad in a very high degree.

In the first place, he drank. We shall come on to that later. And he was a widower, bereft and forsaken of all the world, there was not a soul on earth to love him. His wife, born Lebzelt, had been taken from him six months before, when she had presented him with a child. It was the third child, and it was born dead. The others were dead too, one of diphtheria, the other of nothing in particular, save general insufficiency. And as though that were not enough, he had lost his job, been deprived with contumely of his position and his daily bread — naturally on account of his vice, which was stronger than Piepsam.

Once he had been able to resist it, to some extent, though yielding to it by bouts. But when his wife and child were snatched from him, when he had no work and no position, nothing to support him, when he stood alone on this earth, then his weakness took more and more the upper hand. He had been a clerk in the office of a benefit society, a sort of superior copyist who got ninety marks a month. But he had been drunken and negligent and after repeated warnings had finally been discharged.

Certainly this did not improve Piepsam's morale. Indeed he declined more and more to his fall. Wretchedness, in fact, is destructive to our human dignity and self-respect — it does us no harm to get a little understanding of these matters. For there is much that is strange about them, not to say thrilling. It does the man no good to keep on protesting that he is not guilty, for in most cases he despises himself for his own unhappiness. And self-contempt and bad conduct stand in the most frightful mutual relation: they feed each other, they play into each other's hands, in a way shocking to behold. Thus was it with Piepsam. He drank because he had no self-respect, and he had no self-respect because the continual breakdown of his good intentions ate it away. At home in his wardrobe he kept a bottle with a poisonous-coloured liquor in it, the name of which I will refrain from mentioning. Before this wardrobe Praisegod Piepsam had before now gone literally on his knees, and in his wrestlings had bitten his tongue – and still in the end capitulated. I do not like even to mention such things – but after all they are very instructive.

Now he was taking his way to the churchyard, striking his black stick before him as he went. The gentle breeze played about his nose too, but he felt it not. A lost and most miserable human being, he stared straight ahead of him with lifted brows. – Suddenly he heard a noise behind him and listened; it was a little rustling sound coming on swiftly from the distance. He turned round and stopped. – A bicycle was approaching at full tilt, its pneumatic tyres crunching the gravel; it slowed down because Piepsam stood directly in the way.

A young man perched on the saddle, a youth, a blithe and carefree cyclist. He made no claims to belong to the great and mighty of this earth – oh, dear me, not at all! He rode a cheapish machine, of no matter what make, worth perhaps two hundred marks, at a guess. On it he rode abroad, he came out from the city and the sun glittered on his pedals as he rode straight into God's great out-of-doors – hurrah, hurrah! He wore a coloured shirt with a grey jacket, gaiters, and the sauciest cap in the world, a perfect joke of a cap, brown checks and a button on top. Underneath it a thick sheaf of blond hair stuck out on his forehead. His eyes were blue lightnings. He came on, like life itself, ringing his bell. But Piepsam did not budge a hair's breadth out of the way. He stood there and looked at Life – unbudgeably.

Life flung him an angry glance and went past – whereupon Piepsam too began to move forwards. When Life got abreast of him he said slowly, with dour emphasis:

'Number nine thousand seven hundred and seven.' He clipped his lips together and looked unflinchingly at the ground, feeling Life's angry eye upon him.

Life had turned round, grasping the saddle behind it with one hand and slowly pedalling.

'What did you say?' asked Life.

'Number nine thousand seven hundred and seven,' Piepsam reiterated. 'Oh, nothing. I am going to report you.'

'You are going to report me?' asked Life; turned round still farther and rode still slower, so that it had to keep its balance by straightening the handle-bars.

'Certainly,' said Piepsam, some five or six paces away.

'Why?' asked Life, getting off. It stood there in an expectant attitude.

'You know very well yourself.'

'No, I do not know.'

'You must know.'

'No, I do not know,' said Life, 'and besides, it interests me very little, I must say.' It turned to its bicycle as though to mount. Life certainly had a tongue in its head.

'I am going to report you for riding here on the path to the churchyard instead of out on the highroad,' said Piepsam.

'But, my dear sir,' said Life with a short impatient laugh, turning round again, 'look at the marks of bicycles all the way along. Everybody uses this path.'

'It makes no difference to me,' replied Piepsam. 'I am going to report you all the same.'

'Just as you please,' said Life, and mounted its machine. It really mounted at one go, with a single push of the foot, secured its seat in the saddle, and bent to the task of getting up as much speed as its temperament required.

'Well, if you go on riding here on the foot-path I will certainly report you,' said Piepsam again, his voice rising and trembling. But Life paid no attention at all; it went on gathering speed.

If you could have seen Praisegod Piepsam's face at that moment, it would have shocked you deeply. He compressed his lips so tightly that his cheeks and even his red-hot nose were drawn out of shape. His eyebrows were lifted as high as they would go and he stared after the departing bicycle with a maniac expression. Suddenly he gave a forward rush and covered running the small space between him and Life. He laid hold on the little leather pocket behind the saddle and held fast with both hands. He clung to it with lips drawn out of human semblance, and tugged wild-eyed and speechless, with all his strength, at the moving and wobbling machine. It seemed from the appear-

ances in doubt whether he was seeking with malice afore-
thought to stop it or whether he had been struck with the idea
of mounting behind Life and riding with glittering pedals into
God's great out-of-doors, hurrah, hurrah! No bicycle could
stand the weight; it stopped, it leaned over, it fell.

But now Life became violent. It had come to a stop with one
leg on the ground; it stretched out its right arm and gave Herr
Piepsam such a push in the chest that he staggered several steps
backwards. Then it said, its voice swelling to a threat:

'You are probably drunk, fellow! But if you continue to
try to stop me, my fine lad, I'll just chop you into little bits – do
you understand? I'll tear you limb from limb. Kindly get that
through your head.' Then Life turned its back on Herr Piepsam, pulled its cap furiously down on its brow, and once more
mounted its bicycle. Yes, Life certainly had a tongue in its
head. And it mounted as neatly as before, in one go, settled
into the saddle, and had the machine at once under control.
Piepsam saw its back retreating faster and faster.

He stood there gasping, staring after Life. And Life did not
fall over, no mishap occurred, no tyre burst, no stone lay in the
way. It moved off on its rubber wheels. Then Piepsam began to
shriek and rail; his voice was no longer melancholy at all, you
might call it a roar.

'You are not to go on!' he shouted. 'You shall not go on.
You are to ride out on the road and not here on the way to the
churchyard – do you hear? Get off, get off at once! I will report
you, I will enter an action against you. Oh, Lord, oh, God, if
you were to fall off, if you would only fall off, you rascally windbag, I would stamp on you, I would stamp on your face with
my boots, you damned villain, you –'

Never was seen such a sight. A man raving mad on the way
to the churchyard, a man with his face swollen with roaring, a
man dancing with rage, capering, flinging his arms about,
quite out of control. The bicycle was out of sight by this time,
but still Piepsam stood where he was and raved.

'Stop him, stop him! Ride on the path to the churchyard,
will he? You blackguard! You outrageous puppy, you! You
damned monkey, I'd like to skin you alive, you with the blue

eyes, you silly cur, you windbag, you blockhead, you ignorant ninny! You get off! Get off this very minute! Won't anybody pitch him off in the dirt? Riding, eh? On the way to the church-yard! Pull him down, damned puppy. ... Oh, if I had hold of you, eh? What wouldn't I do? Devil scratch your eyes out, you ignorant, ignorant, ignorant fool!'

Piepsam went on from this to expressions which cannot be set down. Foaming at the mouth, he uttered the most shame-less objurgations, while his voice cracked in his throat and his writhings grew more fantastic. A few children with a fox-terrier and a basket crossed over from the road; they climbed the ditch, surrounded the shrieking man and peered into his distorted face. Some labourers at work on the new houses, just about to take their midday rest, saw that something was going on and joined the group – there were both men and women among them. But Piepsam went on, his frenzy grew worse and worse. Blind with rage he shook his fist at all four quarters of the heavens, whirled round on himself, bounded and bent his knees and bobbed up again in the extremity of his effort to shriek even louder. He did not stop for breath and where all his words came from was the greatest wonder. His face was frightfully puffed out, his top hat sat on the back of his neck, and his shirt hung out of his waistcoat. By now he had passed on from the particular to the general and was making remarks which had nothing at all to do with the situation: references to his own vicious mode of life, and religious allusions which certainly sounded strange in such a voice, mingled as they were with his dissolute curses.

'Come on, come on, all of you!' he bellowed. 'Not only you and you and you but all the rest of you, with your blue-lightning eyes and your little caps with buttons. I will shriek the truth in your ears and it will fill you with everlasting horror. ... So you are grinning, so you are shrugging your shoulders? I drink ... well, yes, of course I drink. I am even a drunkard, if you want to know. What does that signify? It is not yet the last day of all. The day will come, you good-for-nothing vermin, when God shall weigh us all in the balance ... ah, the Son of Man shall come in the clouds, you filth, and His justice is not of this world. He will hurl you into outer darkness, all you light-headed breed, and there shall be wailing and . . .'

He was now surrounded by a crowd of some size. People were laughing at him, some were frowning. More hod-carriers and labourers, men and women, came over from the unfinished buildings. A driver got down from his wagon and jumped the ditch, whip in hand. One man shook Piepsam by the arm, but nothing came of it. A troop of soldiers marched by, turning to look at the scene and laughing. The fox-terrier could no longer contain itself; it braced its forefeet and howled into Piepsam's face with its tail between its legs.

Then Praisegod Piepsam screamed once more with all his strength: 'Get off, get off at once, you ignorant fool!' He described with one arm a wide half-circle – and collapsed. He lay there, his voice abruptly silenced, a black heap surrounded by the curious throng. His wide-brimmed hat blew off, bounced once, and then lay on the ground.

Two masons bent over the motionless Piepsam and considered his case in the moderate and reasonable tone that working-people have. One of them then got on his legs and went off at a run. The other made experiments with the unconscious man. He sprinkled him with water from a tub, he poured out brandy in the hollow of his hand and rubbed Piepsam's temples with it. None of these efforts were crowned with success.

Some little time passed. Then the sound of wheels was heard and a wagon came along the road. It was an ambulance with a great red cross on each side, drawn by two charming little horses. Two men in neat uniforms got down from the box; one went to the back of the wagon, opened it, and drew out a stretcher; the other ran over to the path, pushed away the yokels standing round Piepsam, and with the help of one of them got Herr Piepsam out of the crowd and into the road. He was laid out on the stretcher and shoved into the wagon as one shoves a loaf of bread into the oven. The door clicked shut and the two men climbed back onto the box. All that went off very efficiently, with but few and practised motions, as though in a theatre. And then they drove Praisegod Piepsam away.

THE HUNGRY

(1902)

THERE came the moment when Detlef was struck by the sense of his own superfluity; as though by chance he let himself be borne away by the bustling throng and disappeared from the sight of his two companions without taking leave.

He gave himself to the current which bore him the whole length of the splendid auditorium; not until he knew that he was far away from Lily and the little painter did he resist the tide and stop in his tracks. He was by then near the stage, leaning against the heavily gilt projecting front of a proscenium box, between a bearded baroque caryatid with neck bent to his burden and his female counterpart whose swelling bosoms were thrust out into the hall. He put on as well as he could the air of a complacent observer, lifting his glasses now and then to his eyes – but in the brilliant circle which they swept he avoided one single point.

The fête was at its height. At the back of these swelling boxes eating and drinking were going on at laden tables, gentlemen in black and coloured dress suits, with mammoth chrysanthemums in their buttonholes, bent over the powdered shoulders of fantastically garbed and extravagantly coiffed ladies, talking and pointing down upon the motley and the bustle in the hall below as it formed eddies and currents, got choked and streamed on again, in quick and colourful play.

There were women in flowing robes, with barge-shaped hats fastened in outlandish curves beneath their chins, leaning on tall staves, holding long-handled lorgnons to their eyes. The puffed sleeves of the men came almost to the brims of their grey top hats. Loud jests mounted to the upper tiers, healths were wafted thitherwards in brimming glasses of champagne and beer. People pushed their way up closer to the stage and stood craning their necks to see the screaming turn then being performed. When the curtains rustled together, everybody pushed away again amid laughter and applause. The orchestra blared. The crowd wreathed and sauntered in and out and to and fro. The golden-yellow light, far brighter than day, gave brilliance to every eye; every breast heaved with quickened breath, idly yet avidly drinking in the intoxication of an atmosphere reeking with odours of food and drink, flowers and scent, dust and overheated human flesh.

The orchestra stopped. People stood where they were, arm in arm, looking up at the stage, where a new turn was beginning with a din of sound. Four or five actors in peasant costume were parodying with clarinets and stringed instruments the chromatic wrestlings of the *Tristan* music. Detlef closed his eyes a moment, the lids burned. His senses were so keen that even this wanton distortion of the music could not fail to bring home to him poignantly that yearning for unity which it supremely expresses. It evoked in him overwhelmingly the suffocating melancholy of the lonely man who has lost himself in love and longing for some light and common child of life.

Lily. His soul, in imploring tenderness, shaped the name; his gaze, do what he would, turned towards her distant form. Yes, they were still there, they stood on the spot where he had left them and as the crowd thinned he would catch glimpses of her figure, leaning against the wall in her milk-white, silver-trimmed gown; her head slightly on one side, she talked with the little artist and looked into his eyes with lingering, mischievous gaze. And his eyes were just as blue, just as wide apart and unclouded as her own.

Ah, that prattle of theirs, flowing so blithely from an inexhaustible fount of simple, artless, unassuring gaiety – how could he share in it, he, a slow and serious man whose life was compact of knowledge and dreams, of paralysing insight and the inexorable urge to create! So he had left them, stolen away in a spasm of defiance and despair, in which there mingles a queer sort of magnanimity; stolen away and left these two children of life to themselves. But even at this distance came the strangling jealousy in his throat with the knowledge that they had smiled with relief at being freed of his oppressive presence.

Why had he come, why had he come here again? To move,

with his tormented soul, among these carefree throngs, knowing himself to be with but not of them? Ah, well he knew! Why then this craving for contact with them? 'We lonely ones,' so he had written once in a quiet hour of self-communing, 'we isolated dreamers, disinherited of life, who spend our introspective days remote in an artificial, icy air and spread abroad a cold breath as from strange regions so soon as we come among living human beings and they see our brows marked with the sign of knowledge and of fear; we poor ghosts of life, who are met with an embarrassed glance and left to ourselves as soon as possible, that our hollow and knowledgeable eye may not blight all joy ... we all cherish a hidden and unappeased yearning for the harmless, simple, and real in life; for a little friendly, devoted, familiar human happiness. That 'life' from which we are shut out – we do not envisage it as wild beauty and cruel splendour, it is not as the extraordinary that we crave it, we extraordinary ones. The kingdom of our longing love is the realm of the pleasant, the normal, and the respectable, it is life in all its tempting, banal everydayness that we want. ...'

He looked over at them again as they stood there talking. The whole hall rang with shouts of laughter and the whining of the clarinets, as the passionate, cloying music was being distorted into shrieking sentimentality. 'That is you,' he thought. 'You are warm, mad, sweet and lovely life, that which stands in eternal opposition to the spirit. Think not that it despises you. Think not it feels one single motion of contempt. Ah, no, we abase ourselves, we denizens of the profound, mute with our monstrous weight of knowledge, we stand afar and in our eyes there burns an avid longing to be like you.

'Do we feel pride stirring? Would we deny that we are lonely? Does our self-respect make us boast that the motions of the spirit bring to love a loftier union with life, at all times and in all places? Ah, but with whom, with what? Always only with our like, with the suffering and the yearning and the poor – never with you, you blue-eyed ones who have no need of spirit!'

Now the curtains had fallen again, dancing began afresh. The band crashed and lilted. Couples turned and glided, wove in and out upon the polished floor. And Lily danced with the little painter. How pricelessly her dainty head rose out of the stiff chalice of her silver-embroidered collar! They moved in a constricted space, with effortless, elastic turnings and pacings. His face was turned towards hers, they continued to talk and smile as they moved in obedience to the sweet and trivial measures from the band.

Suddenly the lonely man felt his spirit reach out to grasp and form as with hands. 'After all, you are mine,' he thought, 'and I am above you. Can I not see through your simple souls with a smile? Do I not observe and perpetuate, half in love and half in mockery, each naïve motion that you make? The sight of your artless activities arouses in me the forces of the Word, the power of irony. It makes my heart beat with desire and the lustful knowledge that I can reshape you as I will and by my art expose your foolish joys for the world to gape at.' But then all his defiance collapsed again quite suddenly, leaving only dull longing in its wake. Ah, to be not an artist but a man, if only once, if only on a night like this! If only once to escape the inexorable doom which rang in his ears: 'You may not live, you must create; you may not love, you must know.' Ah, just once to live, to love and to give thanks, to feel and know that feeling is all! Just once to share your life, ye living ones, just once to drink in magic draughts the bliss of the commonplace!

He shuddered and turned away. As he looked at all these charming, overheated faces it seemed to him that they peered into his and then turned away in disgust. He was overpowered by a desire to void the field, to seek out stillness and darkness – yes, he would go away, withdraw without a word, as he had withdrawn from Lily's side; go home and lay his burning, throbbing head upon a cool pillow. He strode to the exit.

Would she see him go? He was so used to this sensation, this going away, this silent, proud, despairing withdrawal from a room, a garden, from any place where society was gathered, with the secret hope of causing even one pang in the light heart of her for whom he longed! He paused, looked across at her again; he implored her in his thoughts. Should he stay, stick it out, should he remain near her, though separated by the length of the hall, remain and await some unhoped-for bliss? No, it would all be in vain. There would be no approach, no understanding, no hope. – 'Go out into the darkness, put your head in your hands and weep, if you can – if in your world of rigid desolation, of ice, of spirit, and of art there are tears left to shed.' – He left the hall.

He felt a burning, gnawing pain in his breast and at the same time a wild and senseless expectation. She *must* see him, must understand, must come, must follow him, even if only out of pity; must come half-way and say to him: Stay here, be glad, I love you. He moved very slowly, although well he knew, was certain to the point of absurdity, that she would not come at all, that little laughing, dancing, chattering Lily!

It was two o'clock. The corridors were empty and behind the long tables in the cloak-room the attendants nodded sleepily. No one but himself thought of going home. He wrapped himself in his cloak, took his hat and stick, and left the theatre.

Long rows of carriages stood on the square; lamps illumined the white mist of the winter night. The horses stood blanketed, with hanging heads; groups of well-bundled coachmen stamped the hard snow to warm their feet. Detlef beckoned to one, and as the man uncovered his horse he waited in the vestibule and let the cool dry air play about his throbbing temples.

The flat after-taste of the champagne made him want a smoke. Mechanically he drew out a cigarette and lighted it. But at the moment when the match went out he saw something strange. He did not at first understand it and stood there puzzled and aghast, with hanging arms. He could not get over it, could not put it out of his mind.

Out of the dark, as his vision recovered from the blindness caused by the flame from the match, there came a red-bearded, hollow-cheeked, lawless face, with horribly inflamed, red-rimmed eyes that stared with sardonic despair and a certain greedy curiosity into his own. The owner of this anguished face stood only two or three paces off, leaning against one of the lamp-posts which flanked the entrance of the theatre, with fists thrust deep into his trouser pockets and the collar of his tattered jacket turned up. His gaze travelled over Detlef's whole figure, from the opera-glass round the neck, down over the fur coat to the patent-leather shoes, then back again to search the other's face with that avid stare. Once the man gave a short, contemptuous snort; then his body relaxed, he shuddered, his flabby cheeks seemed to grow even hollower, while the eyelids quivered and closed and the mouth drooped at the corners with an expression both tragic and malign.

Detlef stood transfixed. He struggled to understand. He had a sudden insight as to how he must look as he stood there; his air of prosperity and well-being as he left the gay gathering, beckoned to the coachman, took the cigarette from his silver box. Involuntarily he lifted his hand in the act to strike his brow. He took a step towards the man, he drew breath to speak, to explain — but what he did was to mount silently into the waiting carriage, almost forgetting, in his distraction, to give the coachman his address. He was confounded by the inadequacy of any explanation he might make.

My God, what an error, what a crass misunderstanding! This starving, outcast man had looked at him with the bitter craving, the violent scorn that spring from envy and longing. Had he not put himself there to be looked at, this hungry man? Had not his shivering body, his tragic and malignant face, been deliberately calculated to make an impression, to give him, Detlef — as an arrogantly happy human being — one moment of misgiving, of sympathy, of distress — But you mistake, my friend — that was not the effect they had. 'You thought to show me a horrifying warning out of a strange and frightful world, to arouse my remorse. But we are *brothers*.

'Have you a weight here, my friend, a burning weight on your breast? How well I know it! And why did you come? Why did you not hug your misery in the shadow instead of taking your stand under the lighted windows behind which are music and laughter? Do not I too know the morbid yearning that drove thee hither, to feed this thy wretchedness, which may just as well be called love as hate?

'Nothing is strange to me of all the sorrow that moves thee — and thou thoughtest to shame me! What is mind but the play of hatred? What art, but yearning in act to create? We are both at home in the land of the betrayed, the hungering, the lamenting, the denying; and common to us both are those hours full of betraying self-contempt, when we lose ourselves in a shameful love of life and of mad happiness.

'Wrong, all wrong!' – And as this pity wholly filled him he felt kindled somewhere deep within an intuition at once painful and sweet. 'Is it only he who errs? Where is the end of error? Is not all longing on earth an error, this of mine first of all, which craves the simple and the instinctive, dumb life itself, ignorant of the enlightenment which comes through mind and art, the release through the Word? Ah, we are all brothers, we creatures of the restlessly suffering will, yet we do not recognize ourselves as such. Another love is needed, another love.'

And when at home he sat among his books and pictures, and the busts ranged along the wall looked down upon him, he felt moved to utter those gentle words:

'Little children, love one another.'

GLADIUS DEI

(1902)

MUNICH was radiant. Above the gay squares and white columned temples, the classicistic monuments and the baroque churches, the leaping fountains, the palaces and parks of the Residence there stretched a sky of luminous blue silk. Well-arranged leafy vistas laced with sun and shade lay basking in the sunshine of a beautiful day in early June.

There was a twittering of birds and a blithe holiday spirit in all the little streets. And in the squares and past the rows of villas there swelled, rolled, and hummed the leisurely, entertaining traffic of that easy-going, charming town. Travellers of all nationalities drove about in the slow little droshkies, looking right and left in aimless curiosity at the house-fronts; they mounted and descended museum stairs. Many windows stood open and music was heard from within: practising on piano, cello, or violin – earnest and well-meant amateur efforts; while from the Odeon came the sound of serious work on several grand pianos.

Young people, the kind that can whistle the Nothung motif, who fill the pit of the Schauspielhaus every evening, wandered in and out of the University and Library with literary magazines in their coat pockets. A court carriage stood before the Academy, the home of the plastic arts, which spreads its white wings between the Türkenstrasse and the Siegestor. And colourful groups of models, picturesque old men, women and children in Albanian costume, stood or lounged at the top of the balustrade.

Indolent, unhurried sauntering was the mode in all the long streets of the northern quarter. There life is lived for pleasanter ends than the driving greed of gain. Young artists with little round hats on the backs of their heads, flowing cravats and no canes – carefree bachelors who paid for their lodgings with colour-sketches – were strolling up and down to let the clear blue morning play upon their mood, also to look at the little girls, the pretty, rather plump type, with the brunette bandeaux, the too large feet, and the unobjectionable morals. Every fifth house had studio windows blinking in the sun. Sometimes a fine piece of architecture stood out from a middle-class row, the work of some imaginative young architect; a wide front with shallow bays and decorations in a bizarre style very expressive and full of invention. Or the door to some monotonous façade would be framed in a bold improvisation of flowing lines and sunny colours, with bacchantes, naiads, and rosy-skinned nudes.

It was always a joy to linger before the windows of the cabinet-makers and the shops for modern articles *de luxe*. What a sense for luxurious nothings and amusing, significant line was displayed in the shape of everything! Little shops that sold picture-frames, sculptures, and antiques there were in endless number; in their windows you might see those busts of Florentine women of the Renaissance, so full of noble poise and poignant charm. And the owners of the smallest and meanest of these shops spoke of Mino da Fiesole and Donatello as though he had received the rights of reproduction from them personally.

But on the Odeonsplatz, in view of the mighty loggia with the spacious mosaic pavement before it, diagonally opposite to the Regent's palace, people were crowding round the large windows and glass show-cases of the big art-shop owned by M. Blüthenzweig. What a glorious display! There were reproductions of the masterpieces of all the galleries in the world, in costly decorated and tinted frames, the good taste of which was precious in its very simplicity. There were copies of modern paintings, works of a joyously sensuous fantasy, in which the antiques seemed born again in humorous and realistic guise; bronze nudes and fragile ornamental glassware; tall, thin earthenware vases with an iridescent glaze produced by a bath in metal steam; *éditions de luxe* which were triumphs of modern binding and presswork, containing the works of the most modish poets, set out with every possible advantage of sumptuous elegance. Cheek by jowl with these, the portraits of artists, musicians, philosophers, actors, writers, displayed to gratify the public taste for personalities. – In the first window, next the book-shop, a large picture stood on an easel, with a crowd of people in front of it, a fine sepia photograph in a wide old-gold frame, a very striking reproduction of the sensation at this year's great international exhibition, to which public attention is always invited by means of effective and artistic posters stuck up everywhere on hoardings among concert programmes and clever advertisements of toilet preparations.

If you looked into the windows of the book-shop your eye met such titles as *Interior Decoration Since the Renaissance, The Renaissance in Modern Decorative Art, The Book as Work of Art, The Decorative Arts, Hunger for Art,* and many more. And you would remember that these thought-provoking pamphlets were sold and read by the thousand and that discussions on these subjects were the preoccupation of all the salons.

You might be lucky enough to meet in person one of the famous fair ones whom less fortunate folk know only through the medium of art; one of those rich and beautiful women whose Titian-blond colouring Nature's most sweet and cunning hand did *not* lay on, but whose diamond parures and beguiling charms had received immortality from the hand of some portrait-painter of genius and whose love-affairs were the talk of the town. These were the queens of the artist balls at carnival-time. They were a little painted, a little made up, full of haughty caprices, worthy of adoration, avid of praise. You might see a carriage rolling up the Ludwigstrasse, with such a great painter and his mistress inside. People would be pointing out the sight, standing still to gaze after the pair. Some of them would curtsy. A little more and the very policemen would stand at attention.

Art flourished, art swayed the destinies of the town, art stretched above it her rose-bound sceptre and smiled. On every hand obsequious interest was displayed in her prosperity, on every hand she was served with industry and devotion. There was a down-right cult of line, decoration, form, significance, beauty. Munich was radiant.

A youth was coming down the Schellingstrasse. With the bells of cyclists ringing about him he strode across the wooden

pavement towards the broad façade of the Ludwigskirche. Looking at him it was as though a shadow passed across the sky, or
cast over the spirit some memory of melancholy hours. Did he
not love the sun which bathed the lovely city in its festal light?
Why did he walk wrapped in his own thoughts, his eyes
directed on the ground?

No one in that tolerant and variety-loving town would have
taken offence at his wearing no hat; but why need the hood of
his ample black cloak have been drawn over his head, shadow-
ing his low, prominent, and peaked forehead, covering his ears
and framing his haggard cheeks? What pangs of conscience,
what scruples and self-tortures had so availed to hollow out
these cheeks? It is frightful, on such a sunny day, to see care
sitting in the hollows of the human face. His dark brows
thickened at the narrow base of his hooked and prominent
nose. His lips were unpleasantly full, his eyes brown and close-
lying. When he lifted them, diagonal folds appeared on the
peaked brow. His gaze expressed knowledge, limitation, and
suffering. Seen in profile his face was strikingly like an old painting preserved at Florence in a narrow cloister cell whence once
a frightful and shattering protest issued against life and her
triumphs.

Hieronymus walked along the Schellingstrasse with a slow,
firm stride, holding his wide cloak together with both hands
from inside. Two little girls, two of those pretty, plump little
creatures with the bandeaux, the big feet, and the unobjectionable morals, strolled towards him arm in arm, on pleasure bent.
They poked each other and laughed, they bent double with
laughter, they even broke into a run and ran away still laughing, at his hood and his face. But he paid them no heed. With
bent head, looking neither to the right nor to the left, he crossed
the Ludwigstrasse and mounted the church steps.

The great wings of the middle portal stood wide open. From
somewhere within the consecrated twilight, cool, dank, incense-
laden, there came a pale red glow. An old woman with inflamed
eyes rose from a prayer-stool and slipped on crutches through
the columns. Otherwise the church was empty.

Hieronymus sprinkled brow and breast at the stoup, bent

the knee before the high altar, and then paused in the centre nave. Here in the church his stature seemed to have grown. He stood upright and immovable; his head was flung up and his great hooked nose jutted domineeringly above the thick lips. His eyes no longer sought the ground, but looked straight and boldly into the distance, at the crucifix on the high altar. Thus he stood awhile, then retreating he bent the knee again and left the church.

He strode up the Ludwigstrasse, slowly, firmly, with bent head, in the centre of the wide unpaved road, towards the mighty loggia with its statues. But arrived at the Odeonsplatz, he looked up, so that the folds came out on his peaked forehead, and checked his step, his attention being called to the crowd at the windows of the big art-shop of M. Blüthenzweig.

People moved from window to window, pointing out to each other the treasures displayed and exchanging views as they looked over one another's shoulders. Hieronymus mingled among them and did as they did, taking in all these things with his eyes, one by one.

He saw the reproductions of masterpieces from all the galleries in the world, the priceless frames so precious in their simplicity, the Renaissance sculpture, the bronze nudes, the exquisitely bound volumes, the iridescent vases, the portraits of artists, musicians, philosophers, actors, writers; he looked at everything and turned a moment of his scrutiny upon each object. Holding his mantle closely together with both hands from inside, he moved his hood-covered head in short turns from one thing to the next, gazing at each awhile with a dull inimical, and remotely surprised air, lifting the dark brows which grew so thick at the base of the nose. At length he stood in front of the last window, which contained the startling picture. For a while he looked over the shoulders of people before him and then in his turn reached a position directly in front of the window.

The large red-brown photograph in the choice old-gold frame stood on an easel in the centre. It was a Madonna, but an utterly unconventional one, a work of entirely modern feeling. The figure of the Holy Mother was revealed as enchantingly feminine and beautiful. Her great smouldering eyes were rimmed with darkness, and her delicate and strangely smiling lips were half-parted. Her slender fingers held in a somewhat nervous grasp the hips of the Child, a nude boy of pronounced, almost primitive leanness. He was playing with her breast and glancing aside at the beholder with a wise look in his eyes.

Two other youths stood near Hieronymus, talking about the picture. They were two young men with books under their arms, which they had fetched from the Library or were taking thither. Humanistically educated people, that is, equipped with science and with art.

'The little chap is in luck, devil take me!' said one.

'He seems to be trying to make one envious,' replied the other. 'A bewildering female!'

'A female to drive a man crazy! Gives you funny ideas about the Immaculate Conception.'

'No, she doesn't look exactly immaculate. Have you seen the original?'

'Of course; I was quite bowled over. She makes an even more aphrodisiac impression in colour. Especially the eyes.'

'The likeness is pretty plain.'

'How so?'

'Don't you know the model? Of course he used his little dress-maker. It is almost a portrait, only with a lot more emphasis on the corruptible. The girl is more innocent.'

'I hope so. Life would be altogether too much of a strain if there were many like this *mater amata*.'

'The Pinakothek has bought it.'

'Really? Well, well! They knew what they were about, anyhow. The treatment of the flesh and the flow of the linen garment are really first-class.'

'Yes, an incredibly gifted chap.'

'Do you know him?'

'A little. He will have a career, that is certain. He has been invited twice by the Prince Regent.'

This last was said as they were taking leave of each other.

'Shall I see you this evening at the theatre?' asked the first. 'The Dramatic Club is giving Machiavelli's *Mandragola*.'

'Oh, bravo! That will be great, of course, I had meant to go to the Variété, but I shall probably choose our stout Niccolo after all. Goodbye.'

They parted, going off to right and left. New people took their places and looked at the famous picture. But Hieronymus stood where he was, motionless, with his head thrust out; his hands clutched convulsively at the mantle as they held it together from inside. His brows were no longer lifted with that cool and unpleasantly surprised expression; they were drawn and darkened; his cheeks, half-shrouded in the black hood, seemed more sunken than ever and his thick lips had gone pale. Slowly his head dropped lower and lower, so that finally the eyes stared upwards at the work of art, while the nostrils of his great nose dilated.

Thus he remained for perhaps a quarter of an hour. The crowd about him melted away, but he did not stir from the spot. At last he turned slowly on the balls of his feet and went thence.

But the picture of the Madonna went with him. Always and ever, whether in his hard and narrow little room or kneeling in the cool church, it stood before his outraged soul, with its smouldering, dark-rimmed eyes, its riddlingly smiling lips – stark and beautiful. And no prayer availed to exorcize it.

But the third night it happened that a command and summons from on high came to Hieronymus, to intercede and lift his voice against the frivolity, blasphemy, and arrogance of beauty. In vain like Moses he protested that he had not the gift of tongues. God's will remained unshaken; in a loud voice He demanded that the faint-hearted Hieronymus go forth to sacrifice amid the jeers of the foe.

And since God would have it so, he set forth one morning and wended his way to the great art-shop of M. Blüthenzweig. He wore his hood over his head and held his mantle together in front from inside with both hands as he went.

The air had grown heavy, the sky was livid and thunder threatened. Once more crowds were besieging the show-cases at the art-shop and especially the window where the photograph of

the Madonna stood. Hieronymus cast one brief glance thither;
then he pushed up the latch of the glass door hung with placards
and art magazines. 'As God wills,' said he, and entered the
shop.

A young girl was somewhere at a desk writing in a big book.
She was a pretty brunette thing with bandeaux of hair and big
feet. She came up to him and asked pleasantly what he would
like.

'Thank you,' said Hieronymus in a low voice and looked her
earnestly in the face, with diagonal wrinkles in his peaked
brow. 'I would speak not to you but to the owner of this shop,
Herr Blüthenzweig.'

She hesitated a little, turned away, and took up her work
once more. He stood there in the middle of the shop.

Instead of the single specimens in the show-windows there
were here a riot and a heaping-up of luxury, a fullness of colour,
line, form, style, invention, good taste, and beauty. Hieronymus
looked slowly round him, drawing his mantle close with both
hands.

There were several people in the shop besides him. At one of
the broad tables running across the room sat a man in a yellow
suit, with a black goat's-beard, looking at a portfolio of French
drawings, over which he now and then emitted a bleating laugh.
He was being waited on by an undernourished and vegetarian
young man, who kept on dragging up fresh portfolios. Diagonally opposite the bleating man sat an elegant old dame, examining art embroideries with a pattern of fabulous flowers in pale
tones standing together on tall perpendicular stalks. An
attendant hovered about her too. A leisurely Englishman in a
travelling-cap, with his pipe in his mouth, sat at another table.
Cold and smooth-shaven, of indefinite age, in his good English
clothes, he sat examining bronzes brought to him by M.
Blüthenzweig in person. He was holding up by the head the
dainty figure of a nude young girl, immature and delicately
articulated, her hands crossed in coquettish innocence upon her
breast. He studied her thoroughly, turning her slowly about. M.
Blüthenzweig, a man with short, heavy brown beard and bright
brown eyes of exactly the same colour, moved in a semicircle

round him, rubbing his hands, praising the statuette with all the terms his vocabulary possessed.

'A hundred and fifty marks, sir,' he said in English. 'Munich art – very charming, in fact. Simply full of charm, you know. Grace itself. Really extremely pretty, good, admirable, in fact.' Then he thought of some more and went on: 'Highly attractive, fascinating.' Then he began again from the beginning.

His nose lay a little flat on his upper lip, so that he breathed constantly with a slight sniff into his moustache. Sometimes he did this as he approached a customer, stooping over as though he were smelling at him. When Hieronymus entered, M. Blüthenzweig had examined him cursorily in this way, then devoted himself again to his Englishman.

The elegant old dame made her selection and left the shop. A man entered. M. Blüthenzweig sniffed briefly at him as though to scent out his capacity to buy and left him to the young bookkeeper. The man purchased a faience bust of young Piero de' Medici, son of Lorenzo, and went out again. The Englishman began to depart. He had acquired the statuette of the young girl and left amid bowings from M. Blüthenzweig. Then the art-dealer turned to Hieronymus and came forward.

'You wanted something?' he said, without any particular courtesy.

Hieronymus held his cloak together with both hands and looked the other in the face almost without winking an eyelash. He parted his big lips slowly and said:

'I have come to you on account of the picture in the window there, the big photograph, the Madonna.' His voice was thick and without modulation.

'Yes, quite right,' said M. Blüthenzweig briskly and began rubbing his hands. 'Seventy marks in the frame. It is unfadeable – a first-class reproduction. Highly attractive and full of charm.'

Hieronymus was silent. He nodded his head in the hood and shrank a little into himself as the dealer spoke. Then he drew himself up again and said:

'I would remark to you first of all that I am not in the position to purchase anything, nor have I the desire. I am sorry to have to disappoint your expectations. I regret if it upsets you.

But in the first place I am poor and in the second I do not love the things you sell. No, I cannot buy anything.'

'No? Well, then?' asked M. Blüthenzweig, sniffing a good deal. 'Then may I ask—'

'I suppose,' Hieronymus went on, 'that being what you are you look down on me because I am not in a position to buy.'

'Oh – er – not at all,' said M. Blüthenzweig. 'Not at all. Only—'

'And yet I beg you to hear me and give some consideration to my words.'

'Consideration to your words. H'm – may I ask—'

'You may ask,' said Hieronymus, 'and I will answer you. I have come to beg you to remove that picture, the big photograph, the Madonna, out of your window and never display it again.'

M. Blüthenzweig looked awhile dumbly into Hieronymus's face – as though he expected him to be abashed at the words he had just uttered. But as this did not happen he gave a violent sniff and spoke himself:

'Will you be so good as to tell me whether you are here in any official capacity which authorizes you to dictate to me, or what does bring you here?'

'Oh, no,' replied Hieronymus, 'I have neither office nor dignity from the state. I have no power on my side, sir. What brings me hither is my conscience alone.'

M. Blüthenzweig, searching for words, snorted violently into his moustache. At length he said:

'Your conscience ... Well, you will kindly understand that I take not the faintest interest in your conscience.' With which he turned round and moved quickly to his desk at the back of the shop, where he began to write. Both attendants laughed heartily. The pretty Fräulein giggled over her account-book. As for the yellow gentleman with the goat's beard, he was evidently a foreigner, for he gave no sign of comprehension but went on studying the French drawings and emitting from time to time his bleating laugh.

'Just get rid of the man for me,' said M. Blüthenzweig shortly over his shoulder to his assistant. He went on writing. The poorly paid young vegetarian approached Hieronymus, smothering his laughter, and the other salesman came up too.

'May we be of service to you in any other way?' the first asked mildly. Hieronymus fixed him with his glazed and suffering eyes.

'No,' he said, 'you cannot. I beg you to take the Madonna picture out of the window, at once and for ever.'

'But – why?'

'It is the Holy Mother of God,' said Hieronymus in a subdued voice.

'Quite. But you have heard that Herr Blüthenzweig is not inclined to accede to your request.'

'We must bear in mind that it is the Holy Mother of God,' said Hieronymus again and his head trembled on his neck.

'So we must. But should we not be allowed to exhibit any Madonnas – or paint any?'

'It is not that,' said Hieronymus, almost whispering. He drew himself up and shook his head energetically several times. His peaked brow under the hood was entirely furrowed with long, deep cross-folds. 'You know very well that it is vice itself that is painted there – naked sensuality. I was standing near two simple young people and overheard with my own ears that it led them astray upon the doctrine of the Immaculate Conception.'

'Oh, permit me – that is not the point,' said the young salesman, smiling. In his leisure hours he was writing a brochure on the modern movement in art and was well qualified to conduct a cultured conversation. 'The picture is a work of art,' he went on, 'and one must measure it by the appropriate standards as such. It has been highly praised on all hands. The state has purchased it.'

'I know that the state has purchased it,' said Hieronymus. 'I also know that the artist has twice dined with the Prince Regent. It is common talk – and God knows how people interpret the fact that a man can become famous by such work as this. What does such a fact bear witness to? To the blindness of the world, a blindness inconceivable, if not indeed shamelessly hypocritical. This picture has its origin in sensual lust and is enjoyed in the same – is that true or not? Answer me! And you too answer me, Herr Blüthenzweig!'

A pause ensued. Hieronymus seemed in all seriousness to demand an answer to his question, looking by turns at the staring attendants and the round back of M. Blüthenzweig turned upon him, with his own piercing and anguishing brown eyes. Silence reigned. Only the yellow man with the goat's beard, bending over the French drawings, broke it with his bleating laugh.

'It is true,' Hieronymus went on in a hoarse voice that shook with his profound indignation. 'You do not dare deny it. How then can honour be done to its creator, as though he had endowed mankind with a new ideal possession? How can one stand before it and surrender unthinkingly to the base enjoyment which it purveys, persuading oneself in all seriousness that one is yielding to a noble and elevated sentiment, highly creditable to the human race? Is this reckless ignorance or abandoned hypocrisy? My understanding falters, it is completely at a loss when confronted by the absurd fact that a man can achieve renown on this earth by the stupid and shameless exploitation of the animal instincts. Beauty? What is beauty? What forces are they which use beauty as their tool today – and upon what does it work? No one can fail to know this, Herr Blüthenzweig. But who, understanding it clearly, can fail to feel disgust and pain? It is criminal to play upon the ignorance of the immature, the lewd, the brazen, and the unscrupulous by elevating beauty into an idol to be worshipped, to give it even more power over those who know not affliction and have no knowledge of redemption. You are unknown to me, and you look at me with black looks – yet answer me! Knowledge, I tell you, is the profoundest torture in the world; but it is the purgatory without whose purifying pangs no soul can reach salvation. It is not infantile, blasphemous shallowness that can save us, Herr Blüthenzweig; only knowledge can avail, knowledge in which the passions of our loathsome flesh die away and are quenched.'

Silence. – The yellow man with the goat's beard gave a sudden little bleat.

'I think you really must go now,' said the underpaid assistant mildly.

But Hieronymus made no move to do so. Drawn up in his hooded cape, he stood with blazing eyes in the centre of the shop and his thick lips poured out condemnation in a voice that was harsh and rusty and clanking.

'Art, you cry; enjoyment, beauty! Enfold the world in beauty and endow all things with the noble grace of style! – Profligate, away! Do you think to wash over with lurid colours the misery of the world? Do you think with the sounds of feasting and music to drown out the voice of the tortured earth? Shameless one, you err! God lets not Himself be mocked, and your impudent deification of the glistering surface of things is an abomination in His eyes. You tell me that I blaspheme art. I say to you that you lie. I do not blaspheme art. Art is no conscienceless delusion, lending itself to reinforce the allurements of the fleshly. Art is the holy torch which turns its light upon all the frightful depths, all the shameful and woeful abysses of life; art is the godly fire laid to the world that, being redeemed by pity, it may flame up and dissolve altogether with its shames and torments. – Take it out, Herr Blüthenzweig, take away the work of that famous painter out of your window – you would do well to burn it with a hot fire and strew its ashes to the four winds – yes, to all the four winds—'

His harsh voice broke off. He had taken a violent backwards step, snatched one arm from his black wrappings, and stretched it passionately forth, gesturing towards the window with a hand that shook as though palsied. And in this commanding attitude he paused. His great hooked nose seemed to jut more than ever, his dark brows were gathered so thick and high that folds crowded upon the peaked forehead shaded by the hood; a hectic flush mantled his hollow cheeks.

But at this point M. Blüthenzweig turned round. Perhaps he was outraged by the idea of burning his seventy-mark reproduction; perhaps Hieronymus's speech had completely exhausted his patience. In any case he was a picture of stern and righteous anger. He pointed with his pen to the door of the shop, gave several short, excited snorts into his moustache, struggled for words, and uttered with the maximum of energy those which he found:

'My fine fellow, if you don't get out at once I will have my packer help you – do you understand?'

'Oh, you cannot intimidate me, you cannot drive me away, you cannot silence my voice!' cried Hieronymus as he clutched his cloak over his chest with his fists and shook his head doughtily. 'I know that I am single-handed and powerless, but yet I will not cease until you hear me, Herr Blüthenzweig! Take the picture out of your window and burn it even today! Ah, burn not it alone! Burn all these statues and busts, the sight of which plunges the beholder into sin! Burn these vases and ornaments, these shameless revivals of paganism, these elegantly bound volumes of erotic verse! Burn everything in your shop, Herr Blüthenzweig, for it is a filthiness in God's sight. Burn it, burn it!' he shrieked, beside himself, describing a wild, all-embracing circle with his arm. 'The harvest is ripe for the reaper, the measure of the age's shamelessness is full – but I say unto you –'

'Krauthuber!' Herr Blüthenzweig raised his voice and shouted towards a door at the back of the shop. 'Come in here at once!'

And in answer to the summons there appeared upon the scene a massive overpowering presence, a vast and awe-inspiring, swollen human bulk, whose limbs merged into each other like links of sausage – a gigantic son of the people, malt-nourished and immoderate, who weighed in, with puffings, bursting with energy, from the packing-room. His appearance in the upper reaches of his form was notable for a fringe of walrus beard; a hide apron fouled with paste covered his body from the waist down, and his yellow shirtsleeves were rolled back from his heroic arms.

'Will you open the door for this gentleman, Krauthuber?' said M. Blüthenzweig; 'and if he should not find the way to it, just help him into the street.'

'Huh,' said the man, looking from his enraged employer to Hieronymus and back with his little elephant eyes. It was a heavy monosyllable, suggesting reserve force restrained with difficulty. The floor shook with his tread as he went to the door and opened it.

Hieronymus had grown very pale. 'Burn –' he shouted once more. He was about to go on when he felt himself turned round by an irresistible power, by a physical preponderance to which no resistance was even thinkable. Slowly and inexorably he was propelled towards the door.

'I am weak,' he managed to ejaculate. 'My flesh cannot bear the force ... it cannot hold its ground, no ... but what does that prove? Burn –'

He stopped. He found himself outside the art-shop. M. Blüthenzweig's giant packer had let him go with one final shove which set him down on the stone threshold of the shop, supporting himself with one hand. Behind him the door closed with a rattle of glass.

He picked himself up. He stood erect, breathing heavily, and pulled his cloak together with one fist over his breast, letting the other hang down inside. His hollow cheeks had a grey pallor; the nostrils of his great hooked nose opened and closed; his ugly lips were writhen in an expression of hatred and despair and his red-rimmed eyes wandered over the beautiful square like those of a man in a frenzy.

He did not see that people were looking at him with amusement and curiosity. For what he beheld upon the mosaic pavement before the great loggia were all the vanities of this world: the masked costumes of the artist balls, the decorations, vases and art objects, the nude statues, the female busts, the picturesque rebirths of the pagan age, the portraits of famous beauties by the hands of masters, the elegantly bound erotic verse, the art brochures – all these he saw heaped in a pyramid and going up in crackling flames amid loud exultations from the people enthralled by his own frightful words. A yellow background of cloud had drawn up over the Theatinerstrasse, and from it issued wild rumblings; but what he saw was a burning fiery sword, towering in sulphurous light above the joyous city.

'Gladius Dei super terram ...' his thick lips whispered; and drawing himself still higher in his hooded cloak while the hand hanging down inside it twitched convulsively, he murmured, quaking: 'cito et velociter!'

THE INFANT PRODIGY
(1903)

T H E infant prodigy entered. The hall became quiet.

It became quiet and then the audience began to clap, because somewhere at the side a leader of mobs, a born organizer, clapped first. The audience had heard nothing yet, but they applauded; for a mighty publicity organization had heralded the prodigy and people were already hypnotized, whether they knew it or not.

The prodigy came from behind a splendid screen embroidered with Empire garlands and great conventionalized flowers, and climbed nimbly up the steps to the platform, diving into the applause as into a bath; a little chilly and shivering, but yet as though into a friendly element. He advanced to the edge of the platform and smiled as though he were about to be photographed; he made a shy, charming gesture of greeting, like a little girl.

He was dressed entirely in white silk, which the audience found enchanting. The little white jacket was fancifully cut, with a sash underneath it, and even his shoes were made of white silk. But against the white socks his bare little legs stood out quite brown, for he was a Greek boy.

He was called Bibi Saccellaphylaccas. And such indeed was his name. No one knew what Bibi was the pet name for, nobody but the impresario, and he regarded it as a trade secret. Bibi had smooth black hair reaching to his shoulders; it was parted on the side and fastened back from the narrow domed forehead by a little silk bow. His was the most harmless childish countenance in the world, with an unfinished nose and guileless mouth. The area beneath his pitch-black mouselike eyes was already a little tired and visibly lined. He looked as though he were nine years old but was really eight and given out for seven. It was hard to tell whether to believe this or not. Probably everybody knew better and still believed it, as happens about so

many things. The average man thinks that a little falseness
goes with beauty. Where should we get any excitement out of
our daily life if we were not willing to pretend a bit? And the
average man is quite right, in his average brains!

The prodigy kept on bowing until the applause died down,
then he went up to the grand piano, and the audience cast a
last look at its programmes. First came a *Marche solonnelle*, then
a *Rêverie*, and then *Le Hibou et les Moineaux* – all by Bibi
Saccellaphylaccas. The whole programme was by him, they
were all his compositions. He could not score them, of course,
but he had them all in his extraordinary little head and they
possessed real artistic significance, or so it said, seriously and
objectively, in the programme. The programme sounded as
though the impresario had wrested these concessions from his
critical nature after a hard struggle.

The prodigy sat down upon the revolving stool and felt with
his feet for the pedals, which were raised by means of a clever
device so that Bibi could reach them. It was Bibi's own piano,
he took it everywhere with him. It rested upon wooden trestles
and its polish was somewhat marred by the constant transpor-
tation – but all that only made things more interesting.

Bibi put his silk-shod feet on the pedals; then he made an
artful little face, looked straight ahead of him, and lifted his
right hand. It was a brown, childish little hand; but the wrist
was strong and unlike a child's, with well-developed bones.

Bibi made his face for the audience because he was aware that
he had to entertain them a little. But he had his own private
enjoyment in the thing too, an enjoyment which he could never
convey to anybody. It was that prickling delight, that secret
shudder of bliss, which ran through him every time he sat at an
open piano – it would always be with him. And here was the
keyboard again, these seven black and white octaves, among
which he had so often lost himself in abysmal and thrilling
adventures – and yet it always looked as clean and untouched
as a newly washed blackboard. This was the realm of music
that lay before him. It lay spread out like an inviting ocean,
where he might plunge in and blissfully swim, where he might
let himself be borne and carried away, where he might go under

in night and storm, yet keep the mastery: control, ordain – he held his right hand poised in the air.

A breathless stillness reigned in the room – the tense moment before the first note came ... How would it begin? It began so. And Bibi, with his index finger, fetched the first note out of the piano, a quite unexpectedly powerful first note in the middle register, like a trumpet blast. Others followed, an introduction developed – the audience relaxed.

The concert was held in the palatial hall of a fashionable first-class hotel. The walls were covered with mirrors framed in gilded arabesques, between frescoes of the rosy and fleshly school. Ornamental columns supported a ceiling that displayed a whole universe of electric bulbs, in clusters darting a brilliance far brighter than day and filling the whole space with thin, vibrating golden light. Not a seat was unoccupied, people were standing in the side aisles and at the back. The front seats cost twelve marks; for the impresario believed that anything worth having was worth paying for. And they were occupied by the best society, for it was in the upper classes, of course, that the greatest enthusiasm was felt. There were even some children, with their legs hanging down demurely from their chairs and their shining eyes staring at their gifted little white-clad contemporary.

Down in front on the left side sat the prodigy's mother, an extremely obese woman with a powdered double chin and a feather on her head. Beside her was the impresario, a man of oriental appearance with large gold buttons on his conspicuous cuffs. The princess was in the middle of the front row – a wrinkled, shrivelled little old princess but still a patron of the arts, especially everything full of sensibility. She sat in a deep, velvet-upholstered arm-chair, and a Persian carpet was spread before her feet. She held her hands folded over her grey striped-silk breast, put her head on one side, and presented a picture of elegant composure as she sat looking up at the performing prodigy. Next to her sat her lady-in-waiting, in a green striped-silk gown. Being only a lady-in-waiting she had to sit up very straight in her chair.

Bibi ended in a grand climax. With what power this wee

manikin belaboured the keyboard! The audience could scarcely
trust its ears. The march theme, an infectious, swinging tune,
broke out once more, fully harmonized, bold and showy; with
every note Bibi flung himself back from the waist as though he
were marching in a triumphal procession. He ended *fortissimo*,
bent over, slipped sideways off the stool, and stood with a smile
awaiting the applause.

And the applause burst forth, unanimously, enthusiastically;
the child made his demure little maidenly curtsy and people in
the front seat thought: 'Look what slim little hips he has! Clap,
clap! Hurrah, bravo, little chap, Saccophylax or whatever your
name is! Wait, let me take off my gloves – what a little devil of
a chap he is!'

Bibi had to come out three times from behind the screen
before they would stop. Some late-comers entered the hall and
moved about looking for seats. Then the concert continued.
Bibi's *Rêverie* murmured its numbers, consisting almost entirely
of arpeggios, above which a bar of melody rose now and then,
weak-winged. Then came *Le Hibou et les Moineaux*. This piece
was brilliantly successful, it made a strong impression; it was an
affective childhood fantasy, remarkably well envisaged. The bass
represented the owl, sitting morosely rolling his filmy eyes;
while in the treble the impudent, half-frightened sparrows
chirped. Bibi received an ovation when he finished, he was
called out four times. A hotel page with shiny buttons carried
up three great laurel wreaths on to the stage and proffered them
from one side while Bibi nodded and expressed his thanks. Even
the princess shared in the applause, daintily and noiselessly
pressing her palms together.

Ah, the knowing little creature understood how to make
people clap! He stopped behind the screen, they had to wait for
him; lingered a little on the steps of the platform, admired the
long streamers on the wreaths – although actually such things
bored him stiff by now. He bowed with the utmost charm, he
gave the audience plenty of time to rave itself out, because
applause is valuable and must not be cut short. '*Le Hibou* is
my drawing card,' he thought – this expression he had learned
from the impresario. 'Now I will play the fantasy, it is a lot

better than *Le Hibou*, of course, especially the C-sharp passage. But you idiots dote on the *Hibou*, though it is the first and the silliest thing I wrote.' He continued to bow and smile.

Next came a *Méditation* and then an *Etude* – the programme was quite comprehensive. The *Méditation* was very like the *Rêverie* – which was nothing against it – and the *Etude* displayed all of Bibi's virtuosity, which naturally fell a little short of his inventiveness. And then the *Fantaisie*. This was his favourite; he varied it a little each time, giving himself free rein and sometimes surprising even himself, on good evenings, by his own inventiveness.

He sat and played, so little, so white and shining, against the great black grand piano, elect and alone, above that confused sea of faces, above the heavy, insensitive mass soul, upon which he was labouring to work with his individual, differentiated soul. His lock of soft black hair with the white silk bow had fallen over his forehead, his trained and bony little wrists pounded away, the muscles stood out visibly on his brown childish cheeks.

Sitting there he sometimes had moments of oblivion and solitude, when the gaze of his strange little mouselike eyes with the big rings beneath them would lose itself and stare through the painted stage into space that was peopled with strange vague life. Then out of the corner of his eye he would give a quick look back into the hall and be once more with his audience.

'Joy and pain, the heights and the depths – that is my *Fantaisie*,' he thought lovingly. 'Listen, here is the C-sharp passage.' He lingered over the approach, wondering if they would notice anything. But no, of course not, how should they? And he cast his eyes up prettily at the ceiling so that at least they might have something to look at.

All these people sat there in their regular rows, looking at the prodigy and thinking all sorts of things in their regular brains. An old gentleman with a white beard, a seal ring on his finger and a bulbous swelling on his bald spot, a growth if you like, was thinking to himself: 'Really, one ought to be shamed.' He had never got any further than 'Ah, thou dearest Augustin' on the piano, and here he sat now, a grey old man, looking on while this little hop-o'-my-thumb performed miracles. Yes, yes, it is a gift of God, we must remember that. God grants His gifts, or He withholds them, and there is no shame in being an ordinary man. Like with the Christ Child. – Before a child one may kneel without feeling shamed. Strange that thoughts like these should be so satisfying – he would even say so sweet, if it was not too silly for a tough old man like him to use the word. That was how he felt, anyhow.

Art ... the business man with the parrot-nose was thinking. 'Yes, it adds something cheerful to life, a little good white silk and a little tumty-ti-ti-tum. Really he does not play so badly. Fully fifty seats, twelve marks apiece, that makes six hundred marks – and everything else besides. Take off the rent of the hall, the lighting and the programmes, you must have fully a thousand marks profit. That is worth while.'

That was Chopin he was just playing, thought the piano-teacher, a lady with a pointed nose; she was of an age when the understanding sharpens as the hopes decay. 'But not very original – I will say that afterwards, it sounds well. And his hand position is entirely amateur. One must be able to lay a coin on the back of the hand – I would use a ruler on him.'

Then there was a young girl, at that self-conscious and chlorotic time of life when the most ineffable ideas come into the mind. She was thinking to herself: 'What is it he is playing? It is expressive of passion, yet he is a child. If he kissed me it would be as though my little brother kissed me – no kiss at all. Is there such a thing as passion all by itself, without any earthly object, a sort of child's-play of passion? What nonsense! If I were to say such things aloud they would just be at me with some more cod-liver oil. Such is life.'

An officer was leaning against a column. He looked on at Bibi's success and thought: 'Yes, you are something and I am something, each in his own way.' So he clapped his heels together and paid to the prodigy the respect which he felt to be due to all the powers that be.

Then there was a critic, an elderly man in a shiny black coat and turned-up trousers splashed with mud. He sat in his free seat and thought: 'Look at him, this young beggar of a Bibi. As an individual he has still to develop, but as a type he is already quite complete, the artist *par excellence*. He has in himself all the artist's exaltation and his utter worthlessness, his charlatanry and his sacred fire, his burning contempt and his secret raptures. Of course I can't write all that, it is too good. Of course, I should have been an artist myself if I had not seen through the whole business so clearly.'

Then the prodigy stopped playing and a perfect storm arose in the hall. He had to come out again and again from behind his screen. The man with the shiny buttons carried up more wreaths: four laurel wreaths, a lyre made of violets, a bouquet of roses. He had not arms enough to convey all these tributes, the impresario himself mounted the stage to help him. He hung a laurel wreath round Bibi's neck, he tenderly stroked the black hair – and suddenly as though overcome he bent down and gave the prodigy a kiss, a resounding kiss, square on the mouth. And then the storm became a hurricane. That kiss ran through the room like an electric shock, it went direct to peoples' marrow and made them shiver down their backs. They were carried away by a helpless compulsion of sheer noise. Loud shouts mingled with the hysterical clapping of hands. Some of Bibi's commonplace little friends down there waved their handkerchiefs. But the critic thought: 'Of course that kiss had to come – it's a good old gag. Yes, good Lord, if only one did not see through everything quite so clearly –'

And so the concert drew to a close. It began at half past seven and finished at half past eight. The platform was laden with wreaths and two little pots of flowers stood on the lampstands of the piano. Bibi played as his last number his *Rhapsodie grecque*, which turned into the Greek national hymn at the end. His fellow-countrymen in the audeince would gladly have sung it with him if the company had not been so august. They made up for it with a powerful noise and hullabaloo, a hot-blooded national demonstration. And the ageing critic was thinking: 'Yes, the hymn had to come too. They have to exploit every vein – publicity cannot afford to neglect any means to its end. I think I'll criticize that as inartistic. But perhaps I am wrong, perhaps that is the most artistic thing of all. What is the artist?

A jack-in-the-box. Criticism is on a higher plane. But I can't say that.' And away he went in his muddy trousers.

After being called out nine or ten times the prodigy did not come any more from behind the screen but went to his mother and the impresario down in the hall. The audience stood about among the chairs and applauded and pressed forward to see Bibi close at hand. Some of them wanted to see the princess too. Two dense circles formed, one round the prodigy, the other round the princess, and you could actually not tell which of them was receiving more homage. But the court lady was commanded to go over to Bibi; she smoothed down his silk jacket a bit to make it look suitable for a court function, led him by the arm to the princess, and solemnly indicated to him that he was to kiss the royal hand. 'How do you do it, child?' asked the princess. 'Does it come into your head of itself when you sit down?' 'Oui, madame,' answered Bibi .To himself he thought: 'Oh, what a stupid old princess!' Then he turned round shyly and uncourtier-like and went back to hi: family.

Outside in the cloak-room there was a crowd. People held up their numbers and received with open arms furs, shawls, and galoshes. Somewhere among her acquaintances the piano-teacher stood making her critique. 'He is not very original,' she said audibly and looked about her.

In front of one of the great mirrors an elegant young lady was being arrayed in her evening cloak and fur shoes by her brothers, two lieutenants. She was exquisitely beautiful, with her steel-blue eyes and her clean-cut, well-bred face. A really noble dame. When she was ready she stood waiting for her brothers. 'Don't stand so long in front of the glass, Adolf,' she said softly to one of them, who could not tear himself away from the sight of his simple, good-looking young features. But Lieutenant Adolf thinks: What cheek! He would button his overcoat in front of the glass, just the same. Then they went out on the street where the arc-lights gleamed cloudily through the white mist. Lieutenant Adolf struck up a little nigger-dance on the frozen snow to keep warm, with hi· hands in his slanting overcoat pockets and his collar turned up.

A girl with untidy hair and swinging arms, accompanied by a

gloomy-faced youth, came out just behind them. A child! she thought. A charming child. But in there he was an awe-inspiring ... and aloud in a toneless voice she said: 'We are all infant prodigies, we artists.'

'Well, bless my soul!' thought the old gentleman who had never got further than Augustin on the piano, and whose boil was now concealed by a top hat. 'What does all that mean? She sounds very oracular.' But the gloomy youth understood. He nodded his head slowly.

Then they were silent and the untidy-haired girl gazed after the brothers and sister. She rather despised them, but she looked after them until they had turned the corner.

A GLEAM

(1904)

HUSH! Let us look into a human soul. On the wing, as it
were, and only in passing; only for a page or so, for we are very
busy. We come from Florence, Florence of the old days, where
we have been dealing with high and tragic and ultimate concerns. And after that – whither? To court, perhaps, a royal
castle? Who knows? Strange, faint-shimmering forms are taking their place on the stage. – Anna, poor little Baroness Anna,
we have little time to spare for you.

Waltz-time, tinkling glasses; smoke, steam, hubbub, voices,
dance-steps. We all know these little weaknesses of ours. Do we
secretly love to linger at life's silliest feasts simply because there
suffering wears bigger, more childlike eyes than in other places?

'*Avantageur!*' cried Baron Harry, the cavalry captain. He
stopped dancing and called the whole length of the hall, one
hand on his hip, the other still holding his partner embraced.
'That's not a waltz, man, it's a funeral march! You have no
rhythm in your body; you just float and sway about without any
sense of time. Let Lieutenant von Gelbsattel play, so that we
can feel the rhythm. Come on down, *Avantageur*! Dance, if you
can do that better!'

And the *Avantageur* stood up, clapped his spurs together,
and without a word yielded the platform to Lieutenant von
Gelbsattel, who straightway began to make the piano ring and
rattle under the blows from his sprawling white fingers.

Baron Harry, we observe, had music in him: waltz music,
march music. He had rhythm, joviality, hauteur, good fortune,
and a conquering-hero air. His gold-braided hussar jacket suited
to a T his glowing young face, unmarked by a single care, a
single thought. He was burnt red, like a blond, though hair and
moustache were dark – a piquant combination that appealed to
the ladies – and the red scar across his right cheek gave a bold
and dashing look to his open countenance. The scar might be

from a wound, or a fall from a horse — in any case it was glorious. He danced divinely.

But the *Avantageur* floated and swayed — to extend the meaning of Baron Harry's phrase. His eyelids were much too large, so that he could never properly open his eyes; also his uniform fitted him rather carelessly and improbably round the waist — and God alone knew how he came to be a soldier. He had not cared much for this affair with the 'Swallows' at the Casino, but even so he had come to it; he had to be careful not to give offence, for two reasons: first, because his origins were bourgeois, and second, because there was a book by him, that he had written or put together, or whatever the word is, a collection of stories, that anybody could buy in a book-shop. It must make people feel a little shy of him, of course.

The hall in the officers' Casino was long and wide — much too large for the thirty people who were disporting themselves in it. The walls and the musicians' platform were decorated with imitation draperies in red plaster, and from the ugly ceiling hung two crooked chandeliers, in which the candles stood askew and dripped hot wax. But the board floor had been scrubbed the whole forenoon by seven hussars told off for the job; and, after all, officers in a little hole like Hohendamm could not expect grandeur. Whatever was otherwise lacking to the feast was amply made up by its characteristic atmosphere; it had the sweetness of forbidden fruit, the reckless charm imparted by the presence of the 'Swallows'. Even the orderlies smirked knowingly as they renewed the supplies of champagne in the ice-tubs beside the white-covered tables which stood ranged along three walls of the room. They looked at each other and then down with a grin, as servants do when they assist irresponsibly at the excesses of their master. And all this with reference to the 'Swallows'.

The Swallows, the Swallows? Well, in short, they were the 'Swallows from Vienna'. Like migratory birds, thirty in the flock, they flew through the country, appearing in fifth-rate variety-theatres and music-halls, where they stood on the stage in easy, unconventional poses and chirped their famous swallows' chorus:

'When the swallows come again
See them fly, *aren't* they fly?'

It was a good song, its humour was not obscure, it was always received with warm applause from the more knowing section of the public.

Well, the Swallows came to Hohendamm and sang in Gugelfing's beer-hall. A whole regiment of hussars were in barracks at Hohendamm, and the Swallows were justified in anticipating a good reception from representative circles. But they got more, they got an enthusiastic one. Evening after evening the unmarried officers sat at the girls' feet, listened to their swallow song, and drank their health in Gugelfing's yellow beer. It was not long before the married officers were there too; one evening Colonel von Rummler appeared in person, followed the programme with the closest interest and afterwards expressed himself with unlimited approval in various places.

So then the lieutenants and cavalry captains conceived a plan to bring about closer contact with the Swallows: to invite a select group of them – say, ten of the prettiest – to a jolly champagne supper in the Casino. The upper orders could not take any public cognizance of the affair, of course; they had to refrain, however sore at heart. Not only the unmarried lieutenants, however, but also the married first lieutenants and cavalry captains took part, and also – this was the nub of the whole matter, the thing that gave it, so to speak, its 'punch' – their wives.

Obstacles and misgivings? First Lieutenant von Levzahn brushed them all away with a phrase: what else, said he, were obstacles for, if not that soldiers might triumph over them! The good citizens of Hohendamm might rage when they heard that the officers were introducing their wives to the Swallows. Of course, they could not have done such a thing themselves. But there were heights, there were aloof and untrammelled regions of existence, where things might freely come to pass that in a lower sphere could only sully and dishonour. It was not as though the worthy natives of Hohendamm were not used to expecting all sort of unexpectednesses from their hussars. The officers would ride along the middle of the pavement, in broad daylight, if it occurred to them so to do. They had done it. One evening pistols had been fired off in the Markplatz – nobody but the officers could have done that. And had anyone dared to murmur? The following anecdote was simply vouched for:

One morning, between five and six o'clock, Captain of Cavalry Baron Harry, feeling pretty jolly, was on his way home from a party, with his friends Captain of Cavalry von Hüh-nemann and Lieutenants Le Maistre, Baron Truchsess, von Trautenau, and von Lichterloh. Riding across the Old Bridge, they met a baker's boy, with a great basket of rolls on his shoul-der, taking his way through the fresh morning air and whist-ling blithely as he went, 'Give me that basket!' commanded Baron Harry. He seized it by the handle, swung it three times round his head, so skilfully that not a roll fell out, and sent it flying out into the stream on a great curve that showed the strength of his arm. At first the baker's boy was scared stiff. Then as he saw his rolls swimming about, he flung up his arms with a yell and behaved as though he had gone out of his mind. The gentlemen amused themselves for a while with his childish despair; then Baron Harry tossed him a gold piece which would have paid three times over for his loss and the officers rode laughing away home. Then the boy realized that these were the nobility and ceased his outcry.

This story lost no time in going the rounds – but who would have ventured to look askance? You might gnash your teeth over the pranks of Baron Harry and his friends, outwardly you took them with a smile. They were the lords and masters of Hohendamm. And now the lords and masters were having a party for the Swallows.

The *Avantageur* seemed not to know how to dance a waltz any better than to play one. For he did not take a partner, but going up to one of the white tables made a bow and sat down near little Baroness Anna, Baron Harry's wife, to whom he addressed a few shy words. The capacity to amuse himself with a Swallow was simply beyond the poor young man. Actually he was afraid of that kind of girl; he fancied that whatever he said to one she looked at him as though she were surprised – and

geur. But music, even the poorest, always
...eechless, relaxed, and dreamy mood – it is
...th these flabby and futile characters; and as the
...a, to whom he was entirely indifferent, made only
...ers to his remarks, they soon fell silent and confined
t...es to gazing into the whirling scene, with the same
somewhat wry smile, strange to say, on both their faces.

The candles flickered and sputtered so much that they became
quite mis-shapen with great blobs of soft wax. Beneath them the
couples twisted and turned in obedience to Lieutenant von
Gelbsattel's inspiring strains. They put out their feet and pointed
their toes, swung round with a flourish, then glided away. The
gentlemen's long legs bent and balanced and sprang again.
Petticoats flew. Gay hussar jackets whirled in abandon; volup-
tuously the ladies inclined their heads, yielding their waists to
their partners' embraces.

Baron Harry held an amazingly pretty young Swallow pressed
fairly close to his braided chest, putting his face down to hers
and looking unswervingly into her eyes. Baroness Anna's gaze
and her smile followed the pair. The long, lanky Lichterloh
was trundling along with a plump and dumpy little Swallow in
an extraordinary décolletage. But Frau Cavalry Captain von
Hühnemann, who loved champagne above all else in life, there
he was, dancing round and round under one of the chandeliers,
completely absorbed, with another Swallow, a friendly creature
whose freckled face beamed all over at the unprecedented
honour done her. 'My dear Baroness,' Frau von Hühnemann
said later to Frau First Lieutenant von Truchsess, 'these girls
are far from ignorant. They know all the cavalry garrisons in
Germany off by heart.' The pair were dancing together because
there were two extra ladies; they were quite unaware that the
other couples had gradually left the field to them until they
were performing all by themselves. At last, however, they saw
what had happened and stood there together in the centre of the
hall overwhelmed from all sides by laughter and applause.

Next came the champagne, and the white-gloved orderlies
ran from table to table pouring out. After that the Swallows

were urged to sing again – they simply had to sing, no matter how out of breath they were.

They stood on the platform that ran along the narrow side of the hall and made eyes at the company. Their shoulders and arms were bare, and they were dressed like the birds they represented, in long dark swallow-tails over pale grey waistcoats. They wore grey clocked stockings, and slippers with very low vamps and very high heels. There were blonde and brunette, there were the fat good-natured and the interestingly lean; there were some whose cheeks were staringly rouged, others with faces chalk-white like clowns. But the prettiest was the little dark one who had almond-shaped eyes and arms like a child's – she it was with whom Baron Harry had just danced. Baroness Anna, too, found that she was the prettiest one, and continued to smile.

The Swallows sang, and Lieutenant von Gelbsattel accompanied them, flinging back his torso and twisting round his head to look, while his long arms reached out after the keys. They sang as with one voice, that they were gay birds, that they had flown the world over and always left broken hearts behind them when they flew away. They sang another very tuneful piece beginning:

> 'Yes, yes, the arm-y,
> How we love the arm-y,'

and ending with the same. And in response to vociferous requests they repeated their Swallow song, and the officers, who knew it by now as well as they did, joined lustily in the chorus:

> 'When the swallows come again
> See them fly – *aren't* they fly?'

The whole hall rang with laughter and song and the stamping and clinking of spurred feet beating out the time.

Baroness Anna laughed too, at all the nonsense and extravagant spirits. She had laughed so much already, all the evening, that her head and her heart ached, and she would have been glad to close her eyes in darkness and quiet had not Harry been so zealous in his pleasures. 'I feel so jolly today,' she had told her neighbour, at a moment when she believed what she said; but the neighbour had answered only by a mocking look, and she had realized that people do not say such things. If you really feel jolly, you act like it; to proclaim the fact makes it sound queer. On the other hand, it would have been quite impossible to say: 'I feel so sad!'

Baroness Anna had grown up in the solitude and stillness of her father's estate by the sea; she was at all times too much inclined to leave out of consideration such home truths as the above, despite her constitutional fear of putting people out and her constitutional yearning to be like them and have them love her. She had white hands and heavy, ash-blonde hair – much too heavy for her narrow face with its delicate bones. Between her light eyebrows ran a perpendicular furrow, which gave a pained expression to her smile.

The truth was, she loved her husband. You must not laugh. She loved him even for the prank with the rolls. With a cowering and miserable love, though he betrayed her and daily abused her love like a schoolboy. She suffered for love of him as a woman does who despises her own weak tenderness and knows that power and the happiness of the powerful are justified on this earth. Yes, she yielded herself to love and its torments as once she had yielded herself to him when in a brief attack of tenderness he wooed her; with the hungry yearning of a lonely and dreamy soul, that craves for life and passion and an outlet for its emotions.

Waltz-time, tinkling glasses – hurly-burly and smoke, voices and dancing steps. That was Harry's world and his kingdom. It was the kingdom of her dreams as well: the world of love and life, the happy commonplace.

Social life, harmless, jolly conviviality – what a frightful thing it is, how enervating, how degrading; what a vain, alluring poison, what an insidious enemy to our peace! There she sat, evening after evening, night after night, a martyr to the glaring contrast between the utter emptiness round about her and the feverish excitement born of wine and coffee, of sensual music and the dance. She sat and looked on while Harry exercised his arts of fascination upon gay and pretty ladies – not because of

their personal charms but because it fed his vanity to have
people see him with them and know what a lucky man he was,
how much in the centre of things, without one single ungratified
longing. His vanity hurt her – and yet she loved it! How sweet
to feel how handsome he was, how young, splendid, and be-
witching! The infatuation of those other women would bring
her own to fever pitch. And when afterwards, at the end of an
evening spent by her in suffering for his sake, he would exhaust
himself in stupid and self-centred expressions of enjoyment,
there would come moments when her hatred and scorn out-
weighed her love; in her heart she would call him a puppy and
a trifler and try to punish him by not talking, by an absurd and
desperate dumbness.

Are we guessing right, little Baroness Anna? Are we giving
words to all that lay behind that poor little smile of yours as the
Swallows sang their song? Behind that pitiable and shameful
state, when you lay in bed afterwards in the grey dawn, thinking of the jests, the witticisms, the repartee, the social charms
you should have displayed – and did not! Dreams come, in that
grey dawn: you, quite worn with anguish, weep on his shoulder, he tries to console you with some of his empty, pleasant,
commonplace phrases, and you are suddenly overcome with the
mockery of your situation: you, lying on his shoulder, are
shedding tears over the whole world!

Suppose he were to fall ill? Are we right in saying that some
small trifling indisposition of his could call up a whole world of
dreams for you, wherein you see him as your ailing child; in
which he lies helpless and broken before you and at last, at last,
belongs to you alone? Do not blush, do not shrink away!
Trouble does sometimes make us think bad thoughts. But after
all you might trouble yourself a little about the young *Avantageur* with the drooping eyelids, sitting there beside you – how
gladly he would share his loneliness with you! Why do you
scorn him? Why despise? Because he belongs to your own
world, not to that other where pride and high spirits reign, and
conscious triumph and dancing rhythm. Truly it is hard not to be
at home in one world or in the other. We know. But there is no
half-way house.

Applause broke in upon Lieutenant von Gelbsattel's final chords. The Swallows had finished their song. They scorned the steps of the platform and jumped down from the front, flopping or fluttering – the gentlemen rushed up to be of help. Baron Harry helped the little brunette Swallow with the childlike arms; he helped her very efficiently and with understanding for such things. He took her by the thigh and the waist, gave himself plenty of time to set her down, then almost carried her to the table, where he brimmed her glass with champagne till it overflowed, and touched his own to it, slowly, meaningfully, gazing into her eyes with a foolish, insistent smile. He had drunk a good deal, and the scar stood out on his forehead, that looked very white next his glowing face. But his mood was a free and hilarious one, unclouded by any passion.

His table stood opposite to Baroness Anna's across the hall. As she sat talking idly with her neighbour she was listening greedily to the laughter over there and sending stolen and reproachful glances to watch every moment – in that painful state of tension which enables a person to carry on a conversation that complies with all the social forms, while actually being elsewhere all the time, and in the presence of the person one is watching.

Once or twice it seemed to her that the little Swallow's eye caught her own. Did she know her? Did she know who she was? How lovely she looked! How provocative, how full of fascination and thoughtless life! If Harry had been in love with her, if he had burned and suffered for her sake, his wife could have forgiven that, she could have understood and sympathized. And suddenly she became conscious that her own feeling for the little Swallow was warmer and deeper than Harry's own.

And the little Swallow herself? Dear me, her name was Emmy, and she was fundamentally commonplace. But she was wonderful too, with black strands of hair framing a wide, sensuous face, shadowed, almond-shaped eyes, a generous mouth full of shining teeth, and those arms like a child's. Loveliest of all were the shoulders – they had a way of moving with such ineffable suppleness in their sockets. Baron Harry took great interest in these shoulders; he would not have them covered, and set up a noisy struggle for the scarf which she would have put about them. And in all this, nobody in the whole hall saw, neither Baron Harry nor his wife nor anyone else, that this poor little waif, made sentimental by the wine she had drunk, had all the evening been casting longing glances at the young *Avantageur* whose lack of feeling for rhythm had caused his demission from the piano-stool. She had been drawn by the way he played, by his drooping lids, she found him noble, poetic, a being from a different world – whereas she was familiar unto boredom with Baron Harry's sort and all its works and ways. She was saddened, she was wretched, because the *Avantageur* cast not a thought in her direction.

The candles burned low and dim in the cigarette smoke and blue wreaths drifted above the company's heads. There was a smell of coffee on the heavy air, and odours and vapours of the feast, made still more heady by the somewhat daring perfume affected by the Swallows, hung about the scene; the white tables and champagne coolers, the men and women, flirting, giggling and guffawing, weary-eyed and unrestrained.

Baroness Anna talked no more, Despair – and that frightful mixture of yearning, envy, love, and self-contempt which we call jealousy and which makes the world no good place at all to live in – had so subdued her heart that she had not power to counterfeit any more. Let him see how she felt, perhaps he would be ashamed – or at least he would have some feeling about her, of whatever kind, in his heart.

She looked across. The game over there was going rather far, everybody was watching and laughing. Harry had thought of a new kind of amorous struggle with the fair Swallow: it consisted in an exchange of rings. Bracing his knee against hers he held her fast to her chair, and snatched and tugged after her hand in a violent effort to open her little clenched fist. In the end he won. Amid noisy applause he wrenched off the narrow circlet she wore – it cost him some trouble – and triumphantly forced his own wedding ring upon her finger.

Then Baroness Anna stood up. Anger and pain, a longing to hide herself away in the dark with her sense of his so dear unworthiness; a desperate desire to punish him by making a

scandal, by forcing him at all costs to acknowledge her presence
– such were the emotions that overpowered her. She pushed
back her chair, and pale as death she walked across the hall
towards the door.

There was a great sensation. People were sobered, they looked
at one another grave-faced. One or two gentlemen called out
Harry's name. All at once it became still in the hall.

Then something very odd happened: the little Swallow –
Emmy – suddenly and decisively espoused the Baroness's
cause. Perhaps she was moved by a natural feminine instinct of
pity for suffering love; perhaps her own pangs for the *Avantageur* with the drooping lids made her see in the little Baroness
a fellow-sufferer. In any case, she acted – to the amazement of
the company.

'You are coarse!' she said loudly, in the hush, and gave the
dumbfounded Harry a great push. Just these three words: 'You
are coarse.' And all at once she was at Baroness Anna's side,
where the latter stood lifting the latch of the door.

'Forgive!' she breathed – softly, as though no one else in the
room were worthy to hear. 'Here is the ring,' and she slipped
Harry's wedding ring into the Baroness's hand. And suddenly
Baroness Anna felt the girl's broad, glowing face bend over this
hand of hers; she felt burning on it a soft and passionate kiss.
'Forgive!' whispered the little Swallow once more, and ran off.

But Baroness Anna stood outside in the darkness, still quite
dazed, and waited for this unexpected event to take on shape
and meaning within her. And it did: it was a joy, so warm, so
sweet, so comfortable that for a moment she closed her eyes.

We stop here. No more, it is enough. Just this one priceless
little detail, as it stands: there she was, quite enraptured and
enchanted, simply because a little chit of a strolling chorus-girl
had come and kissed her hand!

We leave you, Baroness Anna. We kiss your brow and take
our leave; farewell, we must hurry away. Sleep, now. You will
dream all night of the Swallow who came to you, and you will
have a gleam of happiness.

For it brings happiness, it brings to the heart a little thrill and
ecstasy of joy, when two worlds, between which longing plies,
for one fleeting, illusory moment touch each other.

AT THE PROPHET'S
(1904)

STRANGE regions there are, strange minds, strange realms of the spirit, lofty and spare. At the edge of large cities, where street lamps are scarce and policemen walk by twos, are houses where you mount till you can mount no further, up and up into attics under the roof, where pale young geniuses, criminals of the dream, sit with folded arms and brood; up into cheap studios with symbolic decorations, where solitary and rebellious artists, inwardly consumed, hungry and proud, wrestle in a fog of cigarette smoke with devastatingly ultimate ideals. Here is the end: ice, chastity, null. Here is valid no compromise, no concession, no half-way, no consideration of values. Here the air is so rarefied that the mirages of life no longer exist. Here reign defiance and iron consistency, the ego supreme amid despair; here freedom, madness, and death hold sway.

It was eight o'clock of Good Friday evening. Several of those whom Daniel had invited arrived together. Their invitations, written in a peculiar script on quarto paper headed by an eagle carrying a naked dagger in its talons, had summoned them to forgather on this evening for the reading aloud of Daniel's Proclamations. Accordingly they had now met at the appointed hour, in the gloomy suburban street, in front of the cheap apartment-house wherein the prophet had his earthly dwelling.

Some of them knew each other and exchanged greetings. There were the Polish artist and the slender girl who lived with him; a lyric poet; a tall, black-bearded Semite with his heavy, pale wife, who dressed in long, flowing robes; a personage with an aspect soldierly yet somewhat sickly withal, who was a retired cavalry captain and professed spiritualist; a young philosopher who looked like a kangaroo. Finally a novelist, a man with a stiff hat and a trim moustache. He knew nobody. He belonged to quite another sphere and was present by the merest chance, being on good terms with life and having written a book which was read in middle-class circles. He wore an un-assuming air, as one who knew that he was here on sufferance and was grateful. At a little distance he followed the others into the house.

They climbed the stairs, one after the other, with their hands on the cast-iron rail. There was no talking; these were folk who knew the value of the Word and were not given to light speak-ing. In the dim light from the little oil lamps which stood on the window-ledges of the landings they read, as they passed, the names on the doors. The homes and business premises of an insurance official, a midwife, an 'agent', *a blanchisseuse du fin*, a chiropodist – they passed by all these, not contemptuous, yet remote. They mounted the narrow staircase as up a dark shaft, cautiously yet firmly; for from far above, from the very last landing, came a faint gleam, a flickering glimmer from the top-most height.

At length they arrived at their goal under the roof, in the light of six candles in divers candlesticks, burning at the head of the stairs on a little table covered with a faded altar-cloth. On the door, which seemed, as indeed it was, the entrance to an attic, was fastened a large pasteboard shield with the name of Daniel on it in Roman lettering done in black crayon. They rang. A boy in a new blue suit and shiny boots opened to them, a pleasant-looking boy with a broad forehead; he had a candle in his hand and lighted them diagonally across the narrow dark corridor into an unpapered mansard-like space, entirely bare save for a wooden hatstand. With a gesture accompanied by gurgling and babbling sounds but no words the boy invited them to take off their things. When the novelist, inspired by vague sympathy, addressed a question to him it became evident that the lad was dumb. He lighted the guests back across the corridor to another door and ushered them in. The novelist entered last. He was wearing a frock-coat and gloves and had made up his mind to behave as though he were in church.

The moderate-sized room which they entered was pervaded by a ceremonial and flickering illumination from twenty or twenty-five candles. A young girl in a modest frock with white turn-over collar and cuffs, and with an innocent and simple face, stood near the door and gave each guest her hand in turn. This was Maria Josepha, Daniel's sister. The novelist had met her at a literary tea, where she sat bolt upright, cup in hand, and talked of her brother in a clear, earnest voice. Daniel was her adoration.

The novelist looked about for him.

'He is not here,' said Maria Josepha. 'He has gone out, I do not know where. But in spirit he will be with us and follow sentence by sentence the Proclamations which we shall hear read.'

'Who is to read them?' asked the novelist with subdued and reverent mien. He took all this very seriously. He was a well-meaning and essentially modest man, full of respect for all the phenomena of this world, ready to learn and to esteem what was estimable.

'One of my brother's young men, whom we expect from Switzerland,' Maria Josepha replied. 'He is not here yet. He will be present at the right moment.'

On a table opposite the door, with its upper edge resting against the slope of the mansard ceiling, was a large, hastily executed drawing. The candlelight revealed it as a picture of Napoleon, standing in a clumsy and autocratic pose warming his jack-boots at a fire. At the right of the entrance was a shrine or altar whereon, between candles in silver candelabra, was a painted figure of a saint with uplifted eyes and outstretched hands. Before the altar was a prie-dieu. A nearer view disclosed a little amateur photograph leaning at one foot of the saint: a portrait of a young man of some thirty years with pale, retreating brow and bony, vulture-like face, expressive of a ferociously concentrated intellect.

The novelist paused awhile before this picture of Daniel; then he cautiously ventured further into the room. It had a large round table with a polished yellow surface displaying in burnt-work the same design – the eagle with the dagger in its claws – which had been on the invitations. Behind the table were low wooden chairs and lording it over these one elevated seat like a throne, tall, narrow, austere, and Gothic. A long plain bench covered with cheap stuff stood under a low window, occupying the space formed by the meeting of wall and roof. The squat porcelain stove had evidently been giving out too much heat, for the window was open upon a square section of the blue night outside, in whose deeps and distances the bright yellow points of the gas street lamps made an irregular pattern that tailed off into the open country.

But opposite the window the room narrowed to form an alcove lighted more brightly than the rest and furnished half as a cabinet, half as a chapel. On the right side stood a curtained book-shelf with lighted candelabra and antique lamps on top. On the left was a white-covered table holding a crucifix, a seven-branched candle-stick, a goblet of red wine, and a piece of raisin cake on a plate. But at the very front was a low platform beneath an iron chandelier; on it stood a gilded plaster column. The capital of the column was covered with an altar-cloth of blood-red silk, and on that lay a thick folio manuscript – it contained Daniel's Proclamations. A light-coloured paper with little Empire garlands covered the walls and sloping ceiling; death-masks, rose-garlands, and a great rusty sword hung against the walls, and besides the large picture of Napoleon there were about the room various reproductions of Luther, Nietzsche, Moltke, Alexander VI, Robespierre, and Savonarola.

'It is all symbolic,' said Maria Josepha, searching the novelist's reserved and respectful features to see if she could tell what impression the room made on him. Meanwhile other guests had come in, silently, solemnly; they all began to take their places in suitable attitudes on the benches and chairs. Besides the earlier comers there was a designer, a fantastic creature with a wizened childish face; a lame woman, who was in the habit of introducing herself as a priestess of Eros; an unmarried young mother whose aristocratic family had cast her out, and who was admitted into the circle solely on the ground of her motherhood, since intellectual pretensions she had none; an elderly authoress and a deformed musician – in all some twelve persons. The novelist had retreated into the window-alcove, and Maria Josepha sat near the door, her hands close together on her knees. Thus they awaited the young man from Switzerland, who would be present at the right moment.

Suddenly another guest arrived — a rich woman who out of sheer amateurishness had a habit of frequenting such gatherings as this. She came from the city in her satin-lined coupé, from her splended house with the tapestries on the walls and the gialloantico door-jambs; she had come all the way up the stairs and in at the door, sweet-scented, luxurious, lovely, in a blue cloth frock with yellow embroidery, a Paris hat on her red-brown hair, and a smile in her Titian eyes. She came out of curiosity, out of boredom, out of craving for something different, out of amiable extravagance, out of pure universal goodwill, which is rare enough in this world. She greeted Daniel's sister, also the novelist, who had entrée at her house, and sat down on the bench under the window, between the priestess of Eros and the kangaroo-philosopher — quite as though she were used to such things.

'I was almost too late,' said she softly, with her lovely mobile lips, to the novelist as he sat behind her. 'I had people at tea; it was rather dragged out.'

The novelist was slightly overcome; how thankful he was that he had on presentable clothes! 'How beautiful she is!' thought he. 'Actually she is worthy of being her daughter's mother.'

'And Fräulein Sonia?' he asked over her shoulder. 'You have not brought Fräulein Sonia with you?'

Sonia was the rich woman's daughter; in the novelist's eyes altogether too good to be true, a marvellous creature, a consummate cultural product, an achieved ideal. He said her name twice because it gave him an indescribable pleasure to pronounce it.

'Sonia is a little ailing,' said the rich woman. 'Yes, imagine, she has a bad foot. Oh, nothing — a swelling, something like a little inflammation or gathering. It has been lanced. The lancing may not have been necessary but she wanted it done.'

'She wanted it done,' repeated the novelist in an enraptured whisper. 'How characteristic! But how may I express my sympathy for the affliction?'

'Of course, I will give her your greetings,' said the rich woman. And as he was silent: 'Is not that enough for you?'

'No, that is not enough for me,' said he, quite low; and as she had a certain respect for his writing she replied with a smile:

'Then send her a few flowers.'

'Oh, thanks!' said he. 'Thanks, I will.' And inwardly he thought: 'A few flowers! A whole flower-shopful! Tomorrow, before breakfast. I'll go in a droshky.' And he felt that life and he were on very good terms.

Just then a noise was heard outside, the door opened with a quick push and closed, and before the guests there stood in the candlelight a short, thickset youth in a dark jacket suit – the young man from Switzerland. He glanced over the room with a threatening eye, went in an impetuous stride to the platform at the front of the alcove, and placed himself behind the plaster column – all with a certain violence, as though he wished to root himself there. He seized the top quire of the manuscript and began to read straightway.

He was perhaps eight-and-twenty years old, short-necked and ill-favoured. His close-cropped hair grew to a point very far down on the low and wrinkled brow. His face, beardless, heavy, and morose, displayed a nose like a bulldog's, large cheek-bones, sunken cheeks, and thick protruding lips, which seemed to form words clumsily, reluctantly, and as it were with a sort of flaccid contempt. The face was coarse and yet pale. He read too loudly, in a fierce voice which nevertheless had a suppressed tremolo and sometimes faltered for lack of breath. The hand that held the manuscript was broad and red and yet it shook. The youth displayed an odd and unpleasant mixture of brutality and weakness and the matter of his reading was in remarkable consonance with its manner.

The 'Proclamations' consisted of sermons, parables, theses, laws, prophecies, and exhortations resembling orders of the day, following each other in a mingled style of psalter and revelation with an endless succession of technical phrases, military and strategic as well as philosophical and critical. A fevered and frightfully irritable ego here expanded itself, a self-isolated megalomaniac flooded the world with a hurricane of violent and threatening words. *Christus imperator maximus* was his name;

he enrolled troops ready to die for the subjection of the globe; he sent out embassies, gave inexorable ultimata, exacted poverty and chastity, and with a sort of morbid enjoyment reiterated his roaring demand for unconditional obedience. Buddha, Alexander, Napoleon and Jesus — their names were mentioned as his humble forerunners, not worthy to unloose the laces of their spiritual lord.

The young man read for an hour; then panting he took a swallow from the beaker of red wine and began on fresh Proclamations. Beads of sweat stood on his low brow, his thick lips quivered, and in between the words he kept expelling the air through his nose with a short, snorting sound, an exhausted roar. The solitary ego sang, raved, commanded. It would lose itself in confused pictures, go down in an eddy of logical error, to bob up again suddenly and startlingly in an entirely unexpected place. Blasphemies and hosannahs — a waft of incense and a reek of blood. In thunderings and slaughterings the world was conquered and redeemed.

It would have been hard to estimate the effect of Daniel's Proclamations upon their hearers. Some with heads tipped far back looked up to the ceiling with a blank stare; others held their heads in their hands, bowed deep over their knees. The eyes of the priestess of Eros wore a strange veiled look whenever the word 'chastity' was pronounced; and the kangaroo-philosopher now and then wrote something or other with his long crooked forefinger in the air. The novelist sought in vain for a comfortable position for his aching back. At ten o'clock he had a vision of a ham sandwich but manfully put it away.

Towards half past ten the young man was seen to be holding the last sheet of paper in his red, unsteady hand. This was his peroration. 'Soldiers,' he cried, his voice of thunder failing for very weakness, 'I deliver to you for plundering — the world!' He stepped down from the platform, looked at everybody with a threatening glance, and went out of the door, as violently as he had come in.

His audience remained a moment motionless in the last position they had taken up. Then as with a common resolve they rose and departed, each one pressing Maria Josepha's hand with a low-toned word, as she stood once more, chaste and silent, at the door.

The dumb boy was still on duty outside. He lighted the guests into the cloak-room, helped them with their overcoats, and led them down the narrow stair, with the flickering light falling upon it from up there where Daniel's kingdom was; down to the outer door, which he unlocked. One after the other the guests issued into the dismal suburban street.

The rich woman's coupé stood before the house; the coachman on the box between the two clear-shining lanterns carried the hand with the whip in it to his hat. The novelist accompanied the rich woman to her carriage.

'How are you feeling?' he inquired.

'I don't like to talk about such things,' she answered. 'Perhaps he really is a genius or something like that.'

'Yes, after all, what is genius?' said he pensively. 'In this Daniel all the conditions are present: the isolation, the freedom, the spiritual passion, the magnificent vision, the belief in his own power, yes, even the approximation to madness and crime. What is there lacking? Perhaps the human element? A little feeling, a little yearning, a little love? But of course that is just a rough hypothesis.'

'Greet Sonia for me,' said he, after she was seated, as she gave him her hand. He looked anxiously into her face to see how she would take his speaking simply of Sonia and not of 'Fräulein Sonia' or 'your daughter'.

She esteemed his literary talent and so she suffered it, with a smile. 'I will do so,' said she.

'Thanks,' said he, and a bewildering gust of hope swept over him. 'Now I am as hungry as a wolf for my supper.'

Yes, he and life were certainly on good terms!

A WEARY HOUR
(1905)

H E got up from the table, his little, fragile writing-desk; got up as though desperate, and with hanging head crossed the room to the tall, thin, pillar-like stove in the opposite corner. He put his hands to it; but the hour was long past midnight and the tiles were nearly stone-cold. Not getting even this little comfort that he sought, he leaned his back against them and, coughing, drew together the folds of his dressing-gown, between which a draggled lace shirt-frill stuck out; he snuffed hard through his nostrils to get a little air, for as usual he had a cold.

It was a particular, a sinister cold, which scarcely ever quite disappeared. It inflamed his eyelids and made the flanges of his nose all raw; in his head and limbs it lay like a heavy, sombre intoxication. Or was this cursed confinement to his room, to which the doctor had weeks ago condemned him, to blame for all his languor and flabbiness? God knew if it was the right thing – perhaps so, on account of his chronic catarrh and the spasms in his chest and belly. And for weeks on end now, yes, weeks, bad weather had reigned in Jena – hateful, horrible weather, which he felt in every nerve of his body – cold, wild, gloomy. The December wind roared in the stove-pipe with a desolate god-forsaken sound – he might have been wandering on a heath, by night and storm, his soul full of unappeasable grief. Yet this close confinement – that was not good either; not good for thought, nor for the rhythm of the blood, where thought was engendered.

The six-sided room was bare and colourless and devoid of cheer; a whitewashed ceiling wreathed in tobacco smoke, walls covered with trellis-patterned paper hung with silhouettes in oval frames, half a dozen slender-legged pieces of furniture; the whole lighted by two candles burning at the head of the manuscript on the writing-table. Red curtains draped the upper part of the window-frames; mere festooned wisps of cotton they were, but red, a warm, sonorous red, and he loved them and would not have parted from them; they gave a little air of ease and charm to the bald unlovely poverty of his surroundings. He stood by the stove and blinked repeatedly, straining his eyes across at the work from which he had just fled: that load, that weight, that gnawing conscience, that sea which to drink up, that frightful task which to perform, was all his pride and all his misery, at once his heaven and his hell. It dragged, it stuck, it would not budge – and now again ... ! It must be the weather; or his catarrh, or his fatigue. Or was it the work? Was the thing itself an unfortunate conception, doomed from its beginning to despair?

He had risen in order to put a little space between him and his task, for physical distance would often result in improved perspective, a wider view of his material and a better chance of conspectus. Yes, the mere feeling of relief on turning away from the battlefield had been known to work like an inspiration. And a more innocent one than that purveyed by alcohol or strong, black coffee.

The little cup stood on the side-table. Perhaps it would help him out in the impasse? No, no, not again! Not the doctor only, but somebody else too, a more important somebody, had cautioned him against that sort of thing – another person, who lived over in Weimar and for whom he felt a love which was a mixture of hostility and yearning. That was a wise man. He knew how to live and create; did not abuse himself; was full of self-regard.

Quiet reigned in the house. There was only the wind, driving down the Schlossgasse and dashing the rain in gusts against the panes. They were all asleep – the landlord and his family, Lotte and the children. And here he stood by the cold stove, awake, alone, tormented; blinking across at the work in which his morbid self-dissatisfaction would not let him believe.

His neck rose long and white out of his stock and his knock-kneed legs showed between the skirts of his dressing-gown. The red hair was smoothed back from a thin, high forehead; it re-treated in bays from his veined white temples and hung down in thin locks over the ears. His nose was aquiline, with an abrupt whitish tip; above it the well-marked line of the brows almost met. They were darker than his hair and gave the deep-set, inflamed eyes a tragic, staring look. He could not breathe through his nose; so he opened his thin lips and made the freckled, sickly cheeks look even more sunken thereby.

No, it was a failure, it was all hopelessly wrong. The army ought to have been brought in! The army was the root of the whole thing. But it was impossible to present it before the eyes of the audience — and was art powerful enough thus to enforce the imagination? Besides, his hero was no hero; he was contemptible, he was frigid. The situation was wrong, the language was wrong; it was a dry pedestrian lecture, good for a history class, but as drama absolutely hopeless!

Very good, then, it was over. A defeat. A failure. Bankruptcy. He would write to Körner, the good Körner, who believed in him, who clung with childlike faith to his genius. He would scoff, scold, beseech — this friend of his; would remind him of the *Carlos*, which likewise had issued out of doubts and pains and rewritings and after all the anguish turned out to be something really fine, a genuine masterpiece. But times were changed. Then he had been a man still capable of taking a strong, confident grip on a thing and giving it triumphant shape. Doubts and struggles? Yes. And ill he had been, perhaps more ill than now; a fugitive, oppressed and hungry, at odds with the world; humanly speaking, a beggar. But young, still young! Each time, however low he had sunk, his resilient spirit had leaped up anew; upon the hour of affliction had followed the feeling of triumphant self-confidence. That came no more, or hardly ever, now. There might be one night of glowing exaltation — when the fires of his genius lighted up an impassioned vision of all that he might do if they burned on; but it had always to be paid for with a week of enervation and gloom. Faith in the future, his guiding star in times of stress, was dead. Here was the despairing truth: the years of need and nothingness, which he had thought of as the painful testing-time, turned out to have been the rich and fruitful ones; and now that a little happiness had fallen to his lot, now that he had ceased to be an intellectual freebooter and occupied a posi-

tion of civic dignity, with office and honours, wife and children
– now he was exhausted, worn out. To give up, to own himself beaten – that was all there was left to do. He groaned;
he pressed his hands to his eyes and dashed up and down the
room like one possessed. What he had just thought was so
frightful that he could not stand still on the spot where he had
thought it. He sat down on a chair by the further wall and
stared gloomily at the floor, his clasped hands hanging down
between his knees.

His conscience ... how loudly his conscience cried out! He
had sinned, sinned against himself all these years, against the
delicate instrument that was his body. Those youthful excesses,
the nights without sleep, the days in close, smoke-laden air,
straining his mind and heedless of his body; the narcotics with
which he had spurred himself on – all that was now taking its
revenge.

And if it did – then he would defy the gods, who decreed the
guilt and then imposed the penalties. He had lived as he had to
live, he had not had time to be wise, not time to be careful. Here
in this place in his chest, when he breathed, coughed, yawned,
always in the same spot came this pain, this piercing, stabbing,
diabolical little warning; it never left him, since that time in
Erfurt five years ago when he had catarrhal fever and inflammation of the lungs. What was it warning him of? Ah, he knew
only too well what it meant – no matter how the doctor chose
to put him off. He had not time to be wise and spare himself,
no time to save his strength by submission to moral laws. What
he wanted to do he must do soon, do quickly, do today.

And the moral laws? ... Why was it that precisely sin,
surrender to the harmful and the consuming, actually seemed to
him more moral than any amount of wisdom and frigid self-
discipline? Not that constituted morality: not the contemptible
knack of keeping a good conscience – rather the struggle and
compulsion, the passion and pain.

Pain ... how his breast swelled at the word! He drew himself
up and folded his arms; his gaze, beneath the close-set auburn
brows, was kindled by the nobility of his suffering. No man was
utterly wretched so long as he could still speak of his misery in

high-sounding and noble words. One thing only was indispensable; the courage to call his life by large and fine names. Not to ascribe his sufferings to bad air and constipation; to be well enough to cherish emotions, to scorn and ignore the material. Just on this one point to be naïve, though in all else sophisticated. To believe, to have strength to believe, in suffering. ... But he *did* believe in it; so profoundly, so ardently, that nothing which came to pass with suffering could seem to him either useless or evil. His glance sought the manuscript, and his arms tightened across his chest. Talent itself – was that not suffering? And if the manuscript over there, his unhappy effort, made him suffer, was not that quite as it should be – a good sign, so to speak? His talents had never been of the copious, ebullient sort; were they to become so he would feel mistrustful. That only happened with beginners and bunglers, with the ignorant and easily satisfied, whose life was not shaped and disciplined by the possession of a gift. For a gift, my friends down there in the audience, a gift is not anything simple, not anything to play with; it is not mere ability. At bottom it is a compulsion; a critical knowledge of the ideal, a permanent dissatisfaction, which rises only through suffering to the height of its powers. And it is to the greatest, the most unsatisfied, that their gift is the sharpest scourge. Not to complain, not to boast; to think modestly, patiently of one's pain; and if not a day in the week, not even an hour, be free from it – what then? To make light and little of it all, of suffering and achievement alike – that was what made a man great.

He stood up, pulled out his snuff box and sniffed eagerly, then suddenly clasped his hands behind his back and strode so briskly through the room that the flames of the candles flickered in the draught. Greatness, distinction, world conquest and an imperishable name! To be happy and unknown, what was that by comparison? To be known – known and loved by all the world – ah, they might call that egotism, those who knew naught of the urge, naught of the sweetness of this dream! Everything out of the ordinary is egotistic, in proportion to its suffering. 'Speak for yourselves,' it says, 'ye without mission on this earth, ye whose life is so much easier than mine!' And Ambition says: 'Shall my sufferings be vain? No, they must make me great!'

The nostrils of his great nose dilated, his gaze darted fiercely about the room. His right hand was thrust hard and far into the opening of his dressing-gown, his left arm hung down, the fist clenched. A fugitive red played in the gaunt cheeks – a glow thrown up from the fire of his artistic egoism: that passion for his own ego, which burnt unquenchably in his being's depths. Well he knew it, the secret intoxication of this love! Sometimes he needed only to contemplate his own hand, to be filled with the liveliest tenderness towards himself, in whose service he was bent on spending all the talent, all the art that he owned. And he was right so to do, there was nothing base about it. For deeper still than his egoism lay the knowledge that he was freely consuming and sacrificing himself in the service of a high ideal, not as a virtue, of course, but rather out of sheer necessity. And this was his ambition: that no one should be greater than he who had not also suffered more for the sake of the high ideal. No one. He stood still, his hand over his eyes, his body turned aside in a posture of shrinking and avoidance. For already the inevitable thought had stabbed him: the thought of that other man, that radiant being, so sense-endowed, so divinely unconscious, that man over there in Weimar, whom he loved and hated. And once more, as always, in deep disquiet, in feverish haste, there began working within him the inevitable sequence of his thoughts: he must assert and define his own nature, his own art, against that other's. Was that other greater? Wherein, then, and why? If he won, would he have sweated blood to do so? If he lost, would his downfall be a tragic sight? He was no hero, no; a god, perhaps. But it was easier to be a god than a hero. Yes, things were easier for him. He was wise, he was deft, he knew how to distinguish between knowing and creating; perhaps that was why he was so blithe and carefree, such an effortless and gushing spring! But if creation was divine, knowledge was heroic, and he who created in knowledge was hero as well as god.

The will to face difficulties ... Did anyone realize what discipline and self-control it cost him to shape a sentence or follow out a hard train of thought? For after all he was ignorant, un-disciplined, a slow, dreamy enthusiast. One of Caesar's letters was harder to write than the most effective scene – and was it not almost for that very reason higher? From the first rhythmi-cal urge of the inward creative force towards matter, towards the material, towards casting in shape and form – from that to the thought, the image, the word, the line – what a struggle, what a Gethsemane! Everything that he wrote was a marvel of yearning after form, shape, line, body; of yearning after the sunlit world of that other man who had only to open his god-like lips and straightway call the bright unshadowed things he saw by name!

And yet – and despite that other man. Where was there an artist, a poet, like himself? Who like him created out of noth-ing, out of his own breast? A poem was born as music in his soul, as pure, primitive essence, long before it put on a garment of metaphor from the visible world. History, philosophy, pas-sion were no more than pretexts and vehicles for something which had little to do with them, but was at home in orphic depths. Words and conceptions were keys upon which his art played and made vibrate the hidden strings. No one realized. The good souls praised him, indeed, for the power of feeling with which he struck one note or another. And his favourite note, his final emotional appeal, the great bell upon which he sounded his summons to the highest feasts of the soul – many there were who responded to its sound. Freedom! But in all their exaltation, certainly he meant by the word both more and less than they did. Freedom – what was it? A self-respecting middle-class attitude towards thrones and princes? Surely not that. When one thinks of all that the spirit of man has dared to put into the word! Freedom from what? After all, from what? Perhaps, indeed, even from human happiness, that silken bond, that tender, sacred tie ...

From happiness. His lips quivered. It was as though his glance turned inward upon himself; slowly his face sank into his hands. ... He stood by the bed in the next room, where the flowered curtains hung in motionless folds across the win-dow, and the lamp shed a bluish light. He bent over the sweet head on the pillow ... a ringlet of dark hair lay across her cheek, that had the paleness of pearl; the childlike lips were open in slumber. 'My wife! Beloved, didst thou yield to my yearning and come to me to be my joy? And that thou art. ... Lie still and sleep; nay, lift not those sweet shadowy lashes and gaze up at me, as sometimes with thy great, dark, questioning, searching eyes. I love thee so! By God I swear it. It is only that sometimes I am tired out, struggling at my self-imposed task, and my feelings will not respond. And I must not be too utterly thine, never utterly happy in thee, for the sake of my mission.'

He kissed her, drew away from her pleasant, slumbrous warmth, looked about him, turned back to the outer room. The clock struck; it warned him that the night was already far spent; but likewise it seemed to be mildly marking the end of a weary hour. He drew a deep breath, his lips closed firmly; he went back and took up his pen. No, he must not brood, he was too far down for that. He must not descend into chaos; or at least he must not stop there. Rather out of chaos, which is fullness, he must draw up to the light whatever he found there fit and ripe for form. No brooding! Work! Define, eliminate, fashion, complete!

And complete it he did, that effort of a labouring hour. He brought it to an end, perhaps not to a good end, but in any case to an end. And being once finished, lo, it was also good. And from his soul, from music and idea, new works struggled upward to birth and, taking shape, gave out light and sound, ringing and shimmering, and giving hint of their infinite origin – as in a shell we hear the sighing of the sea whence it came.

THE BLOOD OF THE WALSUNGS
(1905)

IT was seven minutes to twelve. Wendelin came into the first-floor entrance-hall and sounded the gong. He straddled in his violet knee-breeches on a prayer-rug pale with age and be-laboured with his drumstick the metal disk. The brazen din, savage and primitive out of all proportion to its purport, re-sounded through the drawing-rooms to left and right, the bil-liard-room, the library, the winter-garden, up and down the house; it vibrated through the warm and even atmosphere, heavy with exotic perfume. At last the sound ceased, and for another seven minutes Wendelin went about his business while Florian in the dining-room gave the last touches to the table. But on the stroke of twelve the cannibalistic summons sounded a second time. And the family appeared.

Herr Aarenhold came in his little toddle out of the library where he had been busy with his old editions. He was continu-ally acquiring old books, first editions, in many languages, costly and crumbling trifles. Gently rubbing his hands he asked in his slightly plaintive way:

'Beckerath not here yet?'

'No, but he will be. Why shouldn't he? He will be saving a meal in a restaurant,' answered Frau Aarenhold, coming noise-lessly up the thick-carpeted stairs, on the landing of which stood a small, very ancient church organ.

Herr Aarenhold blinked. His wife was impossible. She was small, ugly, prematurely aged, and shrivelled as though by tropic suns. A necklace of brilliants rested upon her shrunken breast. She wore her hair in complicated twists and knots to form a lofty pile, in which, somewhere on one side, sat a great jewelled brooch, adorned in its turn with a bunch of white aigrettes. Herr Aarenhold and the children had more than once, as diplomatically as possible, advised against this style of coif-fure. But Frau Aarenhold clung stoutly to her own taste.

The children came: Kunz and Märit, Siegmund and Sieglinde. Kunz was in a braided uniform, a stunning tanned creature with curling lips and a killing scar. He was doing six weeks' service with his regiment of hussars. Märit made her appearance in an uncorseted garment. She was an ashen, austere blonde of twenty-eight, with a hooked nose, grey eyes like a falcon's, and a bitter, contemptuous mouth. She was studying law and went entirely her own way in life.

Siegmund and Sieglinde came last, hand in hand, from the second floor. They were twins, graceful as young fawns, and with immature figures despite their nineteen years. She wore a Florentine cinquecento frock of claret-coloured velvet, too heavy for her slight body. Siegmund had on a green jacket suit with a tie of raspberry shantung, patent-leather shoes on his narrow feet, and cuff-buttons set with small diamonds. He had a strong growth of black beard but kept it so close-shaven that his sallow face with the heavy gathered brows looked no less boyish than his figure. His head was covered with thick black locks parted far down on one side and growing low on his temples. Her dark brown hair was waved in long, smooth undulations over her ears, confined by a gold circlet. A large pearl – his gift – hung down upon her brow. Round one of his boyish wrists was a heavy gold chain – a gift from her. They were very like each other, with the same slightly drooping nose, the same full lips lying softly together, the same prominent cheek-bones and black, bright eyes. Likest of all were their long slim hands, his no more masculine than hers, save that they were slightly redder. And they went always hand in hand, heedless that the hands of both inclined to moisture.

The family stood about awhile in the lobby, scarcely speaking. Then Beckerath appeared. He was engaged to Sieglinde. Wendelin opened the door to him and as he entered in his black frock-coat he excused himself for his tardiness. He was a government official and came of a good family. He was short of stature, with a pointed beard and a very yellow complexion, like a canary. His manners were punctilious. He began every sentence by drawing his breath in quickly through his mouth and pressing his chin on his chest.

He kissed Sieglinde's hand and said:

'And you must excuse me too, Sieglinde – it is so far from the Ministry to the Zoo –'

He was not allowed to say thou to her – she did not like it. She answered briskly:

'Very far. Supposing that, in consideration of the fact, you left your office a bit earlier.'

Kunz seconded her, his black eyes narrowing to glittering cracks:

'It would no doubt have a most beneficial effect upon our household economy.'

'Oh, well – business, you know what it is,' von Beckerath said dully. He was thirty-five years old.

The brother and sister had spoken glibly and with point. They may have attacked out of a habitual inward posture of self-defence; perhaps they deliberately meant to wound – perhaps again their words were due to the sheer pleasure of turning a phrase. It would have been unreasonable to feel annoyed. They let his feeble answer pass, as though they found it in character, as though cleverness in him would have been out of place. They went to table; Herr Aarenhold led the way, eager to let von Beckerath see that he was hungry.

They sat down, they unfolded their stiff table-napkins. The immense room was carpeted, the walls were covered with eighteenth-century panelling, and three electric lustres hung from the ceiling. The family table, with its seven places, was lost in the void. It was drawn up close to the large French window, beneath which a dainty little fountain spread its silver spray behind a low lattice. Outside was an extended view of the still wintry garden. Tapestries with pastoral scenes covered the upper part of the walls; they, like the panelling, had been part of the furnishings of a French château. The dining-chairs were low and soft and cushioned with tapestry. A tapering glass vase holding two orchids stood at each place, on the glistening, spotless, faultlessly ironed damask cloth. With careful, skinny hands Herr Aarenhold settled the pince-nez half-way down his nose and with a mistrustful air read the menu, three copies of which lay on the table. He suffered from a weakness of the solar plexus, that nerve centre which lies at the pit of the stomach and may give rise to serious distress. He was obliged to be very careful what he ate.

There was bouillon with beef marrow, sole *au vin blanc*, pheasant, and pineapple.

Nothing else. It was a simple family meal, But it satisfied Herr Aarenhold. It was good, light, nourishing food. The soup was served: a dumb-waiter above the sideboard brought it noiselessly down from the kitchen and the servants handed it round, bending over assiduously, in a very passion of service. The tiny cups were of translucent porcelain, whitish morsels of marrow floated in the hot golden liquid.

Herr Aarenhold felt himself moved to expand a little in the comfortable warmth thus purveyed. He carried his napkin cautiously to his mouth and cast after a means of clothing his thought in words.

'Have another cup, Beckerath,' said he. 'A working-man has a right to his comforts and his pleasures. Do you really like to eat – really enjoy it, I mean? If not, so much the worse for you. To me every meal is a little celebration. Somebody said that life is pretty nice after all – being arranged so that we can eat four times a day. He's my man! But to do justice to the arrangement one has to preserve one's youthful receptivity – and not everybody can do that. We get old – well, we can't help it. But the thing is to keep things fresh and not get used to them. For instance,' he went on putting a bit of marrow on a piece of roll and sprinkling salt on it, 'you are about to change your estate, the plane on which you live is going to be a good deal elevated' (von Beckerath smiled), 'and if you want to enjoy your new life, really enjoy it, consciously and artistically, you must take care never to get used to your new situation. Getting used to things is death. It is ennui. Don't live into it, don't let anything become a matter of course, preserve a childlike taste for the sweets of life. You see … for some years now I have been able to command some of the amenities of life' (von Beckerath smiled), 'and yet I assure you, every morning that God lets me wake up I have a little thrill because my bed-cover is made of silk. That is what it is to be young. I know perfectly well how

I did it; and yet I can look round me and feel like an enchanted prince.'

The children exchanged looks, so openly that Herr Aarenhold could not help seeing it; he became visibly embarrassed. He knew that they were united against him, that they despised him: for his origins, for the blood which flowered in his veins and through him in theirs; for the way he had earned his money; for his fads, which in their eyes were unbecoming; for his valetudinarianism, which they found equally annoying; for his weak and whimsical loquacity, which in their eyes traversed the bounds of good taste. He knew all this – and in a way conceded that they were right. But after all he had to assert his personality, he had to lead his own life; and above all he had to be able to talk about it. That was only fair – he had proved that it was worth talking about. He had been a worm, a louse if you like. But just his capacity to realize it so fully, with such vivid self-contempt, had become the ground of that persistent, painful, never-satisfied striving which had made him great. Herr Aarenhold had been born in a remote village in East Prussia, had married the daughter of a well-to-do tradesman, and by means of a bold and shrewd enterprise, of large-scale schemings which had as their object a new and productive coal-bed, he had diverted a large and inexhaustible stream of gold into his coffers.

The fish course came on. The servants hurried with it from the sideboard through the length of the room. They handed round with it a creamy sauce and poured out a Rhine wine that prickled on the tongue. The conversation turned to the approaching wedding.

It was very near, it was to take place in the following week. They talked about the dowry, about plans for the wedding journey to Spain. Actually it was only Herr Aarenhold who talked about them, supported by von Beckerath's polite acquiescence. Frau Aarenhold ate greedily, and as usual contributed nothing to the conversation save some rather pointless questions. Her speech was interlarded with guttural words and phrases from the dialect of her childhood days. Märit was full of silent opposition to the church ceremony which they planned to have; it affronted her highly enlightened convictions. Herr Aarenhold also was privately opposed to the ceremony. Von Beckerath was a Protestant and in Herr Aarenhold's view Protestant ceremonial was without any aesthetic value. It would be different if von Beckerath belonged to the Roman confession. Kunz said nothing, because when von Beckerath was present he always felt annoyed with his mother. And neither Siegmund nor Sieglinde displayed any interest. They held each other's narrow hands between their chairs. Sometimes their gaze sought each other's, melting together in an understanding from which everybody else was shut out. Von Beckerath sat next to Sieglinde on the other side.

'Fifty hours,' said Herr Aarenhold, 'and you are in Madrid, if you like. That is progress. It took me sixty by the shortest way. I assume that you prefer the train to the sea route via Rotterdam?'

Von Beckerath hastily expressed his preference for the overland route.

'But you won't leave Paris out. Of course, you could go direct to Lyons. And Sieglinde knows Paris. But you should not neglect the opportunity ... I leave it to you whether or not to stop before that. The choice of the place where the honeymoon begins should certainly be left to you.'

Sieglinde turned her head, turned it for the first time towards her betrothed, quite openly and unembarrassed, careless of the lookers-on. For quite three seconds she bent upon the courteous face beside her the wide-eyed, questioning, expectant gaze of her sparkling black eyes – a gaze as vacant of thought as any animal's. Between their chairs she was holding the slender hand of her twin; and Siegmund drew his brows together till they formed two black folds at the base of his nose.

The conversation veered and tacked to and fro. They talked of a consignment of cigars which had just come by Herr Aarenhold's order from Havana, packed in zinc. Then it circled round a point of purely abstract interest, brought up by Kunz: namely, whether if a were necessary and sufficient condition for b, b must also be the necessary and sufficient condition for a. They argued the matter, they analysed it with great ingenuity, they gave examples; they talked nineteen to the dozen, attacked each other with steely and abstract dialectic, and got no little heated. Märit had introduced a philosophical distinction, that between the actual and the causal principle. Kunz told her, with his nose in the air, that 'casual principle' was a pleonasm. Märit, in some annoyance, insisted upon her terminology. Herr Aarenhold straightened himself, with a bit of bread between thumb and forefinger, and prepared to elucidate the whole matter. He suffered a complete rout, the children joined forces to laugh him down. Even his wife jeered at him. 'What are you talking about?' she said. 'Where did you learn that – you didn't learn much!' Von Beckerath pressed his chin on his breast, opened his mouth, and drew in breath to speak – but they had already passed on, leaving him hanging.

Siegmund began, in a tone of ironic amusement, to speak of an acquaintance of his, a child of nature whose simplicity was such that he abode in ignorance of the difference between dress clothes and dinner jacket. This Parsifal actually talked about a checked dinner jacket. Kunz knew an even more pathetic case – a man who went out to tea in dinner clothes.

'Dinner clothes in the afternoon!' Sieglinde said, making a face. 'It isn't even human!'

Von Beckerath laughed sedulously. But inwardly he was remembering that once he himself had worn a dinner coat before six o'clock. And with the game course they passed on to matters of more general cultural interest: to the plastic arts, of which von Beckerath was an amateur, to literature and the theatre, which in the Aarenhold house had the preference – though Siegmund did devote some of his leisure to painting.

The conversation was lively and general and the young people set the key. They talked well, their gestures were nervous and self-assured. They marched in the van of taste, the best was none too good for them. For the vision, the intention, the labouring will, they had no use at all; they ruthlessly insisted upon power achievement, success in the cruel trial of strength. The triumphant work of art they recognized – but they paid it no homage. Herr Aarenhold himself said to von Beckerath:

'You are very indulgent, my dear fellow; you speak up for intentions – but results, *results* are what we are after! You say:

"Of course his work is not much good – but he was only a peasant before he took it up, so his performance is after all astonishing." Nothing in it. Accomplishment is absolute, not relative. There are no mitigating circumstances. Let a man do first-class work or let him shovel coals. How far should I have got with a good-natured attitude like that? I might have said to myself: "You're only a poor fish, originally – it's wonderful if you get to be the head of your office." Well, I'd not be sitting here! I've had to force the world to recognize me, so now I won't recognize anything unless I am forced to!'

The children laughed. At that moment they did not look down on him. They sat there at table, in their low, luxuriously cushioned chairs, with their spoilt, dissatisfied faces. They sat in splendour and security, but their words rang as sharp as though sharpness, hardness, alertness, and pitiless clarity were demanded of them as survival values. Their highest praise was a grudging acceptance, their criticism deft and ruthless; it snatched the weapons from one's hand, it paralysed enthusiasm, made it a laughing-stock. 'Very good,' they would say of some masterpiece whose lofty intellectual plane would seem to have put it beyond the reach of critique. Passion was a blunder – it made them laugh. Von Beckerath, who tended to be disarmed by his enthusiasms, had hard work holding his own – also his age put him in the wrong. He got smaller and smaller in his chair, pressed his chin on his breast, and in his excitement breathed through his mouth – quite unhorsed by the brisk arrogance of youth. They contradicted everything – as though they found it impossible, discreditable, lamentable, not to contradict. They contradicted most efficiently, their eyes narrowing to gleaming cracks. They fell upon a single word of his, they worried it, they tore it to bits and replaced it by another so telling and deadly that it went straight to the mark and sat in the wound with quivering shaft. Towards the end of luncheon von Beckerath's eyes were red and he looked slightly deranged.

Suddenly – they were sprinkling sugar on their slices of pine-apple – Siegmund said, wrinkling up his face in the way he had, as though the sun were making him blink:

'Oh, by the by, von Beckerath, something else, before we forget it. Sieglinde and I approach you with a request – meta-phorically speaking, you see us on our knees. They are giving the *Walküre* tonight. We should like, Sieglinde and I, to hear it once more together – may we? We are of course aware that everything depends upon your gracious favour –'

'How thoughtful!' said Herr Aarenhold.

Kunz drummed the Hunding motif on the cloth.

Von Beckerath was overcome at anybody asking his permis-sion about anything. He answered eagerly:

'But by all means, Siegmund – and you too, Sieglinde; I find your request very reasonable – do go, of course; in fact I shall be able to go with you. There is an excellent cast tonight.'

All the Aarenholds bowed over their plates to hide their laughter. Von Beckerath blinked with his effort to be one of them, to understand and share in their mirth.

Siegmund hastened to say:

'Oh, well, actually, it's a rather poor cast, you know. Of course we are just as grateful to you as though it were good. But I am afraid there is a slight misunderstanding. Sieglinde and I were asking you to permit us to hear the *Walküre* once more *alone* together before the wedding. I don't know if you feel now that –'

'Oh, certainly. I quite understand. How charming! Of course you *must* go!'

'Thanks, we are most grateful indeed. Then I will have Percy and Leiermann put in for us ...'

'Perhaps I may venture to remark,' said Herr Aarenhold, 'that your mother and I are driving to dinner with the Erlangers and using Percy and Leiermann. You will have to condescend to the brown coupé and Baal and Lampa.'

'And your box?' asked Kunz.

'I took it long ago,' said Siegmund, tossing back his head.

They all laughed, all staring at the bridegroom.

Herr Aarenhold unfolded with his finger-tips the paper of a belladonna powder and shook it carefully into his mouth. Then he lighted a fat cigarette, which presently spread abroad a price-less fragrance. The servants sprang forward to draw away his and Frau Aarenhold's chairs. The order was given to serve coffee in the winter-garden. Kunz in a sharp voice ordered his dog-cart brought round; he would drive to the barracks.

Siegmund was dressing for the opera; he had been dressing for an hour. He had so abnormal and constant a need for purification that actually he spent a considerable part of his time before the wash-basin. He stood now in front of his large Empire mirror with the white enamelled frame; dipped a powder-puff in its embossed box and powdered his freshly shaven chin and cheeks. His beard was so strong that when he went out in the evening he was obliged to shave a second time.

He presented a colourful picture as he stood there, in rose-tinted silk drawers and socks, red morocco slippers, and a wadded house-jacket in a dark pattern with revers of grey fur. For background he had his large sleeping-chamber, full of all sorts of elegant and practical white-enamelled devices. Beyond the windows was a misty view over the tree-tops of the Tiergarten.

It was growing dark. He turned on the circular arrangement of electric bulbs in the white ceiling – they filled the room with soft milky light. Then he drew the velvet curtains across the darkening panes. The light was reflected from the liquid depths of the mirrors in wardrobe, washing-stand, and toilet-table, it flashed from the polished bottles on the tile-inlaid shelves. And Siegmund continued to work on himself. Now and then some thought in his mind would draw his brows together till they formed two black folds over the base of the nose.

His day had passed as his days usually did, vacantly and swiftly. The opera began at half past six and he had begun to change at half past five, so there had not been much afternoon. He had rested on his chaise-longue from two to three, then drunk tea and employed the remaining hour sprawled in a deep leather armchair in the study which he shared with Kunz, reading a few pages in each of several new novels. He had found them pitiably weak on the whole; but he had sent a few of them to the binder's to be artistically bound in choice bindings, for his library.

But in the forenoon he had worked. He had spent the hour from ten to eleven in the atelier of his professor, an artist of

European repute, who was developing Siegmund's talent for drawing and painting, and receiving from Herr Aarenhold two thousand marks a month for his services. But what Siegmund painted was absurd. He knew it himself; he was far from having any glowing expectations on the score of his talent in this line. He was too shrewd not to know that the conditions of his existence were not the most favourable in the world for the development of a creative gift. The accoutrements of life were so rich and varied, so elaborated, that almost no place at all was left for life itself. Each and every single accessory was so costly and beautiful that it had an existence above and beyond the purpose it was meant to serve – until one's attention was first confused and then exhausted. Siegmund had been born into superfluity, he was perfectly adjusted to it. And yet it was the fact that this superfluity never ceased to thrill and occupy him, to give him constant pleasure. Whether consciously or not, it was with him as with his father, who practised the art of never getting used to anything.

Siegmund loved to read, he strove after the word and the spirit as after a tool which a profound instinct urged him to grasp. But never had he lost himself in a book as one does when that single work seems the most important in the world; unique, a little, all-embracing universe, into which one plunges and submerges oneself in order to draw nourishment out of every syllable. The books and magazines streamed in, he could buy them all, they heaped up about him and even while he read, the number of those still to be read disturbed him. But he had the books bound in stamped leather and labelled with Siegmund Aarenhold's beautiful book-plate; they stood in rows, weighing down his life like a possession which he did not succeed in subordinating to his personality.

The day was his, it was given to him as a gift with all its hours from sunrise to sunset; and yet Siegmund found in his heart that he had no time for a resolve, how much less then for a deed. He was no hero, he commanded no giant powers. The preparation, the lavish equipment for what should have been the serious business of life used up all his energy. How much mental effort had to be expended simply in making a proper toilette! How much time and attention went to his supplies of cigarettes, soaps, and perfumes; how much occasion for making up his mind lay in that moment, recurring two or three times daily, when he had to select his cravat! And it was worth the effort. It was important. The blond-haired citizenry of the land might go about in elastic-sided boots and turn-over collars, heedless of the effect. But he – and most explicitly he – must be unassailable and blameless of exterior from head to foot.

And in the end no one expected more of him. Sometimes there came moments when he had a feeble misgiving about the nature of the 'actual'; sometimes he felt that this lack of expectation lamed and dislodged his sense of it. ... The household arrangements were all made to the end that the day might pass quickly and no empty hour be perceived. The next mealtime always came promptly on. They dined before seven; the evening, when one can idle with a good conscience, was long. The days disappeared, swiftly the seasons came and went. The family spent two summer months at their little castle on the lake, with its large and splendid grounds and many tennis courts, its cool paths through the parks, and shaven lawns adorned by bronze statuettes. A third month was spent in the mountains, in hotels where life was even more expensive than at home. Of late, during the winter, he had had himself driven to school to listen to a course of lectures in the history of art which came at a convenient time. But he had had to leave off because his sense of smell indicated that the rest of the class did not wash often enough.

He spent the hour walking with Sieglinde instead. Always she had been at his side since the very first; she had clung to him since they lisped their first syllables, taken their first steps. He had no friends, never had had one but this, his exquisitely groomed, darkly beautiful counterpart, whose moist and slender hand he held while the richly gilded, empty-eyed hours slipped past. They took fresh flowers with them on their walks, a bunch of violets or lilies of the valley, smelling them in turn or sometimes both together, with languid yet voluptuous abandon. They were like self-centred invalids who absorb themselves in trifles, as narcotics to console them for the loss of hope. With an inward gesture of renunciation they doffed aside the evil-smelling world and loved each other alone, for the priceless sake of their own rare uselessness. But all that they uttered was pointed, neat, and brilliant; it hit off the people they met, the things they saw, everything done by somebody else to the end that it might be exposed to the unerring eye, the sharp tongue, the witty condemnation.

Then von Beckerath had appeared. He had a post in the government and came of a good family. He had proposed for Sieglinde. Frau Aarenhold had supported him, Herr Aarenhold had displayed a benevolent neutrality, Kunz the hussar was his zealous partisan. He had been patient, assiduous, endlessly good-mannered and tactful. And in the end, after she had told him often enough that she did not love him, Sieglinde had begun to look at him searchingly, expectantly, mutely, with her sparkling black eyes — a gaze as speaking and as vacant of thought as an animal's — and had said yes. And Siegmund, whose will was her law, had taken up a position too; slightly to his own disgust he had not opposed the match; was not von Beckerath in the government and a man of good family too? Sometimes he wrinkled his brows over his toilette until they made two heavy black folds at the base of his nose.

He stood on the white bearskin which stretched out its claws beside his bed; his feet were lost in the long soft hair. He sprinkled himself lavishly with toilet water and took up his dress shirt. The starched and shining linen glided over his yellowish torso, which was as lean as a young boy's and yet shaggy with black hair. He arrayed himself further in black silk drawers, black silk socks, and heavy black silk garters with silver buckles, put on the well-pressed trousers of silky black cloth, fastened the white silk braces over his narrow shoulders, and with one foot on a stool began to button his shoes. There was a knock on the door.

'May I come in, Gigi?' asked Sieglinde.

'Yes, come in,' he answered.

She was already dressed, in a frock of shimmering sea-green silk, with a square neck outlined by a wide band of beige embroidery. Two embroidered peacocks facing each other above the girdle held a garland in their beaks. Her dark brown hair was unadorned; but a large egg-shaped precious stone hung on a thin pearl chain against her bare skin, the colour of smoked meerschaum. Over her arm she carried a scarf heavily worked with silver.

'I am unable to conceal from you,' she said, 'that the carriage is waiting.' He parried at once:

'And I have no hesitation in replying that it will have to wait patiently two minutes more.' It was at least ten. She sat down on the white velvet chaise-longue and watched him at his labours.

Out of a rich chaos of ties he selected a white piqué band and began to tie it before the glass.

'Beckerath,' said she, 'wears coloured cravats, crossed over the way they wore them last year.'

'Beckerath,' said he, 'is the most trivial existence I have ever had under my personal observation.' Turning to her quickly he added: 'Moreover, you will do me the favour of not mentioning that German's name to me again this evening.'

She gave a short laugh and replied: 'You may be sure it will not be a hardship.'

He put on the low-cut piqué waistcoat and drew his dress coat over it, the white silk lining caressing his hands as they passed through the sleeves.

'Let me see which buttons you chose,' said Sieglinde. They were the amethyst ones; shirt-studs, cuff-links, and waistcoat buttons, a complete set.

She looked at him admiringly, proudly, adoringly, with a world of tenderness in her dark, shining eyes. He kissed the lips lying so softly on each other. They spent another minute on the chaise-longue in mutual caresses.

'Quite, quite soft you are again,' said she, stroking his shaven cheeks.

'Your little arm feels like satin,' said he, running his hand down her tender forearm. He breathed in the violet odour of her hair.

She kissed him on his closed eyelids; he kissed her on the throat where the pendant hung. They kissed one another's hands. They loved one another sweetly, sensually, for sheer mutual delight in their own well-groomed, pampered, expensive smell. They played together like puppies, biting each other with their lips. Then he got up.

'We mustn't be too late today,' said he. He turned the top of the perfume bottle upside down on his handkerchief one last time, rubbed a drop into his narrow red hands, took his gloves, and declared himself ready to go.

He put out the light and they went along the red-carpeted corridor hung with dark old oil paintings and down the steps past the little organ. In the vestibule on the ground floor Wendelin was waiting with their coats, very tall in his yellow paletot. They yielded their shoulders to his ministrations; Sieglinde's dark head was half lost in her collar of silver fox. Followed by the servant they passed through the stone-paved vestibule into the outer air. It was mild, and there were great ragged flakes of snow in the pearly air. The coupé awaited them. The coachman bent down with his hand to his cockaded hat while Wendelin ushered the brother and sister to their seats; then the door banged shut, he swung himself up to the box, and the carriage was at once in swift motion. It crackled over the gravel, glided through the high, wide gate, curved smoothly to the right, and rolled away.

The luxurious little space in which they sat was pervaded by a gentle warmth. 'Shall I shut us in?' Siegmund asked. She nodded and he drew the brown silk curtains across the polished panes.

They were in the city's heart. Lights flew past behind the curtains. Their horses' hoofs rhythmically beat the ground, the carriage swayed noiselessly over the pavement, and round them roared and shrieked and thundered the machinery of urban life. Quite safe and shut away they sat among the wadded brown silk cushions, hand in hand. The carriage drew up and stopped. Wendelin was at the door to help them out. A little group of grey-faced shivering folk stood in the brilliance of the arc-lights and followed them with hostile glances as they passed through the lobby. It was already late, they were the last. They mounted the staircase, threw their cloaks over Wendelin's arms, paused a second before a high mirror, then went through the little door into their box. They were greeted by the last sounds before the hush – voices and the slamming of seats. The lackey pushed their plush-upholstered chairs beneath them; at that moment the lights went down and below their box the orchestra broke into the wild pulsating notes of the prelude.

Night, and tempest. ... And they, who had been wafted hither on the wings of ease, with no petty annoyances on the way, were in exactly the right mood and could give all their attention at once. Storm, a raging tempest, without in the wood. The angry god's command resounded, once, twice repeated in its wrath, obediently the thunder crashed. The curtain flew up as though blown by the storm. There was the rude hall, dark save for a glow on the pagan hearth. In the centre towered up the trunk of the ash tree. Siegmund appeared in the doorway and leaned against the wooden post beaten and harried by the storm. Draggingly he moved forwards on his sturdy legs wrapped round with hide and thongs. He was rosy-skinned, with a straw-coloured beard; beneath his blond brows and the blond forelock of his wig his blue eyes were directed upon the conductor, with an imploring gaze. At last the orchestra gave way to his voice, which rang clear and metallic, though he tried to make it sound like a gasp. He sang a few bars, to the effect that no matter to whom the hearth belonged he must rest upon it; and at the last word he let himself drop heavily on the bear-skin rug and lay there with his head cushioned on his plump arms. His breast heaved in slumber. A minute passed, filled with the singing, speaking flow of the music, rolling its waves at the feet of the events on the stage. . . . . Sieglinde entered from the left. She had an alabaster bosom which rose and fell marvellously beneath her muslin robe and deerskin mantle. She displayed surprise at sight of the strange man; pressed her chin upon her breast until it was double, put her lips in position and expressed it, this surprise, in tones which swelled soft and warm from her white throat and were given shape by her tongue and her mobile lips. She tended the stranger; bending over him so that he could see the white flower of her bosom rising from the rough skins, she gave him with both hands the drinking horn. He drank. The music spoke movingly to him of cool refreshment and cherishing care. They looked at each other with the beginning of enchantment, a first dim recognition, standing rapt while the orchestra interpreted in a melody of profound enchantment.

She gave him mead, first touching the horn with her lips, then watching while he took a long draught. Again their glances met and mingled, while below, the melody voiced their yearning. Then he rose, in deep dejection, turning away painfully, his arms hanging at his sides, to the door, that he might remove from her sight his affliction, his loneliness, his persecuted, hated existence and bear it back into the wild. She called upon him but he did not hear; heedless of self she lifted up her arms and confessed her intolerable anguish. He stopped. Her eyes fell. Below them the music spoke darkly of the bond of suffering that united them. He stayed. He folded his arms and remained by the hearth, awaiting his destiny.

Announced by his pugnacious motif, Hunding entered, paunchy and knock-kneed, like a cow. His beard was black with brown tufts. He stood there frowning, leaning heavily on his spear, and staring ox-eyed at the stranger guest. But as the primitive custom would have it he bade him welcome, in an enormous, rusty voice.

Sieglinde laid the evening meal, Hunding's slow, suspicious gaze moving to and fro between her and the stranger. Dull lout though he was, he saw their likeness: the selfsame breed, that odd, untrammelled rebellious stock, which he hated, to which he felt inferior. They sat down, and Hunding, in two words, introduced himself and accounted for his simple, regular, and orthodox existence. Thus he forced Siegmund to speak of himself – and that was incomparably more difficult. Yet Siegmund spoke, he sang clearly and with wonderful beauty of his life and misfortunes. He told how he had been born with a twin sister – and as people do who dare not speak out, he called himself by a false name. He gave a moving account of the hatred and envy which had been the bane of his life and his strange father's life, how their hall had been burnt, his sister carried off, how they had led in the forest a horrid, persecuted, outlawed life, and how finally he had mysteriously lost his father as well.

... And then Siegmund sang the most painful thing of all: he told of his yearning for human beings, his longing and ceaseless loneliness. He sang of men and women, of friendship and love he had sometimes won, only to be thrust back again into the dark. A curse had lain upon him for ever, he was marked by the brand of his strange origins. His speech had not been as others' speech nor theirs as his. What he found good was vexation to them, he was galled by the ancient laws to which they paid honour. Always and everywhere he had lived amid anger and strife, he had borne the yoke of scorn and hatred and contempt – all because he was strange, of a breed and kind hopelessly different from them.

Hunding's reception of all this was entirely characteristic. His reply showed no sympathy and no understanding, but only a sour disgust and suspicion of all Siegmund's story. And finally understanding that the stranger standing here on his own hearth was the very man for whom the hunt had been called up today, he behaved with the four-square pedantry one would have expected of him. With a grim sort of courtesy he declared that for tonight the guest-right protected the fugitive; tomorrow he would have the honour of slaying him in battle. Gruffly he commanded Sieglinde to spice his night-drink for him and to await him in bed within; then after a few more threats he followed her, taking all his weapons with him and leaving Siegmund alone and despairing by the hearth.

Up in the box Siegmund bent over the velvet ledge and leaned his dark head on his narrow red hand. His brows made two black furrows, and one foot, resting on the heel of his patent-leather shoe, was in constant nervous motion. But it stopped as he heard a whisper close to him.

'Gigi!'

His mouth, as he turned, had an insolent line.

Sieglinde was holding out to him a mother-of-pearl box with maraschino cherries.

'The brandy chocolates are underneath,' she whispered. But he accepted only a cherry, and as he took it out of the waxed paper she said in his ear:

'She will come back to him again at once.'

'I am not entirely unaware of the fact,' he said, so loud that several heads were jerked angrily in his direction ... Down in the darkness big Siegmund was singing alone. From the depths of his heart he cried out for the sword — for a shining haft to swing on that day when there burst forth at last the bright flame of his anger and rage, which so long had smouldered deep in his heart. He saw the hilt glitter in the tree, saw the embers fade on the hearth, sank back in gloomy slumber — and started up in joyful amaze when Sieglinde glided back to him in the darkness.

Hunding slept like a stone, a deafened, drunken sleep. Together they rejoiced at the outwitting of the clod; they laughed, and their eyes had the same way of narrowing as they laughed. Then Sieglinde stole a look at the conductor, received her cue, and putting her lips in position sang a long recitative: related the heart-breaking tale of how they had forced her, forsaken, strange and wild as she was, to give herself to the crude and savage Hunding and to count herself lucky in an honourable marriage which might bury her dark origins in oblivion. She sang too, sweetly and soothingly, of the strange old man in the hat and how he had driven the sword-blade into the trunk of the ash tree, to await the coming of him who was destined to draw it out. Passionately she prayed in song that it might be he whom she meant, whom she knew and grievously longed for, the consoler of her sorrows, the friend who should be more than friend, the avenger of her shame, whom once she had lost, whom in her abasement she wept for, her brother in suffering, her saviour, her rescuer. ...

But at this point Siegmund flung about her his two rosy arms. He pressed her cheek against the pelt that covered his breast and, holding her so, sang above her head — sang out his exultation to the four winds, in a silver trumpeting of sound. His breast glowed hot with the oath that bound him to his mate. All the yearning of his hunted life found assuagement in her; all that love which others had repulsed, when in conscious shame of his dark origins he forced it upon them — in her it found its home. She suffered shame as did he, dishonoured was she like to himself – and now, now their brother-and-sister love should be their revenge!

The storm whistled, a gust of wind burst open the door, a flood of white electric light poured into the hall. Divested of darkness they stood and sang their song of spring and spring's sister, love!

Crouching on the bearskin they looked at each other in the white light, as they sang their duet of love. Their bare arms touched each other's as they held each other by the temples and gazed into each other's eyes, and as they sang their mouths were very near. They compared their eyes, their foreheads, their voices – they were the same. The growing, urging recognition wrung from his breast his father's name; she called him by his: Siegmund! Siegmund! He freed the sword, he swung it above his head, and submerged in bliss she told him in song who she was: his twin sister, Sieglinde. In ravishment he stretched out his arms to her, his bride, she sank upon his breast – the curtain fell as the music swelled into a roaring, rushing, foaming whirlpool of passion – swirled and swirled and with one mighty throb stood still.

Rapturous applause. The lights went on. A thousand people got up, stretched unobtrusively as they clapped, then made ready to leave the hall, with heads still turned towards the stage, where the singers appeared before the curtain, like masks hung out in a row at a fair. Hunding too came out and smiled politely, despite all that had just been happening.

Siegmund pushed back his chair and stood up. He was hot; little red patches showed on his cheek-bones, above the lean, sallow, shaven cheeks.

'For my part,' said he, 'what I want now is a breath of fresh air. Siegmund was pretty feeble, wasn't he?'

'Yes,' answered Sieglinde, 'and the orchestra saw fit to drag abominably in the Spring Song.'

'Frightfully sentimental,' said Siegmund, shrugging his narrow shoulders in his dress coat. 'Are you coming out?' She lingered a moment, with her elbows on the ledge, still gazing at the stage. He looked at her as she rose and took up her silver scarf. Her soft, full lips were quivering.

They went into the foyer and mingled with the slow-moving throng, downstairs and up again, sometimes holding each other by the hand.

'I should enjoy an ice,' said she, 'if they were not in all probability uneatable.'

'Don't think of it,' said he. So they ate bonbons out of their box – maraschino cherries and chocolate beans filled with cognac.

The bell rang and they looked on contemptuously as the crowds rushed back to their seats, blocking the corridors. They waited until all was quiet, regaining their places just as the lights went down again and silence and darkness fell soothingly upon the hall. There was another little ring, the conductor raised his arms and summoned up anew the wave of splendid sound.

Siegmund looked down into the orchestra. The sunken space stood out bright against the darkness of the listening house; hands fingered, arms drew the bows, cheeks puffed out – all these simple folk laboured zealously to bring to utterance the work of a master who suffered and created; created the noble and simple visions enacted above on the stage. Creation? How did one create? Pain gnawed and burned in Siegmund's breast, a drawing anguish which yet was somehow sweet, a yearning – whither, for what? It was all so dark, so shamefully unclear! Two thoughts, two words he had: creation, passion. His temples glowed and throbbed, and it came to him as in a yearning vision that creation was born of passion and was reshaped anew as passion. He saw the pale, spent woman hanging on the breast of the fugitive to whom she gave herself, he saw her love and her destiny and knew that so life must be to be creative. He saw his own life, and knew its contradictions, its clear understanding and spoilt voluptuousness, its splendid security and idle spite, its weakness and wittiness, its languid contempt; his life, so full of words, so void of acts, so full of cleverness, so empty of emotion – and he felt again the burning, the drawing anguish which yet was sweet – whither, and to what end? Creation? Experience? Passion?

The finale of the act came, the curtain fell. Light, applause, general exit. Sieglinde and Siegmund spent the interval as before. They scarcely spoke, as they walked hand-in-hand through the corridors and up and down the steps. She offered him cherries but he took no more. She looked at him, but withdrew her gaze as his rested upon her, walking rather constrained at his side and enduring his eye. Her childish shoulders under the silver web of her scarf looked like those of an Egyptian statue, a little too high and too square. Upon her cheeks burned the same fire he felt in his own.

Again they waited until the crowd had gone in and took their seats at the last possible moment. Storm and wind and driving cloud; wild, heathenish cries of exultation. Eight females, not exactly stars in appearance, eight untrammelled, laughing maidens of the wild, were disporting themselves amid a rocky scene. Brünnhilde broke in upon their merriment with her fears. They skimmed away in terror before the approaching wrath of Wotan, leaving her alone to face him. The angry god nearly annihilated his daughter – but his wrath roared itself out, by degrees grew gentle and dispersed into a mild melancholy, on which note it ended. A noble prospect opened out, the scene was pervaded with epic and religious splendour. Brünnhilde slept. The god mounted the rocks. Great, full-bodied flames, rising, falling, and flickering, glowed all over the boards. The Walküre lay with her coat of mail and her shield on her mossy couch ringed round with fire and smoke, with leaping, dancing tongues, with the magic sleep-compelling fire-music. But she had saved Sieglinde, in whose womb there grew and waxed the seed of that hated unprized race, chosen of the gods, from which the twins had sprung, who had mingled their misfortunes and their afflictions in free and mutual bliss.

Siegmund and Sieglinde left their box; Wendelin was outside, towering in his yellow paletot and holding their cloaks for them to put on. Like a gigantic slave he followed the two dark, slender, fur-mantled, exotic creatures down the stairs to where the carriage waited and the pair of large finely glossy thoroughbreds tossed their proud heads in the winter night. Wendelin ushered the twins into their warm little silken-lined retreat, closed the door, and the coupé stood poised for yet a second, quivering slightly from the swing with which Wendelin agilely mounted the box. Then it glided swiftly away and left the theatre behind. Again they rolled noiselessly and easefully to the rhythmic beat of the horses' hoofs, over all the unevennesses of the road, sheltered from the shrill harshness of the bustling life through which they passed. They sat as silent and remote as they had sat in their opera-box facing the stage – almost, one might say, in the same atmosphere. Nothing was there which could alienate them from that extravagant and stormily passionate world which worked upon them with its magic power to draw them to itself.

The carriage stopped; they did not at once realize where they were, or that they had arrived before the door of their parents' house. Then Wendelin appeared at the window, and the porter came out of his lodge to open the door.

'Are my father and mother at home?' Siegmund asked, looking over the porter's head and blinking as though he were staring into the sun.

No, they had not returned from dinner at the Erlangers'. Nor was Kunz at home; Märit too was out, no one knew where, for she went entirely her own way.

In the vestibule they paused to be divested of their wraps; then they went up the stairs and through the first-floor hall into the dining-room. Its immense and splendid spaces lay in darkness save at the upper end, where one lustre burned above a table and Florian waited to serve them. They moved noiselessly across the thick carpet, and Florian seated them in their softly upholstered chairs. Then a gesture from Siegmund dismissed him, they would dispense with his services.

The table was laid with a dish of fruit, a plate of sandwiches, and a jug of red wine. An electric tea-kettle hummed upon a great silver tray, with all appliances about it.

Siegmund ate a caviar sandwich and poured out wine into a slender glass where it glowed a dark ruby red. He drank in quick gulps, and grumblingly stated his opinion that red wine and caviar were a combination offensive to good taste. He drew out his case, jerkily selected a cigarette, and began to smoke, leaning back with his hands in his pockets, wrinkling up his face and twitching his cigarette from one corner of his mouth to the other. His strong growth of beard was already beginning to show again under the high cheek-bones; the two black folds stood out on the base of his nose.

Sieglinde had brewed the tea and added a drop of burgundy. She touched the fragile porcelain cup delicately with her full, soft lips and as she drank she looked across at Siegmund with her great humid black eyes.

She set down her cup and leaned her dark, sweet little head upon her slender hand. Her eyes rested full upon him, with such liquid, speechless eloquence that all she might have said could be nothing beside it.

'Won't you have any more to eat, Gigi?'

'One would not draw,' said he, 'from the fact that I am smoking, the conclusion that I intend to eat more.'

'But you have had nothing but bonbons since tea. Take a peach, at least.'

He shrugged his shoulders – or rather he wriggled them like a naughty child, in his dress coat.

'This is stupid. I am going upstairs. Good night.'

He drank out his wine, tossed away his table-napkin, and lounged away, with his hands in his pockets, into the darkness at the other end of the room.

He went upstairs to his room, where he turned on the light – not much, only two or three bulbs, which made a wide white circle on the ceiling. Then he stood considering what to do next. The good-night had not been final; this was not how they were used to take leave of each other at the close of the day. She was sure to come to his room. He flung off his coat, put on his fur-trimmed house-jacket, and lighted another cigarette. He lay down on the chaise-longue; sat up again, tried another posture, with his cheek in the pillow; threw himself on his back again and so remained awhile, with his hands under his head.

The subtle, bitterish scent of the tobacco mingled with that of cosmetics, the soaps, and the toilet waters; their combined perfume hung in the tepid air of the room and Siegmund breathed it in with conscious pleasure, finding it sweeter than ever. Closing his eyes he surrendered to this atmosphere, as a man will console himself with some delicate pleasure of the senses for the extraordinary harshness of his lot.

Then suddenly he started up again, tossed away his cigarette and stood in front of the white wardrobe, which had long mirrors let into each of its three divisions. He moved very close to the middle one and eye to eye he studied himself, conned every feature of his face. Then he opened the two side wings and studied both profiles as well. Long he looked at each mark of his race: the slightly drooping nose, the full lips that rested so softly on each other; the high cheek-bones, the thick black, curling hair that grew far down on the temples and parted so decidedly on one side, finally the eyes under the knit brows, those large black eyes that glowed like fire and had an expression of weary sufferance.

In the mirror he saw the bearskin lying behind him, spreading out his claws beside the bed. He turned round, and there was tragic meaning in the dragging step that bore him towards it – until after a moment more of hesitation he lay down all its length and buried his head in his arm.

For a while he lay motionless, then propped his head on his elbows, with his cheeks resting on his slim reddish hands, and fell again into contemplation of his image opposite him in the mirror. There was a knock on the door. He started, reddened, and moved as though to get up – but sank back again, his head against his outstretched arm, and stopped there, silent.

Sieglinde entered. Her eyes searched the room, without finding him at once. Then with a start she saw him lying on the rug.

'Gigi, whatever are you doing there? Are you ill?' She ran to him, bending over with her hand on his forehead, stroking his hair as she repeated: 'You are not ill?'

He shook his head, looking up at her under his brow as she continued to caress him.

She was half ready for bed, having come over in slippers from her dressing-room, which was opposite to his. Her loosened hair flowed down over her open white dressing-jacket; beneath the lace of her chemise Siegmund saw her little breasts, the colour of smoked meerschaum.

'You were so cross,' she said. 'It was beastly of you to go away like that. I thought I would not come. But then I did, because that was not a proper good-night at all. . . .'

'I was waiting for you,' said he.

She was still standing bent over, and made a little moue which brought out markedly the facial characteristics of her race. Then, in her ordinary tone:

'Which does not prevent my present position from giving me a crick in the back.'

He shook her off.

'Don't, don't – we must not talk like that – not that way, Sieglinde.' His voice was strange, he himself noticed it. He felt parched with fever, his hands and feet were cold and clammy. She knelt beside him on the skin, her hand in his hair. He lifted himself a little to fling one arm round her neck and so looked at her, looked as he had just been looking at himself – at eyes and temples, brow and cheeks.

'You are just like me,' said he, haltingly, and swallowed to moisten his dry throat. 'Everything about you is just like me – and so – what you have – with Beckerath – the experience – is for me too. That makes things even, Sieglinde – and anyhow, after all, it is, for that matter – it is a revenge, Sieglinde –'

He was seeking to clothe in reason what he was trying to say – yet his words sounded as though he uttered them out of some strange, rash, bewildered dream.

But to her it had no quality of strangeness. She did not blush at his half-spoken, turbid, wild imaginings; his words enveloped her senses like a mist, they drew her down whence they had come, to the borders of a kingdom she had never entered, though sometimes, since her betrothal, she had been carried thither in expectant dreams.

She kissed him on his closed eyelids; he kissed her on her throat, beneath the lace she wore. They kissed each other's hands. They loved each other with all the sweetness of the senses, each for the other's spoilt and costly well-being and delicious fragrance. They breathed it in, this fragrance, with languid and voluptuous abandon, like self-centred invalids, consoling themselves for the loss of hope. They forgot themselves in

caresses, which took the upper hand, passing over into a tumult
of passion, dying away into a sobbing ...

She sat there on the bearskin, with parted lips, supporting
herself with one hand, and brushed the hair out of her eyes. He
leaned back on his hands against the white dressing-chest,
rocked to and fro on his hips, and gazed into the air.

'But Beckerath,' said she, seeking to find some order in her
thoughts, 'Beckerath, Gigi ... what about him, now?'

'Oh,' he said – and for a second the marks of his race stood
out strong upon his face – 'he ought to be grateful to us. His
existence will be a little less trivial, from now on.'

RAILWAY ACCIDENT

(1907)

TELL you a story? But I don't know any. Well, yes, after all, here is something I might tell.

Once, two years ago now it is, I was in a railway accident; all the details are clear in my memory.

It was not really a first-class one – no wholesale telescoping or 'heaps of unidentifiable dead' – not that sort of thing. Still, it was a proper accident, with all the trimmings, and on top of that it was at night. Not everybody has been through one, so I will describe it the best I can.

I was on my way to Dresden, whither I had been invited by some friends of letters: it was a literary and artistic pilgrimage, in short, such as, from time to time, I undertake not unwillingly. You make appearances, you attend functions, you show yourself to admiring crowds – not for nothing is one a subject of William II. And certainly Dresden is beautiful, especially the Zwinger; and afterwards I intended to go for ten days or a fortnight to the White Hart to rest, and if, thanks to the treatments, the spirit should come upon me, I might do a little work as well. To this end I had put my manuscript at the bottom of my trunk, to-gether with my notes – a good stout bundle done up in brown paper and tied with string in the Bavarian colours. I like to travel in comfort, especially when my expenses are paid. So I patronized the sleeping-cars, reserving a place days ahead in a first-class compartment. All was in order; nevertheless I was excited, as I always am on such occasions, for a journey is still an adventure to me, and where travelling is concerned I shall never manage to feel properly blasé. I perfectly well know that the night train for Dresden leaves the central station at Munich regularly every evening, and every morning is in Dresden. But when I am travelling with it, and linking my momentous destiny to its own, the matter assumes importance. I cannot rid myself of the notion that it is making a special trip today, just on my account, and the unreasoning and mistaken conviction sets up in me a deep and speechless unrest, which does not subside until all the formalities of departure are behind me – the packing, the drive in the loaded cab to the station, the arrival there, and the registration of luggage – and I can feel myself finally and securely bestowed. Then, indeed, a pleasing relaxation takes place, the mind turns to fresh concerns, the unknown unfolds itself beyond the expanse of window-pane, and I am consumed with joyful anticipations.

And so on this occasion. I had tipped my porter so liberally that he pulled his cap and gave me a pleasant journey; and I stood at the corridor window of my sleeping-car smoking my evening cigar and watching the bustle on the platform. There were whistlings and rumblings, hurryings and farewells, and the singsong of newspaper and refreshment vendors, and over all the great electric moons glowed through the mist of the October evening. Two stout fellows pulled a hand-cart of large trunks along the platform to the baggage car in front of the train. I easily identified, by certain unmistakable features, my own trunk; one among many there it lay, and at the bottom of it reposed my precious package. 'There,' thought I, 'no need to worry, it is in good hands. Look at that guard with the leather cartridge-belt, the prodigious sergeant-major's moustache, and the inhospitable eye. Watch him rebuking the old woman in the threadbare black cape – for two pins she would have got into a second-class carriage. He is security, he is authority, he is our parent, he is the State. He is strict, not to say gruff, you would not care to mingle with him; but reliability is writ large upon his brow, and in his care your trunk reposes as in the bosom of Abraham.'

A man was strolling up and down the platform in spats and a yellow autumn coat, with a dog on a leash. Never have I seen a handsomer dog: a small, stocky bull, smooth-coated, muscular, with black spots; as well groomed and amusing as the dogs one sees in circuses, who make the audience laugh by dashing round and round the ring with all the energy of their small bodies. This dog had a silver collar, with a plaited leather leash. But all this was not surprising, considering his master, the gentleman in spats, who had beyond a doubt the noblest origins. He wore a monocle, which accentuated without distorting his general air; the defiant perch of his moustache bore out the proud and stubborn expression of his chin and the corners of his mouth. He addressed a question to the martial guard, who knew perfectly well with whom he was dealing and answered hand to cap. My gentleman strolled on, gratified with the impression he had made. He strutted in his spats, his gaze was cold, he regarded men and affairs with penetrating eye. Certainly he was far above feeling journey-proud; travel by train was no novelty to him. He was at home in life, without fear of authority or regulations; he was an authority himself – in short, a nob. I could not look at him enough. When he thought the time had come, he got into the train (the guard had just turned his back). He came along the corridor behind me, bumped into me, and did not apologize. What a man! But that was nothing to what followed. Without turning a hair he took his dog with him into the sleeping-compartment! Surely it was forbidden to do that. When should I presume to take a dog with me into a sleeping-compartment? But he did it, on the strength of his prescriptive rights as a nob, and shut the door behind him.

There came a whistle outside, the locomotive whistled in response, gently the train began to move. I stayed awhile by the window watching the hand-waving and the shifting lights. ... I retired inside the carriage.

The sleeping-car was not very full, a compartment next to mine was empty and had not been got ready for the night; I decided to make myself comfortable there for an hour's peaceful reading. I fetched my book and settled in. The sofa had a silky salmon-pink covering, an ash-tray stood on the folding table, the light burned bright. I read and smoked.

The sleeping-car attendant entered in pursuance of his duties and asked for my ticket for the night. I delivered it into his grimy hands. He was polite but entirely official, did not even vouchsafe me a good night as from one human being to another, but went out at once and knocked on the door of the next compartment. He would better have left it alone, for my gentleman of the spats was inside; and perhaps because he did not wish anyone to discover his dog, but possibly because he had really gone to bed, he got furious at anyone daring to disturb him. Above the rumbling of the train I heard his immediate and elemental burst of rage. 'What do you want?' he roared. 'Leave me alone, you swine.' He said 'swine'. It was a lordly epithet, the epithet of a cavalry officer – it did my heart good to hear it. But the sleeping-car attendant must have resorted to diplomacy – of course he had to have the man's ticket – for just as I stepped into the corridor to get a better view the door of the compartment abruptly opened a little way and the ticket flew out into the attendant's face; yes, it was flung with violence straight in his face. He picked it up with both hands, and though he had got the corner of it in one eye, so that the tears came, he thanked the man, saluting and clicking his heels together. Quite overcome, I returned to my book.

I considered whether there was anything against my smoking another cigar and concluded that there was little or nothing. So I did it, rolling onward and reading; I felt full of contentment and good ideas. Time passed, it was ten o'clock, half past ten, all my fellow-travellers had gone to bed, at last I decided to follow them. I got up and went into my own compartment. A real little bedroom, most luxurious, with stamped leather wall hangings, clothes-hooks, a nickel-plated wash-basin. The lower berth was snowily prepared, the covers invitingly turned back. Oh, triumph of modern times! I thought. One lies in this bed as though at home, it rocks a little all night, and the result is that next morning one is in Dresden. I took my suitcase out of the rack to get ready for bed; I was holding it above my head, with my arms stretched up.

It was at this moment that the railway accident occurred. I remember it like yesterday.

We gave a jerk – but jerk is a poor word for it. It was a jerk of deliberately foul intent, a jerk with a horrid reverberating crash, and so violent that my suitcase leaped out of my hands I knew not whither, while I was flung forcibly with my shoulder against the wall. I had no time to stop and think. But now followed a frightful rocking of the carriage, and while that went on, one had plenty of leisure to be frightened. A railway carriage rocks going over switches or on sharp curves, that we know; but this rocking would not let me stand up, I was thrown from one wall to the other as the carriage careened. I had only one simple thought, but I thought it with concentration, exclusively. I thought: 'Something is the matter, something is the matter, something is *very much* the matter!' Just in those words. But later I thought: 'Stop, stop, stop!' For I knew that it would be a great help if only the train could be brought to a halt. And lo, at this my unuttered but fervent behest, the train did stop.

Up to now a deathlike stillness had reigned in the carriage, but at this point found tongue. Shrill feminine screams mingled with deeper masculine cries of alarm. Next door someone was shouting 'Help!' No doubt about it, this was the very same voice which, just previously, had uttered the lordly epithet – the voice of the man in spats, his very voice, though distorted by fear. 'Help!' it cried; and just as I stepped into the corridor, where the passengers were collecting, he burst out of his compartment in a silk sleeping-suit and halted, looking wildly round him. 'Great God!' he exclaimed, 'Almighty God!' and then, as though to abase himself utterly, perhaps in hope to avert destruction, he added in a deprecating tone: '*Dear* God!' But suddenly he thought of something else. Of trying to help himself. He threw himself upon the case on the wall where an axe and saw are kept for emergencies, and broke the glass with his fist. But finding that he could not release the tools at once, he abandoned them, buffeted his way through the crowd of passengers, so that the half-dressed women screamed afresh, and leaped out of the carriage.

All that was the work of a moment only. And then for the first time I began to feel the shock: in a certain weakness of the spine, a passing inability to swallow. The sleeping-car attendant, red-eyed, grimy-handed, had just come up; we all pressed round him; the women, with bare arms and shoulders, stood wringing their hands.

The train, he explained, had been derailed, we had run off the track. That, as it afterwards turned out, was not true. But behold, the man in his excitement had become voluble, he abandoned his official neutrality; events had loosened his tongue and he spoke to us in confidence, about his wife. 'I told her today, I did. "Wife," I said, "I feel in my bones somethin's goin' to happen."' And sure enough, hadn't something happened? We all felt how right he had been. The carriage had begun to fill with smoke, a thick smudge; nobody knew where it came from, but we all thought it best to get out into the night.

That could only be done by quite a big jump from the footboard on to the line, for there was no platform, of course, and besides our carriage was canted a good deal towards the opposite side. But the ladies – they had hastily covered their nakedness – jumped in desperation and soon we were all standing there between the lines.

It was nearly dark, but from where we were we could see that no damage had been done at the rear of the train, though all the carriages stood at a slant. But farther forward – fifteen or twenty paces farther forward! Not for nothing had the jerk we felt made such a horrid crash. There lay a waste of wreckage; we could see the margins of it, with the little lights of the guards' lanterns flickering across and to and fro.

Excited people came towards us, bringing reports of the situation. We were close by a small station not far beyond Regensburg, and as a result of a defective point our express had run on to the wrong line, had crashed at full speed into a stationary freight train, hurling it out of the station, annihilating its rear carriages, and itself sustaining serious damage. The great express engine from Maffei's in Munich lay smashed up and done for. Price seventy thousand marks. And in the forward coaches, themselves lying almost on one side, many of the seats were telescoped. No, thank goodness, there were no lives lost. There was talk of an old woman having been 'taken out', but nobody had seen her. At least, people had been thrown in all directions, children buried under luggage, the shock had been great. The baggage car was demolished. Demolished – the baggage car? Demolished.

There I stood.

A bareheaded official came running along the track. The station-master. He issued wild and tearful commands to the passengers, to make them behave themselves and get back into the coaches. But nobody took any notice of him, he had no cap and no self-control. Poor wretch! Probably the responsibility was his. Perhaps this was the end of his career, the wreck of his prospects. I could not ask him about the baggage car – it would have been tactless.

Another official came up – he *limped* up. I recognized him by the sergeant-major's moustache: it was the stern and vigilant guard of the early evening – our Father, the State. He limped along, bent over with his hand on his knee, thinking about nothing else. 'Oh, dear!' he said, 'oh, dear, oh, dear me!' I asked him what was the matter. 'I got stuck, sir, jammed me in the chest, I made my escape through the roof.' This 'made my escape through the roof' sounded like a newspaper report. Certainly the man would not have used the phrase in everyday life; he had experienced not so much an accident as a newspaper account of it – but what was that to me? He was in no state to give me news of my manuscript. So I accosted a young man who came up bustling and self-important from the waste of wreckage, and asked him about the heavy luggage.

'Well, sir, nobody can say anything as to that' – his tone implied that I ought to be grateful to have escaped unhurt. 'Everything is all over the place. Women's shoes –' he said with a sweeping gesture to indicate the devastation, and wrinkled his nose. 'When they start the clearing operations we shall see. ... Women's shoes. ...'

There I stood. All alone I stood there in the night and searched my heart. Clearing operations. Clearing operations were to be undertaken with my manuscript. Probably it was destroyed, then, torn up, demolished. My honeycomb, my spider-web, my nest, my earth, my pride and pain, my all, the best of me – what should I do if it were gone? I had no copy of what had been welded and forged, of what already was a living, speaking thing – to say nothing of my notes and drafts, all that I had saved and stored up and overheard and sweated over for years – my squirrel's hoard. What should I do? I inquired of my own soul and I knew that I should begin over again from the beginning. Yes, with animal patience, with the tenacity of a primitive creature the curious and complex product of whose little ingenuity and industry has been destroyed; after a moment of helpless bewilderment I should set to work again – and perhaps this time it would come easier !

But meanwhile a fire brigade had come up, their torches cast a red light over the wreck; when I went forward and looked for the baggage car, behold it was almost intact, the luggage quite unharmed. All the things that lay strewn about came out of the freight train : among the rest a quantity of balls of string – a perfect sea of string covered the ground far and wide.

A load was lifted from my heart. I mingled with the people who stood talking and fraternizing in misfortune – also showing off and being important. So much seemed clear, that the engine-driver had acted with great presence of mind. He had averted a great catastrophe by pulling the emergency brake at the last moment. Otherwise, it was said, there would have been a general smash and the whole train would have gone over the steep embankment on the left. Oh, praiseworthy engine-driver ! He was not about, nobody had seen him, but his fame spread down the whole length of the train and we all lauded him in his absence. 'That chap,' said one man, and pointed with one hand somewhere off into the night, 'that chap saved our lives.' We all agreed.

But our train was standing on a track where it did not belong, and it behoved those in charge to guard it from behind so that another one did not run into it. Firemen perched on the rear carriage with torches of flaming pitch, and the excited young man who had given me such a fright with his 'women's shoes' seized upon a torch too and began signalling with it, though no train was anywhere in sight.

Slowly and by degrees something like order was produced, the State our Father regained pose and presence. Steps had been taken, wires sent, presently a breakdown train from Regensburg steamed cautiously into the station and great gas flares with reflectors were set up about the wreck. We passengers were now turned off and told to go into the little station building to wait for our new conveyance. Laden with our hand luggage, some of the party with bandaged heads, we passed through a lane of inquisitive natives into the tiny waiting-room, where we herded together as best we could. And inside of an hour we were all stowed higgledly-piggledy into a special train.

I had my first-class ticket – my journey being paid for – but it availed me nothing, for everybody wanted to ride first and my carriage was more crowded than the others. But just as I found me a little niche, whom do I see diagonally opposite to me, huddled in the corner? My hero, the gentleman with the spats and the vocabulary of a cavalry officer. He did not have his dog, it had been taken away from him in defiance of his rights as a nob and now sat howling in a gloomy prison just behind the engine. His master, like myself, held a yellow ticket which was no good to him, and he was grumbling, he was trying to make head against this communistic levelling of rank in the face of general misfortune. But another man answered him in a virtuous tone: 'You ought to be thankful that you can sit down.' And with a sour smile my gentleman resigned himself to the crazy situation.

And now who got in, supported by two firemen? A wee little old grandmother in a tattered black cape, the very same who in Munich would for two pins have got into a second-class carriage. 'Is this the first class?' she kept asking. And when we made room and assured her that it was, she sank down with a 'God be praised !' on to the plush cushions as though only now was she safe and sound.

By Hof it was already five o'clock and light. There we breakfasted; an express train picked me up and deposited me with my belongings, three hours late, in Dresden.

Well, that was the railway accident I went through. I suppose it had to happen once; but whatever mathematicians may say, I feel that I now have every chance of escaping another.

THE FIGHT BETWEEN
JAPPE AND DO ESCOBAR
(1911)

I was very much taken aback when Johnny Bishop told me that Jappe and Do Escobar were going to fight each other and that we must go and watch them do it.

It was in the summer holidays at Travemünde, on a sultry day with a slight land breeze and a flat sea ever so far away across the sands. We had been some three-quarters of an hour in the water and were lying on the hard sand under the props of the bathing-cabins – we two and Jürgen Brattström the ship-owner's son. Johnny and Brattström were lying on their backs entirely naked; I felt more comfortable with my towel wrapped round my hips. Brattström asked me why I did it and I could not think of any sensible answer; so Johnny said with his winning smile that I was probably too big now to lie naked. I really was larger and more developed than Johnny and Brattström; also a little older, about thirteen; so I accepted Johnny's explanation in silence, although with a certain feeling of mortification. For in Johnny Bishop's presence you actually felt rather out of it if you were any less small, fine, and physically childlike than he, who was all these things in such a very high degree. He knew how to look up at you with his pretty, friendly blue eyes, which had a certain mocking smile in them too, with an expression that said: 'What a great, gawky thing you are, to be sure!' The ideal of manliness and long trousers had no validity in his presence – and that at a time, not long after the war, when strength, courage, and every hardy virtue stood very high among us youth and all sorts of conduct were banned as effeminate. But Johnny, as a foreigner – or half-foreigner – was exempt from this atmosphere. He was a little like a woman who preserves her youth and looks down on other women who are less successful at the feat. Besides he was far and away the best-dressed boy in town,

distinctly aristocratic and elegant in his real English sailor suit
with the linen collar, sailor's knot, laces, a silver whistle in his
pocket, and an anchor on the sleeves that narrowed round his
wrists. Anyone else would have been laughed at for that sort of
thing – it would have been jeered at as 'girls's clothes'. But he
wore them with such a disarming and confident air that he
never suffered in the least.

He looked rather like a thin little cupid as he lay there, with
his pretty, soft blond curls and his arms up over the narrow
English head that rested on the sand. His father had been a
German business man who had been naturalized in England
and died some years since. His mother was English by blood, a
long-featured lady with quiet, gentle ways, who had settled in
our town with her two children, Johnny and a mischievous little
girl just as pretty as he. She still wore black for her husband,
and she was probably honouring his last wishes when she
brought the children to grow up in Germany. Obviously they
were in easy circumstances. She owned a spacious house outside
the city and a villa at the sea and from time to time she travelled
with Johnny and Sissie to more distant resorts. She did not
move in society, although it would have been open to her.
Whether on account of her mourning or perhaps because the
horizon of our best families was too narrow for her, she herself
led a retired life, but she managed that her children should have
social intercourse. She invited other children to play with them
and sent them to dancing and deportment lessons, thus quietly
arranging that Johnny and Sissie should associate exclusively
with the children of well-to-do families – of course not in pursuance of any well-defined principle, but just as a matter of
course. Mrs Bishop contributed, remotely, to my own education : it was from her I learned that to be well thought of by
others no more is needed than to think well of yourself. Though
deprived of its male head the little family showed none of the
marks of neglect or disruption which often in such cases make
people fight shy. Without further family connection, without
title, tradition, influence, or public office, and living a life apart,
Mrs Bishop by no means lacked social security or pretensions.
She was definitely accepted at her own valuation and the friend-

ship of her children was much sought after by their young con-
temporaries.

As for Jürgen Brattström, I may say in passing that his father
had made his own money, achieved public office, and built for
himself and his family the red sandstone house on the Burgfeld,
next to Mrs Bishop's. And that lady had quietly accepted his
son as Johnny's playmate and let the two go to school together.
Jürgen was a decent, phlegmatic, short-legged lad without any
prominent characteristics. He had begun to do a little private
business in licorice sticks.

As I said, I was extremely shocked when Johnny told me
about the impending meeting between Jappe and Do Escobar
which was to take place at twelve o'clock that day on the Leuchtenfeld. It was dead earnest – might have a serious outcome, for
Jappe and Do Escobar were both stout and reckless fellows and
had strong feelings about knightly honour. The issue might well
be frightful. In my memory they still seem as tall and manly as
they did then, though they could not have been more than fifteen at the time. Jappe came from the middle class of the city;
he was not much looked after at home, he was already almost
his own master, a combination of loafer and man-about-town.
Do Escobar was an exotic and bohemian foreigner, who did not
even come regularly to school but only attended lectures now
and then – an irregular but paradisial existence! He lived *en
pension* with some middle-class people and rejoiced in complete
independence. Both were people who went late to bed, visited
public-houses, strolled of evenings in the Broad Street, followed
girls about, performed crazy 'stunts' – in short, were regular
blades. Although they did not live in the Kurhotel at Travemünde – where they would scarcely have been acceptable – but
somewhere in the village, they frequented the Kurhaus and
garden and were at home there as cosmopolitans. In the evening,
especially on a Sunday, when I had long since been in my bed in
one of the chalets and gone off to sleep to the pleasant sound of
the Kurhaus band, they, and other members of the young
generation – as I was aware – still sauntered up and down in
the stream of tourists and guests, loitered in front of the long
awning of the café, and sought and found grown-up enter-

tainment. And here they had come to blows, goodness knows
how and why. It is possible that they had only brushed against
each other in passing and in the sensitiveness of their knightly
honour had made a fighting matter of the encounter. Johnny,
who of course had been long since in bed too and was instructed
only by hearsay in what happened, expressed himself in his
pleasant, slightly husky childish voice, that the quarrel was
probably about some 'gal' – an easy assumption, considering
Jappe's and Do Escobar's precocity and boldness. In short, they
had made no scene among the guests, but in few and biting
words agreed upon hour and place and witnesses for the satisfaction of their honour. The next day, at twelve, rendezvous at
such and such a spot on the Leuchtenfeld. Good evening. –
Ballet-master Knaak from Hamburg, master of ceremonies and
leader of the Kurhaus cotillions, had been on the scene and
promised his presence at the appointed hour and place.

Johnny rejoiced wholeheartedly in the fray – I think that
neither he nor Brattström would have shared my apprehensions.
Johnny repeatedly assured me, forming the r far forward on his
palate, with his pretty enunciation, that they were both 'in dead
eahnest' and certainly meant business. Complacently and with a
rather ironic objectivity he weighed the chances of victory for
each. They were both frightfully strong, he grinned; both of
them great fighters – it would be fun to have it settled which of
them was the greater. Jappe, Johnny thought, had a broad chest
and capital arm and leg muscles, he could tell that from seeing
him swimming. But Do Escobar was uncommonly wiry and
savage – hard to tell beforehand who would get the upper hand.
It was strange to hear Johnny discourse so sovereignly upon
Jappe's and Do Escobar's qualifications, looking at his childish
arms, which could never have given or warded off a blow. As
for me, I was indeed far from absenting myself from the spectacle. That would have been absurd and moreover the proceed-
ings had a great fascination for me. Of course I must go, I must
see it all, now that I knew about it. I felt a certain sense of duty,
along with other and conflicting emotions: a great shyness and
shame, all unwarlike as I was, and not at all minded to trust
myself upon the scene of manly exploits. I had a nervous dread

of the shock which the sight of a duel *à outrance,* a fight for
life and death, as it were, would give me. I was cowardly
enough to ask myself whether, once on the field, I might not be
caught up in the struggle and have to expose my own person to
a proof of valour which I knew in my inmost heart I was far
from being able or willing to give. On the other hand I kept
putting myself in Jappe's and Do Escobar's place and feeling
consuming sensations which I assumed to be what they were
feeling. I visualized the scene of the insult and the challenge,
summoned my sense of good form and with Jappe and Do Escobar resisted the impulse to fall to there and then. I experienced
the agony of an overwrought passion for justice, the flaring,
shattering hatred, the attacks of raving impatience for revenge,
in which they must have passed the night. Arrived at the last
ditch, lost to all sense of fear, I fought myself blind and bloody
with an adversary just as inhuman, drove my fist into his hated
jaw with all the strength of my being, so that all his teeth were
broken, received in exchange a brutal kick in the stomach and
went under in a sea of blood. After which I woke in my bed
with ice-bags, quieted nerves, and a chorus of mild reproaches
from my family. In short, when it was half past eleven and we
got up to dress I was half worn out with my apprehensions. In
the cabin and afterwards when we were dressed and went out-
doors, my heart throbbed exactly as though it was I myself who
was to fight with Jappe or Do Escobar, in public and with all
the rigours of the game.

I still remember how we took the narrow wooden bridge
which ran diagonally up from the beach to the cabins. Of course
we jumped, in order to make it sway as much as possible, so
that we bounced as though on a spring-board. But once below
we did not follow the board walk which led along the beach
past the tents and the basket chairs; but held inland in the
general direction of the Kurhaus but rather more leftwards. The
sun brooded over the dunes and sucked a dry, hot odour from
the sparse and withered vegetation, the reeds and thistles that
stuck into our legs. There was no sound but the ceaseless humming of the blue-bottle flies which hung apparently motionless
in the heavy warmth, suddenly to shift to another spot and

begin afresh their sharp, monotonous whine. The cooling effect
of the bath was long since spent. Brattström and I kept lifting
our hats, he his Swedish sailor cap with the oilcloth visor, I my
round Heligoland woollen bonnet – the so-called tam-o'-shanter
– to wipe our brows. Johnny suffered little from heat, thanks to
his slightness and also because his clothing was more elegantly
adapted than ours to the summer day. In his light and comfortable sailor suit of striped washing material which left bare
his throat and legs, the blue, short-ribboned cap with English
lettering on his pretty little head, the long slender feet in fine,
almost heelless white leather shoes, he walked with mounting
strides and somewhat bent knees between Brattström and me
and sang with his charming accent 'Little Fisher Maiden' – a
ditty which was then the rage. He sang it with some vulgar
variation in the words, such as boys like to invent. Curiously
enough, in all his childishness he knew a good deal about
various matters and was not at all too prudish to take them in
his mouth. But always he would make a sanctimonious little
face and say: 'Fie! Who would sing such dirty songs?' – as
though Brattström and I had been the ones to make indecent
advances to the little fisher maiden.

I did not feel at all like singing, we were too near the fatal
spot. The prickly grass of the dunes had changed to the sand
and sea moss of a barren meadow; this was the Leuchtenfeld, so
called after the yellow lighthouse towering up in the far distance.
We soon found ourselves at our goal.

It was a warm, peaceful spot, where almost nobody ever
came: protected from view by scrubby willow trees. On the free
space among the bushes a crowd of youths lay or sat in a circle.
They were almost all older than we and from various strata of
society. We seemed to be the last spectators to arrive. Everybody
was waiting for Knaak the dancing-master, who was needed in
the capacity of neutral and umpire. Both Jappe and Do Escobar
were there – I saw them at once. They were sitting far apart in
the circle and pretending not to see each other. We greeted a
few acquaintances with silent nods and squatted in our turn on
the sun-warmed ground.

Some of the group were smoking. Both Jappe and Do Escobar

held cigarettes in the corners of their mouths. Each kept one eye
shut against the smoke and I instantly felt and knew that they
were aware how grand it was to sit there and smoke before entering the ring. They were both dressed in grown-up clothes, but
Do Escobar's were more gentlemanly than Jappe's. He wore
yellow shoes with pointed toes, a light-grey summer suit, a
rose-coloured shirt with cuffs, a coloured silk cravat, and a
round, narrow-brimmed straw hat sitting far back on his head,
so that his mop of shiny black hair showed on one side beneath
it, in a big hummock. He kept raising his right hand to shake
back the silver bangle he wore under his cuff. Jappe's appearance
was distinctly less pretentious. His legs were encased in tight
trousers with straps under his waxed black boots. A checked cap
covered his curly blond hair; in contrast to Do Escobar's jaunty
headgear he wore it pulled down over his forehead. He sat with
his arms clasped round one knee; you could see that he had on
loose cuffs over his shirt-sleeves, also that his finger-nails were
either cut too short or else that he indulged in the vice of biting
them. Despite the smoking and the assumed nonchalance, the
whole circle was serious and silent, restraint was in the air. The
only one to make head against it was Do Escobar, who talked
without stopping to his neighbours, in a loud, strained voice,
rolling his *r*'s and blowing smoke out of his nose.

I was rather put off by his volubility; it inclined me, despite
the bitten finger-nails, to side with Jappe, who at most addressed
a word or two over his shoulder to his neighbour and for the
rest gazed in apparent composure at the smoke of his cigarette.

Then came Herr Knaak – I can still see him, in his blue
striped flannel morning suit, coming with winged tread from
the direction of the Kurhaus and lifting his hat as he paused
outside the circle. That he wanted to come I do not believe; I
am convinced rather that he had made a virtue of necessity
when he honoured the fight with his presence. And the necessity, the compulsion, was due to his equivocal position in the
eyes of martially- and masculinely-minded youth. Dark-skinned
and comely, plump, particularly in the region of the hips, he
gave us dancing and deportment lessons in the wintertime –
private, family lessons as well as public classes in the Casino;

and in the summer he acted as bathing-master and social mana-
ger at Travemünde. He rocked on his hips and weaved in his
walk, turning out his toes very much and setting them first on
the ground as he stepped. His eyes had a vain expression, his
speech was pleasant but affected, and his way of entering a
room as though it were a stage, his extraordinary and fastidious
mannerisms charmed all the female sex, while the masculine
world, and especially critical youth, viewed him with suspicion.
I have often pondered over the position of François Knaak in
life and always I have found it strange and fantastic. He was of
humble origins, his parents were poor, and his taste for the
social graces left him as it were hanging in the air – not a mem-
ber of society, yet paid by it as a guardian and instructor of its
conventions. Jappe and Do Escobar were his pupils too; not in
private lessons, like Johnny, Brattström, and me, but in the
public classes in the Casino. It was in these that Herr Knaak's
character and position were most sharply criticized. We of the
private classes were less austere. A fellow who taught you the
proper deportment towards little girls, who was thrillingly re-
ported to wear a corset, who picked up the edge of his frock-
coat with his finger-tips, curtsied, cut capers, leaped suddenly
into the air, where he twirled his toes before he came down
again – what sort of chap was he, after all? These were the
suspicions harboured by militant youth on the score of Herr
Knaak's character and mode of life, and his exaggerated airs
did nothing to allay them. Of course, he was a grown-up man
(he was even, comically enough, said to have a wife and children
in Hamburg); and his advantage in years and the fact that he
was never seen except officially and in the dance-hall prevented
him from being convicted and unmasked. Could he do gymnastics? Had he ever been able to? Had he courage? Had he
parts? In short, could one accept him as an equal? He was never
in a position to display the soldier characteristics which might
have balanced his salon arts and made him a decent chap. So
there were youths who made no bones of calling him straight
out a coward and a jackanapes. All this he knew and therefore
he was here today to manifest his interest in a good stand-up
fight and to put himself on terms with the young, though in

his official position he should not have countenanced such goings-on. I am convinced, however, that he was not comfortable – he knew he was treading on thin ice. Some of the audience looked coldly at him and he himself gazed uneasily round to see if anybody was coming.

He politely excused his late arrival, saying that he had been kept by a consultation with the management of the Kurhaus about the next Sunday's ball. 'Are the combatants present?' he next inquired in official tones. 'Then we can begin.' Leaning on his stick with his feet crossed he gnawed his soft brown moustache with his under lip and made owl eyes to look like a connoisseur.

Jappe and Do Escobar stood up, threw away their cigarettes, and began to prepare for the fray. Do Escobar did it in a hurry, with impressive speed. He threw hat, coat, and waistcoat on the ground, unfastened tie, collar, and braces and added them to the pile. He even drew his rose-coloured shirt out of his trousers, pulled his arms briskly out of the sleeves, and stood up in a red and white striped undershirt which exposed the larger part of his yellow arms, already covered with a thick black fell. 'At your service, sir,' he said, with a rolling *r*, stepping into the middle of the ring, expanding his chest and throwing back his shoulders. He still wore the silver bangle.

Jappe was not ready yet. He turned his head, elevated his brows, and looked at Do Escobar's feet a moment with narrowed eyes – as much as to say: 'Wait a bit – I'll get there too, even if I don't swagger so much.' He was broader in the shoulder; but as he took his place beside Do Escobar he seemed nowhere near so fit or athletic. His legs in the tight strapped boots inclined to be knock-kneed and his fit-out was not impressive – grey braces over a yellowed white shirt with loose buttoned sleeves. By contrast Do Escobar's striped tricot and the black hair on his arms looked uncommonly grim and businesslike. Both were pale but it showed more in Jappe as he was otherwise blond and red-cheeked, with jolly, not-too-refined features including a rather turned-up nose with a saddle of freckles. Do Escobar's nose was short, straight, and drooping and there was a downy black growth on his full upper lip.

They stood with hanging arms almost breast to breast, and looked at one another darkly and haughtily in the region of the stomach. They obviously did not know how to begin – and how well I could understand that! A night and half a day had intervened since the unpleasantness. They had wanted to fly at each other's throats and had only been held in check by the rules of the game. But they had had time to cool off. To do to order, as it were, before an audience, by appointment, in cold blood, what they had wanted to do yesterday when the fit was on them – it was not the same thing at all. After all, they were not gladiators. They were civilized young men. And in possession of one's senses one has a certain reluctance to smash a sound human body with one's fists. So I thought, and so, very likely, it was.

But something had to be done, that honour might be satisfied, so each began to work the other up by hitting him contemptuously with the finger-tips on the breast, as though that would be enough to finish him off. And, indeed, Jappe's face began to be distorted with anger – but just at that moment Do Escobar broke off the skirmish.

'Pardon,' said he, taking two steps backwards and turning aside. He had to tighten the buckle at the back of his trousers, for he was narrow-hipped and in the absence of braces they had begun to slip. He took his position again almost at once, throwing out his chest and saying something in guttural and rattling Spanish, probably to the effect that he was again at Jappe's service. It was clear that he was inordinately vain.

The skirmishing with shoulders and buffeting with palms began again. Then unexpectedly there ensued a blind and raging hand-to-hand scuffle with the fists, which lasted three seconds and broke off without notice.

'Now they are warming up,' said Johnny, sitting next to me with a dry grass in his mouth. 'I'll wager Jappe beats him. Look how he keeps squinting over at us – Jappe keeps his mind on his job. Will you bet he won't give him a good hiding?'

They had now recoiled and stood, fists on hips, their chests heaving. Both had doubtless taken some punishment, for they both looked angry, sticking out their lips furiously as much as to say: 'What do you mean by hurting me like that?' Jappe was red-eyed and Do Escobar showed his white teeth as they fell to again.

They were hitting out now with all their strength on shoulders, forearms, and breasts by turns and in quick succession. 'That's nothing,' Johnny said, with his charming accent. 'They won't get anywhere that way, either of them. They must go at it under the chin, with an uppercut to the jaw. That does it.' But meanwhile Do Escobar had caught both Jappe's arms with his left arm, pressed them as in a vice against his chest, and with his right went on pummelling Jappe's flanks.

There was great excitement. 'No clinching!' several voices cried out, and people jumped up. Her Knaak hastened between the combatants, in horror. 'You are holding him fast, my dear friend. That is against all the rules.' He separated them and again instructed Do Escobar in the regulations. Then he withdrew once more outside the ring.

Jappe was obviously in a fury. He was quite white, rubbing his side and looking at Do Escobar with a slow nod that boded no good. When the next round began, his face looked so grim that everybody expected him to deliver a decisive blow.

And actually as soon as contact had been renewed Jappe carried out a coup – he practised a feint which he had probably planned beforehand. A thrust with his left caused Do Escobar to protect his head; but as he did so Jappe's right hit him so hard in the stomach that he crumpled forwards and his face took on the colour of yellow wax.

'That went home,' said Johnny. 'That's where it hurts. Maybe now he will pull himself together and take things seriously, so as to pay it back.' But the blow to the stomach had been too telling, Do Escobar's nerve was visibly shaken. It was clear he could not even clench his fists properly, and his eyes took on a glazed look. However, finding his muscles thus affected, his vanity counselled him to play the agile southron, dancing round the German bear and rendering him desperate by his own dexterity. He took tiny steps and made all sorts of useless passes, moving round Jappe in little circles and trying to assume an arrogant smile – which in his reduced condition struck me as really heroic. But it did not upset Jappe at all – he simply turned round on his heel and got in many a good blow with his right while with his left he warded off Do Escobar's feeble attack. But what sealed Do Escobar's fate was that his trousers kept slipping. His tricot shirt even came outside and rucked up, showing a little strip of his bare yellow skin – some of the audience sniggered. But why had he taken off his braces? He would have done better to leave aesthetic considerations on one side. For now his trousers bothered him, they had bothered him during the whole fight. He kept wanting to pull them up and stuff in his shirt, for however much he was punished he could bear it better than the thought that he might be cutting a ridiculous figure. In the end he was fighting with one hand while with the other he tried to put himself to rights; and thus Jappe was able to land such a blow on his nose that to this day I do not understand why it was not broken.

But the blood poured out, and Do Escobar turned and went apart from Jappe, trying with his right hand to stop the bleeding and with his left making an eloquent gesture behind him as he went. Jappe stood there with his knock-kneed legs spread out and waited for Do Escobar to come back. But Do Escobar was finished with the business. If I interpret him aright he was the more civilized of the two and felt that it was high time to call a halt. Jappe would beyond doubt have fought on with his nose bleeding; but almost as certainly Do Escobar would equally have refused to go on, and he did so with even more conviction in that it was himself that bled. They had made the claret run out of his nose – in his view things should never have been allowed to go so far, devil take it! The blood ran between his fingers onto his clothes, it soiled his light trousers and dripped on his yellow shoes. It was beastly and nothing but beastly – and under such circumstances he declined to take part in more fighting. It would be inhuman.

And his attitude was accepted by the majority of the spectators. Herr Knaak came into the ring and declared that the fight was over. Both sides had behaved with distinction. You could see how relieved he felt that the affair had gone off so smoothly.

'But neither of them was brought to a fall,' said Johnny, surprised and disappointed. However, even Jappe was quite satis-